"I...have a son."

His hand suspended midair, the paper hanging there between them, Reese looked at her.

"His name's Elliott. He's... During the day he's... There were only two places in the United States that offered the kind of nonresident counseling and education that he needs, and the other one is on the East Coast. I'd have to recertify and..."

She had a son. He dropped his hand to his side. His Faye. The woman he'd thought would be the mother of his children...had a son.

"He's severely at risk, Reese. To move him now, after he's started the program... To move him from Southern California, the only home he's ever known... Please. Give me a second chance to show you that I have what it takes to be reliable. I'm good at my job. Really good. You've seen my credentials and performance reports. I won't let you, your department or Santa Raquel down."

"Severely at risk," he repeated. "What does that mean?"

Dear Reader,

I'm so glad you're joining us in Santa Raquel. I love this town, the beach, the people and, of course, The Lemonade Stand, *Where Secrets are Safe*.

The scary thing is that abuse comes in many forms. From different, often unpredictable, sources. It comes verbally, physically, emotionally. And sometimes... sexually.

The really, really good news is that in every city there are places where caring people help victims of abuse recover. Places where victims can find healing. Where many can find hope and the ability to open their hearts and love again.

This story is particularly close to my heart. I can tell you from firsthand knowledge that women suffer as Faye did more often than you'd ever expect. I can also say, unequivocally, that with love, kindness and the right man, women like Faye do find pure joy again. The world is filled with survivors. Women who know and value their strengths. Who reach out to other women who've been where they've been and are struggling to get where they are. Women who care.

Please come on in to The Lemonade Stand. Join us. As a collective group, we're going to make the world a beautiful, safe place. One heart at a time.

I love to hear from my readers. Please find me at Facebook.com/tarataylorquinn and on Twitter, @tarataylorquinn. Or join my open Friendship board on Pinterest, Pinterest.com/tarataylorquinn/friendship!

All the best,

Tara

www.TaraTaylorQuinn.com

USA TODAY Bestselling Author

TARA TAYLOR QUINN

The Fireman's Son

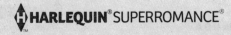

H HARLEQUIN® SUPERROMANCE®

Recycling programs
for this product may
not exist in your area.

ISBN-13: 978-0-373-64025-6

The Fireman's Son

Printed in U.S.A.

Having written over eighty novels, **Tara Taylor Quinn** is a *USA TODAY* bestselling author with more than seven million copies sold. She is known for delivering intense, emotional fiction. Tara is a past president of Romance Writers of America. She has won a Readers' Choice Award and is a five-time finalist for an RWA RITA® Award, a finalist for a Reviewers' Choice Award and a Booksellers' Best Award. She has also appeared on TV across the country, including *CBS Sunday Morning*. She supports the National Domestic Violence Hotline. If you or someone you know might be a victim of domestic violence in the United States, please contact 1-800-799-7233.

Books by Tara Taylor Quinn

HARLEQUIN SUPERROMANCE

Where Secrets are Safe

Wife by Design
Once a Family
Husband by Choice
Child by Chance
Mother by Fate
The Good Father
Love by Association
His First Choice
The Promise He Made Her
Her Secret Life

Shelter Valley Stories

Sophie's Secret
Full Contact

HARLEQUIN HEARTWARMING

Family Secrets

For Love or Money
Her Soldier's Baby
The Cowboy's Twins

MIRA BOOKS

The Friendship Pact
In Plain Sight

Visit the Author Profile page at Harlequin.com for more titles.

For the ones who know Faye's story intimately—
you are stronger than you know.

This is your reminder.

CHAPTER ONE

REESE BRISTOW WOULD not normally race to the scene of a small fire on the beach in the middle of the night. He was the newly appointed Santa Raquel Fire Chief. One truck of junior firefighters could handle the call half asleep.

Still, there he was, in jeans and a T-shirt, racing up the beach behind men in full gear carrying hoses he hoped they wouldn't need to use.

If they could smother the fire instead of drench it, there'd be more evidence.

And that was why Reese was there. To get a look at the initial evidence firsthand.

Holding back to give the suited men ample room, he watched his team. Three in turnout wear, one in paramedic blues. Even suited up and from the rear, he could tell who was who. Brandt, his second-in-command, was the tall one who ran with the bent knees of a track star. Riley had the shoulders of a football player. And Mark, at five-one, was the smallest firefighter he'd ever known.

Gaze moving to the paramedic, Reese frowned. He didn't recognize the guy—or more specifically the rounded derriere that filled out those blues like a man wouldn't.

The new hire. He'd vetted her file, but Brandt had done the interviewing and hiring. Reese had spent much of the past week between his office, scenes and a forensic lab in LA trying to find anything that would help him solve the rash of small fires being set around Santa Raquel.

As one of Southern Cal's wonder-boy fire investigators, he was not doing so wonderfully. Pathetic, considering he was the man who'd been in national news for his work on a fire that had killed most of a family. The husband and father was the only surviving member. He'd claimed he'd jumped out his bedroom window when he awoke to the flames. All evidence had pointed to an accident. All of it. No matter how many times Reese had looked at it. But he'd had a hunch.

Made into a strong suspicion when he heard that the survivor had completed a fire training course years before in another state under a different name.

It turned out the husband had set the fire himself. The guy had made one mistake. When he'd broken the window to jump out—which he'd broken after the fire was set—he'd left the glass on the ground just as it had fallen. Glass that wasn't as shattered, or as sooty, as it would have been if the fire had been burning as hot and as close as the guy claimed when he took his sail.

Reese had discovered the guy's wife was leaving him. He'd been willing to break a leg jumping out of a second-story window to kill her and their kids so she couldn't start over without him.

"We've got this one, boss!" Mark's voice traveled the short distance down the beach as Reese jogged toward them. He could barely see smoke or flames now. Hoses on the ground, Brandt and Riley were working the fire, while Mark and the new hire stood ready to jump in if needed.

Reese went straight for the one person he didn't know, holding his hand out as he approached. "Reese Bristow," he said. "Sorry we have to meet at a scene in the middle of the night. My understanding was that you didn't start shift until tomorrow."

He'd planned to meet her at the station in the morning. Have a pseudo-interview with her. She'd already accepted the job. He already knew her credentials were fine. He just liked to know every member of his team.

And he knew he didn't like it when one of them hesitated before shaking his hand. When she didn't meet his gaze.

If she'd been focused on the scene, he might have shrugged off the brief gaffe. The fact that she was looking toward the sand when she reached for his hand a couple of seconds late bothered him.

"Hi, Reese."

What the hell?

A new employee didn't…

The voice…he knew it…

With his hand holding hers, he reared back a few inches. Studying her in the shadows. Damning the darkness.

What in the hell was her name? He pictured her file on his desk.

Faye Walker.

The only Faye he'd ever known had been Faye Browning and…

She was staring at him now. His men, the tamped-down fire…it all faded out in the tepid beach air. Her hair was longer. A lot longer. Still dark. He couldn't make out the blue in her eyes, but he remembered it well. And the way they glinted with emotion when they looked at him.

Emotion that the moonlight couldn't hide.

"Faye?"

What in the hell was she doing on his beach? In EMT clothing? With his team?

Heads were going to roll.

Starting with hers.

"I thought you'd at least call," she was saying. Making no sense at all. "I wouldn't take the job until Brandt assured me that you'd seen my file and approved the employment…"

Last he'd heard, Faye Browning had been in

her second year of a four-year nursing program at UC Berkeley.

He'd been at Southern Cal in LA.

"You *did* know, didn't you?" Her voice trailed off.

His horror must have been showing.

He'd glanced at Faye Walker's credentials and work history. And trusted Brandt with the rest. If he'd felt a need to do more, he'd have conducted the interview himself.

"You didn't know…"

"Okay, boss, she's all yours," Mark said, approaching him and *Faye* and motioning to the smoldering embers behind them.

"On first glance it's just like all the rest," Brandt said, joining them. "Gasoline. Matches. Nothing but ashes left, so considering how quickly we got here and put it out, there couldn't have been that much to burn to begin with…"

"Or that they used a lot more gasoline, in a wider sphere…" Reese said, turning his back on the paramedic he couldn't deal with in that moment. "It's a bigger radius," he said, coming up on the fire.

"Yeah." Brandt stood with him. The rest of the crew was a few feet back. Reese heard soft murmuring among them. And hoped to God it was about fires.

If she thought for one second she was going to

come here and upend his life again, she'd be out on her ass so fast…

"And closer to property that could catch and do actual damage," Brandt said, reminding Reese that his second-in-command was still standing there assessing the mess on the beach.

"It's escalating," Reese said, confirming a fear that he and Brandt had already discussed.

"Clearly it's not homeless people trying to stay warm." Brandt's tone did not lack for sarcasm. The theory had appeared in the media a month or so back, when they'd had a cold spell at night, colder than usual for Santa Raquel in June.

"It's also not kids." Reese rebutted the other theory that had been passing through the town by word of mouth. "They'd have grown bored by now and…"

"We were here fast enough tonight to catch them if there'd been a group of them."

Because Reese had had sentinels on the beach. And the Santa Raquel police force was vigilantly watching the town for signs of smoke.

Disproving theories one and two only left them with number three. Someone was giving them a warning. Something bigger was ahead.

And it was his job to find the clue to what that might be and stop the perpetrator before it happened.

"You and the others…you can head back. Get

some rest," he said. "I've got my evidence kit in the car. I'll take it from here."

Brandt nodded. Reese felt the other man's stare and knew it was because of his curt tone. He also knew he couldn't do anything about it.

"So you met the new girl," Brandt said. "Smith had a couple of drinks at a party tonight. He couldn't come out."

With a glance, Reese communicated what they both knew. Smith was history. The paramedic had known he was on call, and lives depended on his self-control and good choices. "At least he had the decency to say so," Reese allowed. To make amends for his earlier tone. He wasn't usually a total ass.

And because he realized that Brandt had taken his tone for displeasure over the fact that he'd been blindsided by a crewmember he wasn't expecting.

If only the other man knew.

"Go on, get some rest," he said now, jerking his head toward the others. He needed Brandt and the guys to go.

He needed *her* to go.

He needed his kit, fresh air and a few hours with smoldering embers on the beach.

Then, maybe, he'd trust himself to get rid of Santa Raquel Fire Department's newest employee with the level of professionalism expected of its chief.

SO...THAT WENT WELL. Faye's sarcasm rang loud and clear in her mind as she trekked across the beach with her brand-new coworkers.

She was on a mission. Had a very clear plan. She'd considered every step in-depth prior to implementation. She'd allowed for every eventuality. Taken measures to ensure that nothing went wrong.

"You told me he approved of my employment," she said to Brandt Rollins, hurrying to catch up with him instead of lagging behind with the other two.

She knew Brandt best. Other than a quick introductory hello to the two that night and a few others when she'd taken a tour of the station as part of her final interview, he was the only one she knew.

Other than Reese, of course.

"He did."

Right. Which was why he'd been shocked to see her that night. And not pleasantly so.

Not that she'd expected he would be pleased. The fact that he'd agreed to her hire without having it out with her had shocked her. It was a part of the plan that had gone far better than anything she'd imagined.

Now she knew why.

"You gave him my whole file. With the photo and all?"

"I put it on his desk. But he likes me to pull out

the credential and experience sheet and attach it to the top. I'm the one in charge of hiring. He trusts me to do my job."

Now she was pissing off the one guy who actually liked her.

Reese had every reason to hate her. And those were the reasons he knew about. She now suspected there could be one more. Worse than the others.

He'd only seen her credentials. All earned and issued under the name Faye Walker, EMT. He'd known Faye Browning, studying to be an RN.

"Don't worry if you think he didn't like you," Brandt said as they reached cement and he stomped the sand off his boots. "It's not you he was pissed at."

Oh, she was pretty sure it was.

But, until Reese said differently, she had to make certain that no one knew she'd ever known him.

If her plan was going to work—and it had to— she had to let her ex-lover call the shots. Until her son had time to heal and she had answers. Then she'd be back in charge. And could take Elliott and quietly slip away.

"How can you be so sure he didn't take an instant dislike to me?" she asked. Because it seemed like something she might have asked if she'd never met the boss before.

They were at the truck and Brandt stripped off

the top half of his gear. The others were still several yards behind.

"Because I know why he was pissed and it didn't have anything to do with you."

She frowned. Completely sure Brandt was wrong, but curious about why he thought he was right.

"Why was he pissed?"

"Because he gave the paramedic you're covering for a second chance and the guy blew it."

It was the best news she'd heard in a while.

Nodding, she climbed up into the truck. Buckled herself in. And allowed herself to take a deep breath.

Reese Bristow had not only become the fire investigator and chief he'd always said he'd be, but he'd grown into a man who gave second chances.

Her plan might just work out fine after all.

CHAPTER TWO

THE SCOPE OF the fire was a ten-yard diameter. Ashes composed one yard of that. The rest of the fire had been caused by a burn-off of gasoline. The fuel stopped just a few feet from a dry field leading directly to an abandoned house. Given the abandoned home's distance from other residences on the private beach, it was likely no one would have been hurt, but considerable damage might have been done.

The first fire, set almost a month ago, had been a three-yard diameter. Set down by the water. The arsonist had only been testing his tools then.

What Reese didn't yet know was why. How. Or who.

What he really didn't understand was what in the hell Faye Browning...*Walker*...was doing working for his department. Or in Santa Raquel, period.

He measured. Took notes.

She hadn't been surprised to see him. She'd been surprised that he'd been surprised to see *her*.

What was it she'd said? *"I thought you'd at least call."*

Why in the hell would he have called her? Ever again?

She'd been his girlfriend, through high school and two years of college. His lover during the college years. In his mind, there'd been no doubt that they were going to marry, raise a family, grow old together. No doubt that she was his one and only.

And then in one weekend, it had all shattered. She'd gone out with another guy. And the very next day had called Reese to tell him they were through. No talking. No chances. Just done.

With gloves on, he handled, bagged and tagged the ashes that he'd be taking to LA. He was using the forensic lab where he'd studied during college. Doing a lot of the work himself.

The fires felt personal.

Santa Raquel was his town now.

She wasn't a nurse. Why? It was all she'd ever wanted to be. Just like his passion had been fire investigations. Firefighting. On the front line protecting his home state from the wildfires that threatened it during the dry season.

That's why, even when she was awarded her scholarship to UC Berkeley, he'd gone to Southern Cal, LA. Because their fire management program was the best in the state.

And now she wasn't even a nurse?

She'd married. Her name was Walker.

She was married. *Walker.* Did the guy know his wife had just moved to the town where her ex-lover had settled? Did he know she was *working* for him?

The audacity of that one burned his blood.

Did she know he'd been married? Did she think that somehow made them even?

Not even close, lady. Not even close.

He walked the beach, his state-of-the-art flashlight leading the way. If the guy had so much as spilled a drop of gasoline, he wanted to find it. It would tell him which direction he'd come from. Or left by. He checked the dried brush on the other side of the fire.

He searched for three hours but found nothing of significance.

Was no closer to discovering his arsonist.

But he had a solid plan for Faye Walker.

She was going to be axed. Immediately.

"ELLIOTT?" LEAVING HER son's bedroom, Faye searched the apartment. She'd rented the upstairs of an antebellum home just two blocks from the beach. The rooms, with their high ceilings, new paint and pristine wooden floors, were beautiful, but the clincher on the deal for her had been the landlady.

Suzie Preston, a widow in her sixties, lived on the first floor and had offered her services as babysitter anytime Faye was called into work. Suzie volunteered in the library at The Lemonade Stand, a unique women's shelter in Santa

Raquel. The place had become Elliott's current daytime habitat.

"Elliott?" She glanced into the bathroom to make sure her eight-year-old hadn't sleepwalked to the toilet to relieve himself and stayed there.

Suzie had met her on the landing as she'd walked up the second flight of the wide, winding, bannistered staircase that could have been in any number of old films. She'd said the boy hadn't made a peep during the hour and a half Faye had been gone.

"Elliott!" Not sure whether to be pissed at her son's deliberate lack of response or worried about finding him before he hurt himself, she sped toward the living room and kitchen.

Her son, thick sandy hair askew, looked up at her with eyes as blue as hers. His expression as dark as Frank Walker's had been the last time he'd left bruises on her arm with his strong grasp...

"Why didn't you answer me?"

Elliott spooned another mouthful of cereal between his lips, slurping. Dripping onto the small Formica table, too.

She sat down next to him. He didn't acknowledge her presence. Not all that unusual when he was in a mood, but there was always a tell. A flinch. A tightening around his mouth. He was only eight. Not yet capable of completely sealing himself off.

Unless he was asleep. Like now. Hard to believe that a child could sit at the table with his eyes open, eating a bowl of cereal and be asleep—but such was her life.

Looking out through the thin black bars on the large window overlooking the gorgeous, flowered backyard, Faye issued a silent thank-you.

For them. The bars. They were the second reason she'd chosen this home. Suzie had told her the bars had been put on the upper windows by her great-grandmother, after a child had almost fallen out one hot summer day.

The bars were tasteful. Decorative, expensive wrought iron that matched the fencing around the house and the rails on the front porch downstairs.

They were what let her sleep at night. Elliott was locked in. There was an alarm system on the front door in case he did manage to find a key and get himself out of their door. And the bars kept him from throwing himself out as he'd tried to do the first night after they'd left his father.

They'd been in a hotel. On the fourth floor. She'd awoken to the sound of the balcony door opening, and she'd had to rip him from a deathly clutch on the balcony rail. The next morning, he'd wondered how his forearms had gotten bruised. He'd remembered none of it.

She'd checked both of them into a women's shelter. She'd had nowhere else to go, no one to turn to, no idea what to do. That had been in

Mission Viejo, where she'd fled when she'd left Frank Walker.

Almost two years had passed since then.

Elliott was fine with the divorce. Never asked to see his father. Never spoke of him.

But he was still sleepwalking.

And he was still angry with her.

Because she hadn't stopped his father from hurting her, because she'd stayed.

For starters.

So here they were in Santa Raquel. Elliott had been referred to The Lemonade Stand as one of two choices for daily education with domestic violence counseling and emotional supervision. Technically he was homeschooled at the shelter.

Reese Bristow had made the town the only choice. For her own healing.

And perhaps for Elliott, as well.

The boy finished his cereal. Carried the bowl with both hands to the sink, as she'd taught him when he was about two so he wouldn't drop it and raise his father's ire. Stopping by the table on his way past it, he wiped at the dribble of milk on its surface with his pajama sleeve. And then he was gone.

Back to bed.

She'd been told not to wake him during these episodes. She should watch out for his safety, but unless he was hurting himself, she should just let him be.

He'd be up again in a couple of hours. Getting ready for her to take him to the Stand. Probably wanting breakfast. Not remembering a thing about his middle-of-the-night snack.

Sitting at the table, thinking about the past few hours, about Elliott, about seeing Reese again for the first time in nine very, very long years, she considered getting some sleep, too.

With tears dripping slowly down her face, she put herself to bed.

On the couch in her son's room.

"MOM, COME ON, we're going to be late!" Was it just her imagination or was Elliott's tone starting to sound like Frank's?

"I've got ten more minutes," she told him, leaning over the sink to apply concealer under both eyes. She'd smoothed on extra foundation, too. And eyeliner. And lipstick.

"Who ever heard of an EMT showing up at a crash in makeup gunk?" Shaking his head, the thick hair he preferred to wear down past his ears flopping, he turned and left her room.

Frank had always insisted on a military cut. For himself. And for their son.

Though Elliott had more stuff—furniture and toys—Faye had taken the larger of the two bedrooms when they'd moved in the week before. Mostly because she'd loved the claw-foot tub in the adjoining bath. Loved that the room had an adjoining bath.

Almost as much as she'd been opposed to Elliott having one. At least if he had to cross the hall to go in the night, she'd have a better chance of hearing him.

"Mom!" he called from the other end of the apartment, near the front door.

Pulling on a clean set of the standard blue utility pants and shirt she'd been issued, Faye was nervous but excited. She slipped into the ugly black EMS boots she'd purchased as soon as she'd graduated from training four years before and reminded herself that she was not only worthy, she was capable.

And had five minutes to spare.

Surprisingly, Elliott was not standing impatiently by the front door. So far, he liked going to The Lemonade Stand. There were two other boys there his age. Both had mothers who were victims. He'd taken quite a liking to one of the older boys, as well.

Maybe that older boy could be someone Elliott could look up to? Someone who'd be able to reach the little guy inside of Elliott—the little guy who'd spent years listening to the sounds of his mother's sexual abuse without her knowing he could hear it?

"Ell?" She turned the corner toward the kitchen. He'd already had breakfast. She'd fixed it—a lighter rendition than usual—and then run for the shower while he ate. The Lemonade Stand provided balanced and delicious meals, so he didn't need to take a lunch.

The boy turned around as she came into the room. She noticed his hesitant expression, like he wasn't sure of his reception. And then she saw the paper plate he held in both hands. He'd made her a bagel with what looked like a half-scrambled, half-fried, somewhat-raw egg on it.

"You don't have to eat it if you don't want," he said, shrugging as he held the plate up to her. "I just…" He shrugged again. "It's your first day and all."

He'd made breakfast for her.

Her precious, precious angel boy had made her breakfast.

Because it was her first day…and all.

They were going to be okay. She knew for certain now that Reese knew about her. She hadn't received a call telling her not to come into work. Which meant she was still employed.

The rest—her plan, Elliott's future—would all fall into place now.

When she could speak without tears clogging her throat, she thanked her son, careful not to let too much emotion spill onto him and make him withdraw. Taking the sandwich with her as they left the apartment, she ate every single bite.

CHAPTER THREE

SLEEP MIGHT HAVE been good. But it wasn't the first time he'd shown up at work without it. Wouldn't be the last.

When a fire was raging out of control and there weren't enough fighters with the necessary training, sleep wasn't an option.

Today Reese had a personal fire raging and he wasn't going to rest until he'd put it out. Faye Walker was not going to have a first day of work. Not one second to settle in. He wanted her out.

He was waiting in the station when he saw her get out of an older, light gray, four-door sedan and head toward him.

Mark, who was in the middle of forty-eight hours on, walked past with a cup of coffee. Reese had sent Brandt home. He didn't need his second caught in the cross fire that could very well happen after he'd had his moment with the woman who'd invaded his den.

"Send the new hire to my office as soon as she gets here," he told Mark and strode in that direction himself, sure that his employee was staring after him. If he'd waited thirty more seconds, he could have told her himself.

If her aim was to force him to keep her on, or threaten to sue for wrongful termination if he didn't, then let her bring it on. He wasn't going to fire her in front of witnesses.

She wasn't staying.

One thing didn't make sense. If she'd meant to trap him, she wouldn't have assumed he knew about her hire. But that phone call thing...why would she expect him to call? Unless she thought he didn't have the balls to fire her face-to-face.

He'd gone home long enough to shower and shave, run a comb through his hair. It was shorter now than when she'd known him. He'd shaved his mustache since she'd last seen him, too. Tabitha had hated it. Said it poked her when he kissed her.

He'd had one clean uniform left. Technically Mondays were his day off. Laundry day, among other things. Instead, he was planning a trip to LA just as soon as he'd finished with the business at hand.

That was all Faye Walker was to him. Business.

And he was a master at handling his job. Which was why, at twenty-nine, he'd already made fire chief.

The knock came as expected. Sharp. Short. No hesitation.

I have to break up with you, Reese. I'm sorry.

She'd left a damned text message. Four years

together, plans for a lifetime and he didn't even warrant an in-person breakup?

Or a phone call?

He'd texted back: *Okay, why?*

Nine years before, that had meant pushing number buttons on a flip phone for corresponding letters. No quick task for a guy with big hands.

That had been shaking.

There's someone else...

He hadn't responded to that. There'd been no point.

"Come in," he called now. He stood a few feet from the door, blocking the chairs in front of his desk, hands in his pockets.

There was no need for her to sit. She wasn't staying.

"Reese, Mark said you wanted to see me..."

Her eyes were as blue as he remembered. And seemed to have all kinds of things to say to him.

He remembered that about her, too. It had been the promises she'd made with those eyes, as much as any words she'd ever given him, that had held him captive.

There'd been only one night he hadn't been there for her. A night after he'd almost been hurt in a fire. He'd been facing death for the first time. Asking himself if there was more he might want out of life before he died...

"You're going to fire me," she said before he got a word out of his mouth.

Damn her. Reading his mind when she was his girlfriend was one thing. But now…there had to be something illegal about that. Invading a person's mind against their will.

"I am." She'd broken up with him in a few words. He could fire her the same way.

At least he'd given her the respect of doing it in person.

He could have texted her. Told her not to bother coming in.

"I'm going to beg you not to do so," she said, standing there with her hands at her sides. Not at all challenging.

And yet he felt…pushed.

Reese didn't like feeling pushed. Most particularly not by a five-foot-three-inch woman with a cute ass and a cheating heart.

"Beg all you want," he said, meaning to hand her the paperwork he'd already filled out.

As he turned to pick up the page lying on his desk, she said, "Please, Reese, I need this job." The pleading in her voice did his injured heart good.

He picked up the sheet and turned back to her. But he didn't immediately hand it over.

Turned out, he wanted her to ask him again. To prolong the moment. He'd had no idea he was such a sick bastard.

But he also couldn't believe that Faye Browning had just walked back into his life expecting to work for him as though they'd never loved each other to distraction.

Probably because she hadn't loved him that way.

"It's not just for me, although, of course, I need the money, but this job, here in particular…it's… important, Reese. Truly important."

She was looking him right in the eye. Not fidgeting. Not even blinking.

The woman was honestly and sincerely begging him.

It kind of threw him for a loop and he had to remind himself that she'd texted him to break up with him. Because she'd met another man.

"Your husband doesn't make enough to pay your bills?" That was it. Remember Mr. Walker. Had she cheated on him, too? And how many in between him and Reese?

"I'm divorced." That seemed to mean more to her than it did to him.

He almost told her he was sorry to hear it. But he wasn't. What he was, was pissed. Pissed that she was there at all.

And pissed that he hadn't kicked her out yet.

"Just out of curiosity, who broke it off? Him or you?"

If she said the guy had left her…if she really was alone and in need…

"I did."

Of course she did.

And then came to beg him to take her in?

Uh-uh. No way. In hell.

Or out of it. He held the termination paper out to her.

He was done with her.

"I…have a son… Reese."

His hand suspended midair, the paper hanging there between them, he looked at her.

"His name's Elliott. He's… During the day he's… There were only two places in the country that offered the kind of nonresident counseling and education that he needs, and the other one is on the east coast. I'd have to recertify and…"

She had a son. His hand dropped to his side. His Faye. The woman he'd thought would be the mother of his children…had a son.

"He's severely at risk, Reese. To move him now, after he's started the program… To move him from Southern California, the only home he's ever known… Please. Give me a second chance to show you that I have what it takes to be reliable. I'm good at my job. Really good. You've seen my credentials and performance reports. I won't let you, your department or Santa Raquel down."

He heard the last part. Couldn't focus on it.

"Severely at risk," he repeated. "What does that mean?"

When she ran her tongue over her lips, he almost turned his back on her. If she thought she was going to play him with that old maneuver…

Her kid probably wasn't at risk at all…

"He's at The Lemonade Stand."

He froze. "The Lemonade Stand's for victims of domestic violence," he said.

She nodded.

She'd asked for a divorce. And the kid was with her.

"Your ex hit your son?"

She shook her head.

Then who had? Surely not her. Faye might be a cheater but she was most definitely not someone who would strike out in anger. Ever. She'd had the most trusting, giving, generous, nurturing heart…

"Who then?"

"Me." For the first time since she'd entered the room, her gaze dropped from his, falling to the floor.

"*You* hit your son?" The world had gone from ridiculous to unrecognizable. Who was this woman? What had happened to drive her to do such a thing?

She shook her head. Shuddered. And then looked up again, something new in her eyes as she looked at him. "No, Reese, my ex-husband hurt me, not our son."

Our son. That answered that then. She'd been married to her son's father.

"How old is he?" He'd never felt so…uncomfortable…in his life. "Your boy, I mean."

"Eight."

The word hit him hard, right in the gut.

"You married the guy you dumped me for."
There was just no classy way to get that out there.

She nodded.

"And had his son."

She nodded a second time. Looking him straight in the eye.

His disrespect for her lessened a little as he tried to figure out what to do with her. How to get rid of her.

The man she'd married had hurt her, she'd said. He was trying his damnedest not to process that part.

"Are you at The Lemonade Stand, too, then?" It was a resort-type place with more housing than most shelters, including cabins for families to live in alone. Or for a mother and one child to share with another mother and one child.

But...Faye was working for him. She wasn't a woman finding protection at a shelter...

The realization hit at the same time she shook her head. "I did go to a shelter, briefly," she told him. "But just until I could get some counseling. Get my bearings. I'm not in... Frank...there's no danger there."

In spite of himself, Reese cared. If some bastard was going to be coming after Faye...

"Frank didn't...abuse me...in the traditional way," she told him. "And he's not angry that I left. He was glad I walked out and took Elliott with me."

"He *wanted* you to take his son?"

Her eyes dropped again. "Frank had antiquated ideas about men and child rearing. He didn't raise a hand to Elliott. He just ignored him."

Reese didn't get it. Not any of it.

Faye being here...her son not being abused but being at the Stand... Faye as a victim of domestic abuse.

And then there was Reese, losing a wife he didn't really love to a car accident that shouldn't have happened. Finding out after his wife was dead that she'd been six weeks pregnant.

Life wasn't supposed to have turned out that way.

But one thing was clear...he and Faye...their ship had sailed. He was sorry Frank Walker had turned out to be a bastard. Honestly sorry.

But that didn't change the fact that Faye had cheated on Reese. Cheated him out of the life— the family—she'd promised they'd have together.

"Elliott wasn't abused, physically, but he... heard...what was going on between his father and me," Faye said, breaking the silence that was leading to him picking up the piece of paper on his desk. "He...my son...has issues. Ones that could ruin his life if we don't get them under control. It's believed that his best chance of success is to spend at least the next semester being homeschooled at the Stand, with specialized counseling, and see if we can break through his walls and help him work through things."

Issues. Specialized. Things. He could imagine. But he didn't really understand.

The vagueness left him unsettled.

"You're not a nurse."

She shook her head. "No, I'm not."

He knew that. He'd read her file.

"But I'm a damned good EMT." She'd grown more outspoken than he remembered her. Stronger.

And yet, she'd always had the strength to move mountains. It had just been a quiet strength.

"A single mother with a troubled son." He shook his head. She'd given him the legitimate out he needed to get rid of her. "There's no way you can be relied upon to work the kind of hours your position is meant to fill," he said. "On call three nights a week. Twelve-hour shifts."

He understood her desperation. But surely even Faye knew that he couldn't cover for her—even if he'd had a mind to.

"I've got that all worked out." She told him about her landlord, Suzie Preston, who worked at the Stand. She was in the library but only because she was retired. The woman had been a counselor at a domestic violence shelter for more than thirty years.

Her eyes begged him. They knew him. Knew he wouldn't turn her away.

But he couldn't have her here. Day after day. Even when she wasn't on duty, he'd know that she'd be back.

For a brief second, he considered quitting. Moving on.

Except that he'd signed a contract. To renege on that for no good professional reason would be a permanent black mark on his record.

In the end, he did what they both had known he would do.

He nodded.

He saw the tears that sprang to her eyes and swore silently.

Out loud all he said was, "Stay out of my way, Faye. I mean that. You've got the job but as far as anyone knows, you and I do not and never have known each other."

She nodded, pursing her lips as though biting back a smile.

"I mean it. No one here knows my past prior to Tabitha." He wasn't going to have people watching him.

Wasn't going to have gossip.

And most certainly wasn't going to have anyone getting the idea into their heads that Faye could somehow heal the gaping hurt caused by his wife's death.

She couldn't.

Because as ashamed as he was to admit it, it wasn't his wife's death that had caused the chasm within him.

It was Faye's cheating that had torn at his heart.

And his unborn child's death that had ripped it in half.

"I understand," Faye said now, reaching for the door handle. "I expected as much. Which was why I expected you to call me before I came to work."

He would have dismissed her, but she'd already stepped out.

And not a second too soon. He needed a drink. Maybe more than one. Didn't matter that it was eight o'clock in the morning. He'd been up all night.

Life had a strange way of dealing its cards. Faye was a cheater who had a child. He was a man who'd been cheated on, with a dead wife on his conscience—and a lost child because of it.

Reaching for his keys, he thought of the beer in his fridge. Then he remembered the evidence bags locked in his trunk. He wasn't going home to drink. He was going to LA.

Maybe he'd spend the night there.

Away from Faye and all of the memories she'd brought back into his world.

Even the good ones were bad now, tainted because they hadn't meant enough to her.

Going out for UC's homecoming had been more

important to her than he'd been. Than their four years together had been.

He'd gotten her message loud and clear.

He wasn't ever going to need to hear it again.

CHAPTER FOUR

HIS HAND SLID across her breast. Cradling it. So soft. So tender. As though it was precious to him.

She shivered. Wondered if she was naked. If he was. In bed, but not sure how she'd gotten there, or even where "there" was, she snuggled closer to him, smelling the musky scent on his skin. Wanting to be closer yet. Finding warmth to soothe her coldness.

His departure was imminent. Fear surrounded his leaving. He couldn't go. She couldn't stop him. She had to stop him. Couldn't. Had to...

Faye didn't know where she was. Drenched, shaking, she stared into the darkness—recognized the small glow of light off to the right...

"Mom?"

Elliott!

Shooting up, she reached for him. Remembered at the last minute not to touch. She could startle him awake.

"You were crying."

He came closer. Sat on the side of her bed. Like most nights, she was in her own room. His gaze was focused.

Touching her cheeks, she felt the wetness there. Knew he saw it.

"I...was...dreaming," she said. Her son was awake. She had to think. Shake off the torturous dream. Convince him that she was fine.

That the years of him waking in the night to the sound of his mother's tears were over.

God, let them be over.

He looked so young standing there...his eyes wide. Innocent. Concerned.

"I'm sorry I woke you," she said, taking his hand. Half expecting him to pull away. To see his blank expression reappear as he walled himself off from her.

Instead, he moved closer, leaning toward her until her arms couldn't help but circle around him and pull him to her. He didn't resist.

He was tired. She was, too. Tired of not being able to just make Elliott's world right. Tired of being strong all alone.

Tired of avoiding Reese the past couple of days as she settled into a job that she otherwise would have loved.

Tired of all the regrets.

So she took the rare gift he'd offered her. Sliding down in the bed, she settled her son against her, laid her head on her pillow and closed her eyes.

Morning would come.

And with it, her strength would return.

ON THURSDAY, REESE pulled into the station with an infusion of energy. He'd had a bit of a hit from the LA lab results—the print from a popular brand of running shoe, men's size ten. Maybe not enough to pursue all the way to a suspect, but it was a start.

And Faye Walker was off for the next four days.

There'd been no other fires in the area since Sunday night. So while his crew had been kept unfortunately busy with a couple of car accidents, it had been a relatively slow week, without a lot of paperwork.

That alone made for a happy day. He had a meeting with the city manager and a couple of inspections awaiting his attention as he also served as the city's construction inspector. In departments as small as his, they couldn't afford too many full-time employees. Part of the reason he'd been awarded the job of chief was because of his multiple qualifications.

Three members of his crew were inside the station, wiping down a newly cleaned truck. Cyrus, the only paramedic left on his crew that he wanted to be around, was checking medical supplies. By nine o'clock, all of the equipment would be checked, as it was every day, seven days a week, and then, barring calls, the men would be in the fitness room, working out.

He'd have liked to join them. If all went well, he'd make it for the afternoon session. Staying in shape was a huge part of their jobs. And a personal must for him.

"You've got a phone call," Doris, their receptionist, called, the receiver still in hand. "Holding on four."

His raised eyebrow was all the question he needed to ask. "I saw you pull in," she said from her desk in the first office inside the door. "And I had a feeling you'd want to take it."

She'd piqued his curiosity.

"Chief Bristow," he said, the phone to his ear as he closed his office door.

"I'm sorry to bug you, um, sir…Chief…"

Reese pulled back and looked at the receiver. What kind of prank was Doris pulling, putting a kid through to him? Certain that his receptionist would have already determined there was no emergency, that she would never have put a kid on hold had there been one, that if there'd been one, the call would have come in through 9-1-1 and police dispatch, not the station's number…

"Who is this?" he asked, trying to figure out the joke. It wasn't like his men to play around at work. When it came to fire safety, he was a pretty serious guy.

But he'd already let one employee go that week—Chester Smith—the paramedic who'd been drinking while on call.

"I can't say," the young voice told him. "At least… I gotta know what happens, first."

"Do you know who you're talking to?" How well had Doris screened this call?

"Yes, um, you just said. You're Chief Bristow. It's...who I asked for."

Sitting behind his desk, he glanced at the folders on top of it. His good mood rapidly dissipating, he thought about sending the call back out to his receptionist.

He wasn't all that great with kids. Didn't spend any time around them, but didn't particularly want to offend one, either. Joke or not.

"What do you gotta know?" he asked, purposely using the kid's vernacular. He assumed he was talking to a boy but wasn't altogether sure.

"If I...confess...do I gotta go to jail right away? Or do I get to explain to my mom?"

He sat forward. And then stood. What in the hell were they dealing with here?

It had to be a joke. But the boy didn't sound like he was kidding.

Which would make it the best kind of joke...

"You sure you don't need to be talking to the police?" he asked, to buy himself another second or two.

"No, um, it's you."

He nodded and adjusted his tie. He would put on working blues later after his meeting with the city manager.

"I can't answer your questions until I know what we're talking about," he said. And then, in case this was for real, added, "But if you're under eighteen, then yes, you can talk to your mom. It's the law. No one can question you without your mom or dad's permission."

Maybe this was a test. Of what, he had no idea.

Knew the thought was out there.

"I don't got a dad."

Or an English teacher, either, apparently.

"But you're under eighteen."

"I'm eight."

The same age as Faye's son? Not that he'd remembered or anything.

All week long, every thought had come back to her. If he ate something they'd shared in the past, he'd remember whether or not she'd liked it. After four years together, they'd eaten pretty much everything together, which meant every time he took a bite those past few days...

He stood still, putting a hand in his pocket.

"You going to tell me what you did?" Joke or no, this had to end.

"I set a fire."

He glanced around the office as though the whole station had heard.

Did Doris know? And if so, why in the hell hadn't she given him a heads-up?

"You did."

"Yes."

Was this his escalating fire threat? An eight-year-old in a size-ten tennis shoe?

He shook his head. "How many of them?"

"Just one."

Not his threat. At least not entirely.

"Did you have help?"

"Maybe."

They'd dismissed the idea that they were dealing with kids. Maybe too soon?

"Where did you set the fire?" he asked, thinking of the various unsolved small-fire crime scenes.

"In a trash can in the boys' bathroom."

Reese ran a hand through his hair. "Not outside?" he asked.

"No. Then it wouldn't be contained."

He hadn't heard an "um" in a couple of minutes. And the kid's grammar had improved. Because he was more comfortable now in speaking with him?

Or because he was repeating what he'd heard from someone else? *Contained* was an industry description.

"Who told you it had to be contained?"

"No one."

"How'd you know, then?"

He had to find out the kid's identity. Find out where he was. Send a crew out.

Heading out of his office, he motioned for Doris to get him the caller ID as the childish voice answered his question.

"My mom."

"You mother taught you a fire had to be contained?"

"She didn't exactly teach me. She just says stuff and I hear it."

"Who's your mom?"

The long silence gave him pause.

"What's your name, son?"

"It's not her fault. And it wasn't s'posed to leave that black mark in the bottom of the can. They weren't s'posed to find out."

"But they did."

"Yeah. This morning when I got here, there was a meeting with all the kids. And no one should hafta get in trouble 'cause of me. 'Specially my mom, too."

Reese started to relax. He was fairly certain that the call was legitimate and that caller ID would tell them the boy was calling him from the elementary school.

Not abreast with current parenting theories, he would have to tread carefully while he tried to figure out what to do.

The boy was obviously a good kid. He'd called the fire chief to confess, after all. But he must be troubled—he'd set the fire to begin with.

Back in his office, with the door shut, he asked, "Does she know you set the fire?"

"Uh-uh."

Still perplexed as to why he was getting this call, Reese asked, "Are you ready to tell me your name?"

"Can my mom not be in trouble?"

"Why would she be in trouble?"

"Um…'cause you're her boss and all."

Reese sat down. Hard.

CHAPTER FIVE

"I DON'T KNOW what's wrong with me…" Leaning forward, her elbows on her knees, hands clasped together, Faye sat on Sara's couch and looked at the other woman. Sara's shoulder-length blond hair framed her face and pretty blue eyes in a way that made Faye feel like she was talking to an angel.

Or her personal rendition of one.

Maybe it was just that she needed a guardian angel right then.

"Nothing's wrong with you," said The Lemonade Stand's full-time counselor.

Faye wasn't seeing Sara on an official basis. Faye had a weekly appointment with Dr. Bloom Larson for her own counseling. She'd just dropped off Elliott and found herself in Sara's office.

"Oh…something's wrong," Faye said now.

Sara, leaning back against her desk, smiled at her. And shook her head.

"You're alive, Faye," she said. "Feeling sexual desire is a normal part of life."

"Not for me it isn't. Not since…"

She stopped. Thought of the previous night's

dream, with feelings that were so mixed up. Glorious and panic-inducing at the same time.

Wonderful mixed with devastating.

"What Frank did to you…it's had an effect on you, Faye. You know that."

She did. She'd been through counseling. "I thought I'd never feel sexual desire again." Mostly, she'd been fine with the prognosis. She had no intention of having another man in her life, so sex was pretty much a nonissue to her.

"You might not. Not in the way you think…"

"But last night…"

"Was showing you that your ability to feel sexual desire is not completely dead."

"Why now?" The words hurt her throat. But she had to know. For the rest of her life, there would be no more hiding. She'd promised Elliott.

And herself.

"My guess?" Sara asked.

Faye nodded.

"Reese takes you back to a time before Frank. To a time when you were on fire with desire."

She stared.

"Am I wrong?"

Faye wanted to jump up and leave the room. Laugh the whole thing off. She just shook her head.

"It doesn't mean that you'd feel those same feelings now," Sara said, a warning note to her voice. "If he were to touch you, I mean."

Okay. The tightening in her chest subsided a bit. She drew in a complete—and calming—breath.

"It's just a trigger from the past. Not an indication of current—"

"What are you asking me?"

"The dream," Faye said. "It doesn't have to mean I'm still in love with him, right? Just that seeing him sparked a 'muscle memory' kind of response from my psyche in terms of sex."

"Exactly."

Well, thank God.

"I woke up crying."

"That's what you said."

"Elliott was there. Awake."

"Yes."

"So…you'll talk to him today?" Because she didn't know how to help her own son. She had to rely on professionals.

"Just like every day."

"Thank you." She stood.

"Faye?"

"Yeah?"

"Be careful."

She nodded. Then turned back to her. "Why do you say it like that?" Like she was really concerned.

Sara wasn't smiling anymore. "Because you're vulnerable. And I don't think you're letting yourself see that. These feelings for Reese—whether they're real or just regression—*feel* real. And he's right here. In your life."

"You think I'll fall prey and sleep with him?" If only Sara knew how far from possible that was. Reese hadn't so much as met her eye in the two days they'd been around the station together. He hadn't been on any of their rescue calls. And when he'd come into the training room and seen her there, he'd made an excuse and turned around and left.

"I think that you could find yourself in a situation where you think what you're feeling is real and make love with him..."

"Not going to happen."

"The more you deny the possibility, the more at risk you are."

"I'm not denying the possibility of my own feelings going haywire. I'm not planning to trust them to guide me." She didn't do that even on a good day anymore. Except when she was working.

The paramedic, she trusted implicitly. The woman, not at all.

"I just know that Reese isn't going to let us get even close to a near encounter."

"And what if he does?" Sara asked.

Faye knew the answer to that one. "I'm grabbing Elliott and running for the hills."

She wasn't going down the man road again. Particularly not until her son was man enough to watch out for himself.

HE'D TOLD HER to stay the hell out of his life. So why in the hell was Reese standing around in a too-small conference room, watching his palms sweat, while he waited to meet the kid who should have been his?

No. The one who should have been his had been his, at least for the few weeks his wife had been pregnant. Even if he hadn't known about it.

Faye's child had not been meant to be his. Her defection had told him that. You'd think, after almost ten years, he'd have gotten that one down straight.

He was meeting the kid alone. Whether or not the boy's mother knew about it was none of his concern. Lila McDaniels—managing director of The Lemonade Stand—had set the whole thing up. Reese had called the Stand as soon as he'd recovered from talking to the boy.

Faye had said Elliott had problems and that he spent his days at the Stand. And now here was Reese, through no wish of his own, having agreed to meet with the boy and hear what he had to say.

Someone thought it was best for Elliott.

Reese damn sure knew it wasn't best for him.

Meeting Faye's kid was about the last thing he wanted to do, right down there with having his toenails pulled off one by one without anesthetic.

Maybe one below that.

At the moment, physical pain, in any amount, seemed preferable to—

He turned sharply as the door opened.

Lila, with her gray bun and wearing a gray suit, stood there. She had her hand on the shoulder of a thin, sandy-haired boy with determination on his face.

He looked straight at Reese, almost as if daring him to take him right to jail. The blue in those eyes, so like his mother's, prevented Reese from moving at all.

Faye's son.

The boy that he'd thought would be his own. Already half grown up.

"I'll leave you two, then," Lila said, nodding at Reese as she ushered the boy in and then closed the door.

Reese and Lila had known each other since before Reese had taken the job as Santa Raquel's fire chief. He'd had a meeting with her at the request of the city manager and chief of police. All public services, and most particularly rescue services, were available to provide any help the Stand might need.

While no members of Reese's staff were on the High Risk team that coordinated social services, counselors, doctors and teachers in an effort to prevent domestic violence deaths, Reese was well aware of the team. He reported to them anytime anything suspicious came across his desk.

"Are you here to take me to jail?" The boy tilted his chin up, skinny arms crossed as he stood here in a striped polo shirt and brown baggy shorts. As if to say he didn't care.

The way his lip trembled gave him away but Reese wasn't going to let on to that. At least not yet.

Lila had asked him if he'd talk to the boy. Try to find out anything he could about what he'd burned, where he'd gotten the matches, why he'd set the fire.

So far, the boy was refusing to speak to anyone else.

"I don't carry handcuffs," Reese said now. He was the man here. Elliott was just a scared little kid.

And it sure as hell wasn't the kid's fault his mother had chosen another man. He pulled out a chair. Sat. Motioned for Elliott to do the same.

Without hesitation, the boy did so and tilted his chin up again. Like he was some kind of cool dude who wasn't going to be intimidated.

Reese wasn't sure what to do. Truth was, he had no plan at all. He was there as a favor to Lila. Nothing more.

"Tell me about the fire."

"I already told you."

"Tell me again."

"I did it."

"Where?"

"In the trash can in the boys' bathroom by where we do gym."

"Why that bathroom?" As Reese started focusing on his purpose for being there, the questions came easier. He was an investigator. A damn good one.

Elliott shrugged. His clothes looked new, as did the leather sandal he was tapping rapidly on the commercial tile floor. "It was furthest from anybody."

"So you didn't want anyone to get hurt."

He was there to get the kid to trust him. To talk. Nothing else.

"Uh-uh."

"But you know fire's dangerous."

"'Course I know. My mom's told me about a hundred times that…" He broke off.

"You broke your mother's rules."

Elliott's chin came up again. "Yes."

"Why?"

"'Cause she's not always right. 'Cause she thinks she knows best but she doesn't."

Interesting.

But in terms of the investigation?

"So you think setting a fire in the boys' bathroom trash can was right?"

"Sorta."

"How can something 'sorta' be right?"

"You can't tell anyone."

"I can't promise not to. Not until I hear what you have to say."

Elliott shook his head. "When we talk in there, no one can say what we say."

Reese studied the boy, investigating a possible subject. He had to consider the fact that he knew, from Elliott's mother as well as from Lila, that the boy was in a dangerous place. That the rest of his life could well depend on his time at the Stand.

Counseling sessions were confidential.

"Did your fire have something to do with something that happened during one of your group meetings with Sara?"

He had no idea if the kids knew they were in counseling, but he knew that Sara Havens was overseeing Elliott. Lila had told him that Sara was the one who'd recommended that Reese be allowed to speak alone with the boy. Because Elliott had reached out to him.

Elliott's nod gave Reese a curious kind of confidence. He had this.

In spite of extenuating circumstances that would not be named.

"Sara didn't tell you to start a fire."

He shook his head.

"What did she say?"

Elliott stared at him.

"She told Lila to call me in to speak with you. I'm sure they told you that," Reese said at the boy's continued silence.

Elliott nodded.

"So she expects you to speak to me, which means you can say what you say in there."

The boy's brow furrowed. He puckered his lips. And then said, "Sometimes we write stuff. To get it out."

"What kind of stuff?"

Elliott shrugged. He was patting the side of his leg over and over with the tips of his right fingers. "Bad stuff."

"Okay."

The boy sat there.

"So you wrote about starting a fire."

Elliott's gaze seemed to be seeking something from him as he once again shook his head.

"You wrote bad stuff."

The boy nodded again.

"And?"

"A way to stop it from bugging you is to write it and then throw it away."

Understanding dawned.

"But you didn't throw yours away."

Elliott shook his head.

"Why not?"

He shrugged.

"I'm not asking you what you wrote, Elliott, I'm asking why you didn't just throw it away in the trash can. Why did you start a fire with it?" He was certain he was right about this part.

"Because I didn't think just throwing it away where it still could be read would be good enough."

A thought many mature adults had, as well. Adults who had the means to find access to a fire pit, a fireplace, a burn barrel...

"Where'd you get the matches?"

"I can't tell you."

"Why not?"

"Because I'm not a snitch."

"Did someone steal them for you?"

"No."

"Did someone else give you the idea to burn what you wrote?"

Another shrug. "Can I just go to jail now?"

The boy was not going to give up his source. Reese's job was done here.

Except...

"Why did you call me?"

"So you don't fire my mom."

"Why would I do that?"

"Because she said that I have to be really good and not make her late on work days, that we can't mess up at all, because bosses fire people and then we'd have to move because there aren't any other EMT jobs here except yours."

Reese was still recovering from the sentence, nowhere near finding a response to it, when the boy said, "And because you're the fire chief. Mom always says if I'm ever in trouble to go straight to the principal. Or to Lila. You know, the boss. I'm not supposed to talk to strangers or trust people we don't know, even if they're adults."

Because his father could send someone for him?

Faye had said they weren't in danger. But that didn't mean she didn't have residual trust issues stemming from what she'd been through.

What she'd been through…

He pushed the thought away.

"I wanted you to know it's not her fault," the boy finished. "Can we go now?"

Reese leaned forward, elbows on his knees, saw his hands shaking and clasped them together. He and Faye used to sit in front of each other, face-to-face, that way, clasping hands when they were talking about serious things.

The memory flashed by out of nowhere.

He sat back.

"You aren't going to jail, Elliott," he said. "You're going to stay right here. Your punishment is up to Lila and Sara. And your mom." Then he stood. "But if I ever hear of you so much as having matches again, we'll have to rediscuss this."

The boy was in danger. Thinking he could get away with playing with matches was not cool.

Elliott's blue eyes were wide now as he nodded. "So I'm not going to be in trouble with you?"

"Not this time."

"And my mom? Is she in trouble?"

"Not at all. She didn't do anything wrong."

He nodded, his lips puckering in a new way now. A little-boy way.

Like he might be about to cry.

Reese yanked open the door, relieved to see both Sara and Lila on the other side. With a nod to both of them, he strode out.

Lila could call him to find out what he knew. When she was ready.

In the meantime, he was ready for a tall one.

CHAPTER SIX

I CAN'T BELIEVE Elliott set a fire. I can't believe it. I cannot believe he did that...

Faye paced by the side door on Reese's house, back and forth, back and forth. Waiting for him to get home. If he was even coming home.

She worried about a lot of things where Elliott was concerned—the fact that he harbored such resentment against her sometimes. The possibility that he'd learned to disrespect her from Frank's example.

The chance that he could have some genetic predisposition to anger, as Frank had. The need to know if that was possible.

Where was Reese? He'd left the station. She'd called to find out.

She'd have gone to work to find him two hours ago—when she'd heard from Lila and Sara about what had been going on that day—except that he'd laid down the law. No one was supposed to know they knew each other.

Or rather, had known each other.

The always-serious, always-businesslike, strict guy Reese was now wasn't the man she'd known.

But then, she probably didn't even remotely resemble the girl he'd once known.

One thing about him was the same—besides his apparent appeal where her screwed-up sexual psyche was concerned—he was fair.

She hoped.

Would he let her keep her job?

What had he thought of Elliott? She'd spent so many hours mentally playing out that moment when Elliott and Reese came face-to-face. Would Elliott like him?

Would Reese care at all?

Or would Elliott just be someone else's child, with no attachment value whatsoever?

Had Reese liked him?

When his shiny blue truck pulled into the drive, she welcomed the interruption from thoughts that served no purpose. Stepping away from the house, she waited for him to notice her. She'd purposely left her car parked down the block, not wanting him to see it and turn around before she had her shot at him.

The scowl on his face as he climbed down from his truck didn't bode well.

"I know, you don't want to see me," she said, approaching him with her hand out in front of her like a stop sign. "But I can't talk to you at work, and I was afraid you'd hang up on me if I called and…"

"You're right, I would have." He walked past

her and toward his door. "You can show yourself out," he said, climbing the two cement steps and putting his key in the lock.

She wasn't in. Was he maybe more rattled than he was letting on?

The house had a lovely front porch by the front door. But the side door was by the garage.

She'd known that was the one he'd use.

Some things hadn't changed.

"Reese…"

He was still in uniform…all official looking in dress pants and shirt with his tie over one arm.

"If you want to keep your job, I suggest that you leave now."

He said the words in the most congenial tone. Still, her feelings might have been hurt if not for the first part. *If you want to keep your job.*

He wasn't firing her.

She turned before he could see the tears of sheer relief that flooded her eyes. "Thank you," she said, and pretty much ran back to her car.

HE WAS NOT going to get involved between her and her son. Hadn't asked a single question.

It wasn't his business.

He didn't want to know.

If the kid was punished…if they found out where he got the matches… What had Elliott written that was so bad he'd had to destroy it?

None of it was anything he needed to worry himself about.

And Faye...

She did her job well. Damn well, according to Brandt, who had her riding with him most of the time. Calm and cool in the most hideous circumstances...and compassionate, too.

She'd started an IV on a screaming four-year-old in seconds, finding the vein immediately. Dealt with the mother, whose face had been severely damaged by the crash, and had done CPR on an elderly occupant of the car. Everyone was still alive.

And that had just been one accident.

His second-in-command had told him that if he was ever dying on the side of the road, he'd want Faye to be the one who came to rescue him.

Reese was busy not thinking about her on Friday night, just past ten, when his scanner beeped. There were reports of a fire out of control near a backyard on a cul-de-sac five miles from him. No one was home. There was no sign of anyone near the fire.

His perp was back.

Reese wasn't on call but had consumed only half a beer. He could be at the scene. Pouring the rest down the drain, he grabbed his gear, suited up at home and headed to the site.

The truck was there ahead of him. Brandt. Mark. Riley.

And Faye.

Cyrus had switched with her so he could attend a family event. Reese had seen the change come through on the calendar.

As before, his guys had the fire put out with little effort, but Reese didn't like what he saw. They'd had to use the hose this time.

"He doused a bigger area with gas," Brandt said as Reese approached. The rest of the crew were standing back, watching, knowing better than to contaminate his crime scene with so much as a footprint that wasn't needed.

Their boots were distinct—far different from a size-ten running shoe—but they could still ruin an imprint.

"And he's moved to private property," Reese said.

"Which is bad, considering that we now have to start giving serious consideration to the fact that people are likely to get hurt if this continues..." Brandt's concerned tone echoed what Reese had already been thinking.

"But it's going to make it harder for him to continue without someone seeing something," Reese added.

Police were already canvassing the neighborhood. They'd left the fire scene to Reese. Evidence bag in hand, he took a step closer.

For now, with the scenes so small, he preferred to be alone. They were a small-town fire department. Paid, not volunteer. If they wanted to stay that way, everyone needed to pull extra weight.

And Brandt did more than his share.

Truth be told, Reese liked the fieldwork. He hadn't fully realized just how much of his time would be taken up with administrative duties when he took the job. He didn't mind them most of the time, but they'd hired him for his wildfire, investigative and inspection skills, too. That was the work he loved.

Kneeling near the burning embers, similar to last week's but in a larger pile than the previous week, he noticed what he thought was a small piece of something white. He shined his flashlight. There was nothing but ashes in the center of the clear gas burn that snaked out for several feet. Except that fleck of white. He had to get to it without disturbing the circle.

Camera in hand, he snapped pictures first. Plenty of them.

He took shots of the doused grass and dirt that hadn't burned. He had samples packed up to prove they'd been doused, but he already knew. He'd smelled them while he'd processed them.

Now…to get to that…

"Reese?"

Shit. He almost dropped his camera.

The truck hadn't left yet. Brandt would still be conferring with the police detail and any witnesses. The last thing he'd expected was to hear Faye's voice right behind him.

"What?" His bark was brusque. She should know better than to disturb him at a crime scene.

"I just…"

The tone of her voice was anything but brusque. She looked…scared?

"What is it?" Where the softness suddenly entering his tone had come from he had no idea. He hadn't thought he had it left in him to be soft.

Had rather hoped there was none left.

"I recognized someone…"

"Where?" He was all business now. Taking her shoulder, he turned her so that her back was to the others. "Who?"

"Back there." She pointed to the crowd of neighbors gathered behind the taped-off crime scene.

"He was standing off by himself…you know… like we're trained to watch for…"

Technically, as an EMT she wasn't trained to notice a possible suspect in the back of the crowd watching his work…but he wasn't surprised that Faye would pick up on the jobs going on around her.

And take on whatever responsibility she could.

No. He shook his head. The Faye he thought he'd known hadn't existed. And this wasn't about her, anyway.

"Who was it?"

"A kid from The Lemonade Stand. Kyle Dawson." She sounded scared. "He's older than they usually allow to stay there, and he's in a bungalow with his mother. I think he's being home-schooled there. But I just saw him. I know it was him."

"It's dark, Faye. And…"

"He's taken Elliott under his wing, Reese. My son really looks up to him…"

And Elliott had had matches. He'd started a fire…

"He's a victim," she said, her tone pleading. Prompting another memory flash. Senior year of high school. Captain of the football team had made fun of Faye's dad's beat-up car in the parking lot. Reese had been ready to deck him. Her dad, a janitor, was an honest man. A good guy who worked a lot and who was raising Faye all by himself. Faye had stopped him from taking the kid out. Telling him that the kid's own dad had just skipped town, leaving him and his mother and little sister without support.

He wondered what had happened to Len Browning. Where he'd been when Faye's husband had been abusing her…

Shaking his head, Reese admonished himself for the inappropriate trip down memory lane. A dead-end road.

"I'll put a call in to Lila," he said, pulling his phone out of the holster on his belt.

She nodded. Took a couple of steps back, watching him, as though she wanted to say more.

But as he started to speak into the phone, Faye turned around and left him to it.

CHAPTER SEVEN

FAYE COULDN'T SLEEP. Not even on the couch in Elliott's room. She just couldn't shut down the worries clouding her mind. The fear slicing through her heart.

Was Elliott's Lemonade Stand mentor their serial arsonist?

She'd been so grateful when Kyle had taken Elliott under his wing. Had felt like their luck was finally changing when Elliott had responded so positively to the older kid. She hated the thought of him in trouble.

Dots connected of their own accord.

Elliott had gotten his matches from someone he was protecting. Even Sara Havens couldn't get him to ante up on that one.

Was her son being led astray at the very place where she'd taken him for guidance?

Life seemed to explode out of control right before her eyes. Kyle was a resident at the Stand. His mother needed to be there. Elliott was only there as part of a special counseling and education program for at-risk kids.

But there was another program he could attend.

On the east coast.

Was she going to have to pull up again and move to such an unfamiliar place? Recertification in another state would take time. Where would she work in the meantime?

And that assumed the shelter in New Jersey would even take her son, or that they could work with her on the fee for having him there.

The Lemonade Stand was essentially free to her—she could donate when she was able.

She'd been considering talking to someone about a position on the High Risk team. Fire and Rescue didn't have a representative on the team…

But she was going to have to leave.

She couldn't expose Elliott to any more risk.

He'd set a fire, for God's sake! A fire, of all things. She'd told him over and over about the dangers. He knew that she worked with people who risked their lives every single time a fire got out of control.

Turning over on the slippery leather couch so she could better see her son, watch him while he slept just like she'd done when he was a baby, she feared all of the things that were affecting his life. Feared everything that was out of her control.

Like her father's death. Who'd have thought a man as gentle and giving, as clean-living as Len Browning, would end up being beaten to death a block from his own home for the measly ten dollars he'd had in his wallet?

She and Frank had only been married a year. Elliott was less than six months old. Len had never even seen him. He'd disapproved of Frank, so Frank had banned him from their home.

In those days Faye had been trying to convince herself she loved her husband. Had been trying to be a good wife. Learn how to be a good mother. She'd told herself they had time for hearts to soften, imagined Frank one day welcoming her father into their home. She'd thought then that her dad would see Frank was a good husband. And Frank would see how much she missed her dad. How much she needed him in his life.

Elliott moved. Faye froze. Waited to see if he'd settle back to a restful sleep. Or get up.

He didn't know about the fire she'd been at earlier that night. He'd already been asleep when the call had come in.

He didn't get up. And eventually she fell into a restless on-and-off doze that took her to morning.

KYLE DAWSON DID not set the fire. After Reese called Lila McDaniels, he'd come in to interview the young man. It was after midnight on Friday. The boy and his mother were waiting for him when he arrived at The Lemonade Stand after he finished processing the scene.

"My aunt's husband just left her," the fourteen-year-old said. "Mom had to go to her and I couldn't let her go out alone."

Mandy Dawson nodded. "He was with my sister and I the entire time," she said, one of the saddest looks Reese had ever seen on her face. Like a woman who'd lost all hope. "He's afraid to let me out of his sight."

But Faye had seen the boy outside.

"When the next-door neighbor called, saying there was a fire, Kyle jumped up and ran out to see," Mandy said, looking at her son with moist eyes. "My sister and I were actually excited to see him act like a normal kid again—even for a second."

"I'm a normal kid, Mom..." The boy watched his mom with the concern of a much older man. Then he turned to Reese. "Mom's...my grandfather...and then my dad...she doesn't defend herself."

"I didn't want them to hurt Kyle," the woman said. And Reese knew he was in way over his head.

No, Reese, my ex-husband hurt me, not our son.

What did you do with that?

The beast he was trained to fight raged by certain rules. You just had to assess the weather and the mood of the fire, then apply the right process. There was never a fire that they wouldn't win against. It was just a matter of how long you had to fight and how much damage you could or couldn't prevent in the meantime.

But this...

"And now here we sit," Mandy said, looking at

Reese, her eyes still wet with unshed tears. "Because Kyle ran outside, he's suddenly a suspect? What has he ever done? My son's a great student. He's never been in any kind of trouble. He's a good boy…"

Reese was done here.

"He's not in trouble," he said. But just to be certain, he had to ask, "What size shoe do you wear?"

"Nine, why?"

"No reason."

He looked at the boy, knowing that he could fix at least one small portion of Mandy Dawson's hopelessness. "We're questioning everyone who was outside tonight," he said. "Because you are both residents here, we wanted to make certain you got back safely, first and foremost. We're just looking for anything you might have seen, however innocuous, anything you might have noticed or that caught your attention, for whatever reason. A candy wrapper on the ground. A person standing alone—"

"I know that my father's white truck was nowhere to be seen, and that he wasn't outside with the other people standing around…"

The boy had been looking for signs of his father. He hadn't noticed anything that could help Reese. The fire truck had just been arriving when he'd run outside. He'd noticed plenty while he'd been standing there, just not anything that might point to a perp. Clearly Kyle was interested in the business of fighting fires. If Reese had hired someone to report on the activities of his crew, if he'd been running a secret performance review, he'd have just received a great one.

Reese thanked Kyle and his mother for their time, apologized for having created any unnecessary angst by requesting a meeting with them and left.

He spent the entire drive home resisting the temptation to go back. To ask if he could do anything to help. He spent the next hour at home, telling himself not to call Faye. He was out of his league on this one.

There was nothing he could do.

The urges he was feeling were his own issue—a product of living with bone-deep regret. Of having lost someone close to him because he hadn't been aware enough. Hadn't done enough.

His skills lay in firefighting.

It was best if he just stuck with that.

FAYE WAS OFF all weekend and spent every waking moment with her son. Trying to fill the two days with happy memories, as though they could wipe out years of frightening ones.

He wanted to go to the beach, so they spent both days there. She made picnic lunches. Bought him a boogie board and herself an umbrella with a weighted stand. She bought sunscreen and beach towels—all things they'd had in their old life but she'd left behind.

Elliott was fine with the plans—as long as they didn't include her.

"I'm not sitting with you," he said as she packed up their gear on Saturday morning. He'd come into the kitchen in his new fluorescent green and blue suit with a drab green T-shirt, carrying his new boogie board. She'd picked up the oversize shoulder bag with her blanket, two beach towels and the book she wanted to read.

"Fine."

He didn't usually sit when they went to the beach. He played in the water.

The cooler sat on the counter, filled with ice and food. Another bag held drinks and cups and paper towels. "Could you get the cooler, please?" she asked him, putting her purse on her opposite shoulder. "It will fit on top of your board."

"No."

"Elliott."

"You wanted the dumb picnic, you carry it."

The whole "happy memory" plan in mind, she picked up the cooler.

"Could you at least get the bag?"

"No."

"Elliott!"

"No. I don't want that junk. I shouldn't hafta carry it."

His disrespect couldn't be ignored. Sara had made that point very clear. "We don't have to go."

"Fine."

Dropping his new board on the floor, he stepped on it, and then off, dropping into a chair, his arms on the table. "I didn't want to go to the stupid beach, anyways," he said.

"I thought you did."

"Not with you, I didn't."

Two years' worth of battling his hateful words still hadn't thickened her skin enough to prevent their sting.

"But you want to go."

He shrugged.

"And you'll get hungry and not want to have to come home with me for lunch. You like peanut butter and jelly sandwiches, which is what I packed."

He didn't budge, his expression sour.

"So...you carry the cooler down with your lunch and I won't walk beside you once we get to the beach. Or put your towel down by my blanket."

Muttering something under his breath, Elliott took the cooler from her, put it on his board and stood sullenly by the door, waiting for her to unlock it and set him free.

SUNDAY DIDN'T GO much better. He didn't think he should have to make his bed because Sundays were days of rest.

"Making your bed keeps the sheets clean for when you climb back between them," she told him. Sara had told her to set boundaries, to give him rules and chores—not too many, but enough—and then to stick to them. To build a source of security, and also a sense that she meant what she said. That her word was something upon which he could rely.

But it was Sunday. After spending the day before utterly alone at the beach watching her son in the water, watching him sit on his towel several feel from hers while he ate his sandwiches and walking behind him back to the car, she was tired.

She didn't want to fight with him, and an unmade bed wasn't a big deal.

But keeping her word was.

"Bed made before breakfast," she said. "Come on, Elliott, you know the rules."

"Yeah, like you think beds aren't dirty." The words were soft. Barely reaching her. But their slap took her air.

He'd heard her say words Frank had made her say. She hadn't known then. She did now. *More, Frank. I'm a dirty girl in a dirty bed.*

Turning her back so he wouldn't see the sudden flood of tears, she said, "I'm making pancakes. When your bed is made, you can join me for breakfast. If you choose not to make it, you will not be eating this morning."

He was in the kitchen before the first pancake was off the griddle.

He didn't apologize. An hour later, when she was back in the kitchen and once again packed and ready for a day at the beach, he picked up the bag with the drinks and paper towels and put it on his boogie board. He left the cooler for her to carry.

Faye didn't thank him, didn't say a word. She didn't want to push him to the point where she'd be forced to make them stay home. The idea of spending all day cooped up in their apartment with him was too much to contemplate.

She could force him to go shopping with her but knew that if she did, he'd very likely just make rude comments to and about her the entire time—loud enough for others to hear.

With the blanket bag on one shoulder and her purse on the other, Faye picked up the cooler. She walked a couple feet behind her son when they arrived at the beach. Kept an equal distance when she ate her sandwiches. He ate every bite of his.

She watched him play. He made friends with a couple of brothers that were about his age and laughed so loud in the waves she could hear him from her spot on the beach.

And Sunday night, as she waited for him to climb into bed—he wouldn't let her tuck him in—and turn out the light in his room, he gave her three words that made all of the effort worthwhile.

"Today was fun."

The words sang her to sleep and took her to work on Monday. They were still ringing in her ears when she picked Elliott up from The Lemonade Stand Monday afternoon. Still in uniform, she'd be heading back to the station for the rest of her twelve-hour shift as soon as she dropped him at home with Suzie. She'd be on call all night, as well.

Reese, thank goodness, was off on Mondays. At least she'd been able to relax as she did her chores at the station, worked out and helped prepare the noon meal. There'd been no looking over her shoulder or worrying about being hit with completely inappropriate and unwanted sexual feelings at the unexpected sight of him in the distance.

She'd barely stepped inside the private section of the Stand when Elliott approached, his backpack slung over his shoulder, and said, "Let's go," in a tone that didn't bode well.

Head slightly bent, he didn't look at her. When he brushed against her on his way to the door, he didn't do so gently.

If Lila or Sara had been present, he'd have been reprimanded for that. Faye knew she was expected to say something, as well. And she would.

Sometime before her son went to bed.

But more pressing than her son's long-term counseling was finding out what had upset him.

She had to deal with one before she could have any effect on the other.

He didn't immediately and automatically listen to her, as he did Sara and Lila. That hurt her feelings more than it should.

Reminding herself that Elliott loved her, she pushed the automatic unlock button on her key fob so he could get in the car as soon as he reached it.

If he thought he was going to subject her to another sullen and silent ride home, he had another think coming. She had to go back to work. And she wasn't leaving him this way.

Her son was angry with her for letting his father hurt her. At himself for being angry with her. At the world for giving him a father who was mean instead of loving to his mother.

She looked weak in his eyes for not stopping what was going on behind closed doors. And her weakness was a huge source of his insecurity.

Reminding herself of what they were dealing with—as she'd been counseled repeatedly to do over the past two years—Faye got in the car ready to speak.

"How could you?" Elliott practically spat the words. His blue eyes, once so sweet and trusting when they looked up at her, were more like points of glass.

Laced with bitterness.

Nothing an eight-year-old should be experiencing, let alone shooting toward his mother.

"How could I what?" she asked, banking down the hurt feelings to focus on him.

"You told on Kyle."

"Elliott…"

"You did. I know you did." The boy was looking straight at her, his thin shoulders far too little to bear all of the weight he continued to put upon them.

She'd spoken with Lila briefly that morning to find out what the situation would be with the older boy. She'd wanted to prepare Elliott for the other boy's absence if nothing else.

Lila had assured her that everything was fine. She claimed Kyle had had nothing to do with the fire and that he and his mother were still at the Stand.

"I don't…" She couldn't lie to him. She knew what he was talking about. She just didn't know how much he knew.

"Can you calm down enough to tell me about it? And then I'll tell you what I did or did not do."

"There was a fire Friday night by his aunt's house. He and his mom had a safe trip to visit her for something…"

Safe trip. It was one of the terms they sometimes used with kids to describe trips away from protective custody during at-risk domestic violence times. A term most kids never heard. The fact that it had become a normal part of her eight-year-old son's vocabulary hurt her heart.

"He went out to look and then when they got back to the Stand, he had to go talk to Chief Bristow in a little room with his mom there."

"Maybe that was just to see if he knew anything."

Elliott shook his head. "You told, Mom. Kyle never saw anyone he knew so no one else could have told on him. It had to be you."

She took a deep breath. "You said Kyle is in trouble," she said. "What kind of trouble is he in?"

The little boy's shrug was telling—most particularly to a mother who used to be able to read him like a book.

"He's not in trouble, is he?" she pressed.

Elliott shrugged again and folded his arms against his chest as he stared out the front windshield.

"You're a snitch." The boy's tone had softened considerably. His chin rested against his chest. "You snitched on my friend."

"I told Chief Bristow that I recognized Kyle," she said. She'd promised him the truth and she was not in a position to go backward on the climb to rebuild his trust. "But I did so for his sake as much as anything else," she said. "I was concerned about him being out on the street where his father could have had access to him." She didn't figure then was the time to tell her son that officials believed the fire was part of a serial arsonist's work.

Elliott looked at her.

She started the car and drove home, feeling his stare the whole way.

When she pulled into their apartment's drive, he didn't immediately reach to undo his seat belt.

"Look, Elliott. I'm not perfect by any means. But I did the right thing Friday night. And I would do it again." They'd told her to be firm. To be consistent. To set boundaries.

He sat still, staring out the front window.

And she forgot counseling for a second. "You hate it that I didn't tell on Dad for what he was doing."

"So?"

"So, I wasn't a snitch then. And it was wrong."

His gaze swung toward her and she continued.

"Sometimes you have to tell," she went on. "And if there's a possibility that someone could get hurt, you have to tell every time. That's something I know now."

She'd known it then, too. She just hadn't realized that the price of staying had been far greater than the one they'd paid for leaving.

She hadn't known that Elliott had been affected by, or even known about, Frank's abuse. She'd been trying to give her son a secure home, with nice things, all the bills paid, a loyal father who came home every night. She'd hoped that as Elliott grew out of boyhood into pre-manhood that

Frank would take over—or at least take an interest in the child he'd fathered.

She'd thought a lot of erroneous things back then.

"Did you tell Kyle I told on him?" she asked now, wondering what kind of position her son had put himself in. Wondering if the bond with the older boy would pit them both against her.

"No. 'Course not," Elliott said. He opened the door and got out.

He didn't speak to her again as she settled him upstairs in their apartment with Suzie. Not even when she told him good-night and that she loved him.

But she heard Suzie's voice behind her.

"That's your mother. A good man responds when his mother speaks to him. And little boys who need their mother's love are allowed to accept it. No matter what."

She was smiling as she skipped down the stairs.

She might feel sometimes like she was facing her battles all alone.

But she wasn't.

She should remember that.

CHAPTER EIGHT

THERE'D BEEN A house fire over the weekend. Reese completed his inspection report on Tuesday. Faulty wiring. No gasoline on the premises.

While he hated to see anyone go through the trauma of losing irreplaceable belongings, he'd been relieved to know that arson wasn't involved.

On Tuesday, he got the report back from LA regarding Friday night's fire. He'd been planning to process the evidence himself, but with the weekend fire he'd been unable to do so. The fleck of shiny white he'd pulled out of the small pile of burned ash turned out to be paint that had flaked off from something.

What kind, he didn't yet know.

But it was something else to add to size-ten tennis shoes. Something else that taunted him, dangling just out of reach when he had trouble sleeping at night.

Still, thoughts of the arsonist were preferable to thinking about Faye Walker. Or her son.

On Wednesday, he ran into her in the station's kitchen. He'd been leaving with a cup of coffee in hand. Dressed in black Lycra shorts, a black tank bra and a white muscle shirt over top, she'd clearly just come from the fitness room. Her hair was pulled back, her skin was flushed, her forehead covered with beads of sweat.

He was swamped with memories. Specifically, a vision of her after making crazy love with him on a pool table in a frat house. She'd been visiting him for the weekend. They'd found the house empty after a bike ride along the coast. She'd been dressed pretty much the same—she'd hoisted herself onto the table, scooted back and dared him.

In less than ten seconds, he'd pulled her shorts down to her ankles and had brought her to almost instant satisfaction.

Had he been nuts? Had she been?

"Did you find out where your son got the matches?" He blurted the words to cover up the rest of what was going on in his mind.

He didn't want to know any more about the boy. Didn't even want to think of him.

Pictures of what might have been, of Faye and her son at home, in the kitchen, watching a movie, on the sand at the beach—would only make life messy. And hard.

She'd been backing up, as though to turn tail and run. But stopped and looked at him.

He didn't get her expression. Had never seen the doubt and uncertainty mixed in with her usual strength.

"No," she said. That was all. Nothing else.

She turned to go. He wanted to call her back. To say what? To what end?

They were strangers. Had nothing to discuss. House rule.

Because this was his house.

FAYE WAS STILL shaking inside from her encounter with Reese when she lay in bed that night. On call for another eight hours, she didn't dare take so much as an aspirin to help her sleep. What she needed to do was relax.

Not think about how close she'd been to throwing her arms around Reese when they'd had their near collision that morning.

He'd asked about Elliott and her heart had started beating such a fierce tattoo she'd thought she might have to sit down.

Did he think about them? Did he care maybe even a tiny bit about her and her son?

She couldn't want him to. Didn't dare want him to.

And yet…

No. It was only latent feelings from her pre-abused days. Going back to muscle memory from when she was emotionally undamaged.

Sara had warned her. She was vulnerable.

She had to stay aware. Keep control of her feelings through strong mental determination. Not let herself be convinced by a psyche that yearned for easier, happier times.

She would not let that happen. She'd die first.

Her son had barely spoken to her when she'd called him at bedtime, as she did every night she was at the station before he went to sleep. He'd said enough to keep Suzie from calling him out, but that was it. He was withdrawing from her. She could feel it and she was panicking.

Eyes closed, she concentrated on a series of mental relaxation techniques she'd learned over the years. Not just because of Frank, but because she worked a high-adrenaline, high-drama job. Finding and maintaining her center was paramount to being successful in her career.

"Let me out!"

Faye was out of bed before her eyes had completely sprung open, through her open door and across the hallway to her son's room.

Elliott stood at the barred window, clawing at the curtains. "Let me out!" he screamed again.

It took everything she had not to wake him. To bring him back from whatever hell he'd sunk into. To hold his arms to his sides until the panic within him calmed.

Standing back, watching for any sign that he could hurt himself, she prayed for his angst to end, for peace to settle over his young soul and lead him gently back to bed.

"Let. Me. Out!" The growl was not a sound Faye recognized. It was as though the body standing there did not belong to her son. He grabbed the curtains, pulling at them as hard as he could. Yanking as though to pull the rod off the wall. "Let. Me. Out!"

She couldn't just stand there. Crossing the room, she took hold of the curtain, just above Elliott's desperate clutch. She withstood his jerks, a countermeasure to the damage he could do. Her arms ached but she didn't know what else to do.

She hoped that he was going to grow out of the nightmares—brought on, his counselors agreed, by the fact that Frank had abused her at night. The sound had woken their son, who'd lain alone in his bed and listened to every vile word as Frank described what he was doing to her. And told her over and over that she liked it.

After another couple of yanks—during which she was thankful for the fitness training her job required—Elliott let go of the curtain. As though he'd merely been up to go to the bathroom, he moved sleepily back to his bed. Lay down. And continued to sleep.

Gently pulling the covers from beneath him, Faye arranged them around his small body, smiling at the car pajamas he'd chosen. She'd been afraid, when she'd bought them, that he'd think they were too childish for him. Instead, they were his go-to choice.

Her little boy was still in there.

They just had to find a way to set him free.

A BAD ACCIDENT occurred on the freeway just above the Santa Raquel exit in the very early hours of Thursday morning. Reese heard about it from Brandt, who called him just past six—Reese was already out of the shower, in the middle of shaving.

"Three cars, all guys, mostly college aged," he said. "Looked like maybe they were drag racing. Alcohol was clearly a factor…"

Santa Raquel Police Department's issue, not his, thankfully.

"Any fatalities?"

"Two. And one injured, non–life threatening. That's actually why I'm calling…"

He'd wondered. Every crash was newsworthy—a fatality more so. But it would wait until he got into work. He and Brandt were pretty good about respecting time off. Everyone had to have downtime. Time to regroup.

"Faye was on call…"

His heart sank. If she'd screwed up, been unable to get there, he'd have no choice but to take measures.

"The fatalities were pretty clear and she went straight for the injured…"

She'd made it to the scene.

No reason for him to feel relief to know that one of his employees had made it to work.

"The guy was clearly under the influence and scared out of his wits. We got him out of the car and on a stretcher, but he went for Faye when she was starting an IV in the back of the bus…"

In his bathroom, with shaving cream on his face, Reese stopped cold. Stood there looking at the man in the mirror, not recognizing the fear in his eyes.

"You're telling me Faye was hurt?" And it hadn't been the first words out of Brandt's mouth?

"No, boss, of course not. You'd have been called at the scene…"

Of course he would have. It was protocol in the event of an employee injured on the job. He nodded to the guy in the mirror.

"She handled it like the pro she is. But he swung at her a couple of times. Connected once just below her left eye, but she said not with much force. I just thought you'd want a sit-down, especially with her being new and all…"

Any time a member of his team dealt with something tougher than usual, he called for one-on-one meetings. Firefighters were trained to be tough. He wasn't going to send his people off to the shrink every time they had a hard day. But he did insist on his own personal assessment, just in case someone needed to seek help.

"Is she still at the station?" he asked.

Of all people to be with a violent victim, it had to be Faye? A woman who'd survived years of partner abuse and come out on the other side? Taking charge of her life. Moving on. Helping people. Raising a little guy all on her own? An at-risk little guy...

"Yeah, she's here," Brandt said.

He swallowed.

"Have her set up a meeting with me for later today before she leaves."

It's what he'd do with any of his crew.

Just not something that normally consumed his thoughts until it happened.

PRETTY MUCH THE last thing Faye wanted to do on Thursday was have a private meeting with her boss.

Hard to imagine that Reese would want to meet with her alone.

Surely he wasn't going to fire her for having an altercation with a victim? The man had been flailing—fighting off her attempts to save his life. She'd had no choice but to forcibly restrain him.

But all the way back to the station that afternoon after seeing to Elliott, she played the scene over in her mind. Had she been too tired? She'd barely fallen back to sleep after Elliott's nightmare when the call had come in.

Adrenaline had kicked in as it always did when she was on the job. She'd followed protocol.

Reese's truck was in his parking spot as she pulled in. She took a last glance in the rearview mirror, checking to see that her makeup completely covered the bruise forming under her left eye. She'd had a couple of hours' sleep before taking Elliott to the Stand that morning.

Not sure what to wear for the inquisition, she'd gone in to change when she dropped off Elliott, opting for black pants and a white, somewhat dressy button-down top, made of silk and tight at the waist with a flare to the hip. She hoped it spoke of strength. And success. More than that, she liked how she looked in it. At the moment, how she felt mattered most.

Because she was off shift as soon as she finished her meeting with Reese, she'd left her hair down and ran her hand through it now, throwing it back over her shoulder as she approached his door.

She still had a job. If, in an hour, she didn't, she'd deal with that then.

Heart thumping, she raised her hand to knock. On Reese's door.

Her Reese's door.

Hand suspended, she stopped.

How cruel could fate be to bring them to this moment?

She reminded herself that she was vulnerable. That her psyche, in its effort to heal, would catapult her back and make her think something was real when it was just a figment of her imagination.

Shaking her head, she knocked.

CHAPTER NINE

WHEN SHE FIRST walked into his office, Reese hardly recognized Faye. He couldn't remember a single time he'd seen her in dress pants. She'd worn jeans. Shorts. And dresses. Right?

Or was time being merciful and allowing him to forget something?

"You wanted to see me?"

Her hair was down. In the weeks she'd been back, he'd only ever seen it in a ponytail.

There was a definite darkening under her left eye—in spite of her attempt to hide it with heavier makeup.

Like she'd hidden years of her husband's abuse?

He'd been reading up on domestic violence over the past few days, prompted by his meeting with Kyle and Mandy Dawson. And, dammit, Faye.

"Yes," he said, standing and motioning to a chair in front of his desk. "Please have a seat."

They both sat.

Keep it official. Do your job. Live your life. Let her live hers.

"Listen, Reese, I don't know what you heard, but I followed protocol all the way…"

He hoped he didn't show that she'd put him off his mark. The last thing he'd expected was for her to come in on the defensive.

He'd been trying to figure out how to nurture her without actually doing so. To check up on her without appearing to care.

"You think you're here for a reprimand?" he asked, hearing the surprise in his voice in spite of his best attempt to suppress it.

"Aren't I?"

He shook his head. Looked for words. Didn't find any he liked.

"Then why am I here?"

"It's customary," he said, sitting back in his chair as she sat forward. "Any time a member of the team has a call that is more challenging than usual, that member has a sit-down with the chief."

He heard himself. Wondered if he'd ever sounded as pompous with any of the other members of his crew.

"With me," he corrected. "I just wanted to make sure you're okay."

"You did?" She didn't smile. But her expression relaxed.

And she looked…stunningly beautiful.

No!

She looked…rigidly…out of place.

"Well." She stood. "I'm fine. And if that's all, I'd like to get a few errands done before it's time to fix Elliott's dinner."

What the hell? He was in charge here. He was the one who would call an end to the meeting.

"That's not all," he said and looked at her chair. He was acting like an ass. And was not all that fond of himself at the moment.

She sat.

He felt better.

And like even more of an ass.

"The whole idea of the meeting is for me to chat with you. For me to get a sense of how you're doing. Not for you to tell me you're fine. If all I'd needed was to hear that, I could have called. Or sent an email. Or text." He was trying to treat her like any other employee, but was pretty certain he failed. The damned history between them...

He had her number programmed into his phone, because he had all of his employees' numbers programmed in. They worked on schedule, but they were still emergency personnel. If he needed someone on his staff to handle a particularly difficult job, he needed to be able to reach them immediately.

"I get that you'd need to do that with other employees," she said, "but you know me. I'm looking you in the eye and telling you I'm fine. You should know that it's true."

She might have him there.

But...

"You look tired."

"I was called out in the middle of the night."

"The first day we met in this office was after a middle of the night call. You didn't look tired then."

When she glanced down at her lap, he knew he was doing more than being an ass. He was actually doing his job. Noticing something about an employee that was slightly off.

The realization was not only a relief, it instilled his normal confidence. Something that only one person had ever been able to strip away from him: the woman sitting in front of him.

"So?" he asked, not being the least bit generous by giving her any space. He looked straight at her. Pinned her with his forthrightness.

As he'd do with any other employee he thought was holding out on him.

"So what?"

"The darkening under your eyes. Like you're not getting enough sleep…" he said. Except he'd meant to ask her about what had happened out on the road early that morning. He'd found that getting people to talk about the tough day usually relieved the immediate pressure of it, let his team member get it out and deal with it. Or it could show him where the issue might be.

"I didn't get much sleep last night. Before the call."

Was she dating someone already? Had he been in her bed when she'd been called into work?

Immediately recognizing the inappropriate

waywardness of his thought, he reined himself in. Severely.

"Any particular reason?" More on track. He allowed himself that one.

"Elliott had a nightmare."

Something about the way she said that, the way her hand clutched the wooden arm of the chair, the way her chin tightened, had his gut tightening up, too.

"A nightmare?"

"Yeah."

"What…did he climb into bed with you? Wake you up?" It was what kids did, right?

She shook her head. Looked him in the eye. And seemed to come to some kind of decision.

"I told you my son was at risk," she said.

He nodded.

"Part of the reason we know that is because he sleepwalks."

Reese had sleepwalked as a kid, or so he'd been told. It had passed. "A lot of kids do," he offered, congratulating himself for staying on the "just like with every other employee" track.

"Elliott does it a lot. Sometime it's not that alarming. He'll get himself something to eat. Or go to the bathroom. The nightmares are induced by a feeling of insecurity. Sometimes to take care of that, all he needs is to meet a perceived physiological need…"

Oh yeah. He was in over his head now.

So much so, Reese wanted to end the interview. Recommend counseling. Before he screwed something up.

He didn't ever get too close. He'd learned.

"Sometimes…but not last night?" He looked at the woman across from him and couldn't bring himself to dismiss her.

She shook her head.

"Sometimes his only goal is to get out."

"Get out?"

She nodded.

He tried to imagine what that meant.

"It's his way of trying to escape what he can't handle. A trauma he can't deal with. A sense of inadequacy or insecurity."

He heard her words. And heard something else, too. "He's trying to escape the fact that he heard his father hurting his mother and couldn't do anything to stop your pain," he guessed. He'd been doing some reading.

"And escape the fact that I didn't do anything to stop it, either."

Her words were a shock to him. Apparently he hadn't done enough reading.

"You?" he asked. "You were the victim."

Of course, but a kid might not be able to make that distinction…

He had no idea how old her son had been when he'd first heard his father hurting his mother.

Didn't want to know, either.

TMI was not his way. Especially not with her. He had a very clear view of his own limitations.

She seemed to agree, as she didn't respond.

"So...last night...was it simple physiological function, or a need to get out?"

He already knew the answer. Her entire demeanor was like a billboard, telling Reese, a man who'd known her well, more than a boss needed to know.

She'd had a rough night before the call because her son had been in pain.

They were both already under professional care for the issue.

Even with a bad night, she'd done her job well. Impeccably well. And other than the bags under her eyes, she was perfectly contained and looking him in the eye. As her boss, that should be all that concerned him.

"What does he do when he's trying to 'get out'?" He swore silently even as he asked the question.

Chin up, she looked right at him, reminding him for a second of her son. "Last night he was trying to pull the curtains off the rod. After first attempting to break through the bars on the windows."

It was almost like she was trying to shock him.

It was working.

"You have to put bars on your windows?"

"They came that way. If they hadn't, I'd have had to live on the ground floor."

"He doesn't ever try anything as simple as going out the front door?"

"Before we moved in, I had a dead bolt installed that is keyed from the inside as well as the outside," she said. And then added, "But oddly enough, no, he's never tried to go out the front door."

"He's a little kid," Reese said. And then wondered if he'd sounded insulting. "He can't be more than seventy pounds," he added.

"You wouldn't know it when he's sleepwalking. It took all my strength to keep hold of the curtain so he didn't pull the rod down and hurt himself."

He had a feeling it hadn't been the first time. She'd imparted the news so nonchalantly.

He wanted to do something.

To change her circumstances.

To make a difference.

He was her boss.

It wasn't his place.

He didn't want to take that place.

Ever. Again.

So…he stood. Nodded. Reminded himself that she was getting professional help. That she didn't need him. Told her that if she ever needed anything, to give him a call. Said that even though the bruise looked small and low enough, he thought she should get the eye checked, just in case.

He told her she'd done a great job the night before and that he was very pleased with her work at the station. He even went so far as to tell her he was glad that she'd come to work for them.

And then he ushered her out.

Just as he'd have done with any other employee.

Though he didn't normally feel half sick for the rest of the day with any other employee. Normally, he went on with his next task and didn't look back.

Reese looked back all evening long, feeling queasy.

That night, as he lay in bed, he wanted to call her. Just to make sure she was getting a good night's rest.

The ludicrousness of the thought occurred to him almost immediately.

He wondered about taking a nice long vacation.

CHAPTER TEN

OF COURSE FAYE had the dream again on Thursday night. It was never exactly the same. That would be too easy—easier to get used to, easier to ignore.

Instead, Reese would appear in different ways. At different times. In the dream on Thursday night, she'd been at the beach alone. She was happy, though. Anticipating something just around the corner, an event coming up or someone walking up the beach. She didn't know. It was dark, the sand lit by moonlight, but there was no sense of danger. Fear didn't exist. A gentle breeze blew and the colorful sundress she was wearing swirled against her calves. Almost like she was dancing with the waves.

And out of the water came Reese. Dripping wet and completely naked. She stood there, watching him. Knowing.

Just knowing.

And then she'd woken up—crying again.

And not knowing a damned thing.

The dream wasn't why she met with Sara on Friday morning. She was there for her weekly meeting about Elliott, sitting with Sara on the couch in the counselor's small office.

Sara and Lila had full say where Elliott was concerned during the hours he was at the Stand. She'd signed paperwork accordingly. They could act on his behalf, make decisions on his behalf regarding his physical and emotional care. When something big happened, like the fire her son had set in the trash can, she was informed right away.

Everything else waited for these weekly sessions, which were usually on Friday mornings after she dropped Elliott off.

She'd worn one of her favorite summer dresses for the meeting. Calf length, tie-dyed cotton. Maybe because of how she'd felt in her dream, being a young woman on the beach knowing no fear.

Sara, in white linen capri pants and a black-and-white, short-sleeved blouse, brought her usual calm to the room.

In her quiet tone, she told Faye about Elliott's schoolwork. He'd done everything he'd been asked to do, read an extra book and was getting good grades.

"His attitude with his teacher and with the rest of the staff here has been impeccable, if you don't count the fact that he refuses to engage in any kind of casual or personal conversation," Sara added. "He's eating well, though he has his definite dislikes."

"He told me you had hot dogs one day this week."

"They had a picnic in the trees beyond the Garden of Renewal," Sara said. "There were hamburgers, too, so he had plenty to eat…"

Faye didn't doubt that for a second. Elliott was a healthy eater.

Thinking about it made her feel good. Like she was getting something right.

Or maybe it was the fact that thinking about something good took her mind away from all that was wrong.

"He's not interacting as well as I'd like with the other kids," Sara said, her expression not changing. They dealt with facts in this office in a manner that made them seem less threatening. At least, that was Faye's take on the sessions.

"Except for Kyle."

Sara shook her head. "Even with Kyle, this week. He seems to have pulled back from all of his associations."

"I'm assuming, since you're mentioning this, you asked him about it?"

Sara nodded. "I did. He said that he didn't want to get anyone else in trouble."

"Because I told Reese I'd seen Kyle?"

Faye had told Sara she was working for a man she used to date because of the dreams she'd been having. Sara shrugged now. "It could be because you recognized Kyle. But I'm not sure that's all it is. He seems to be separating himself purposefully. He waits for everyone to sit at lunch and then finds a place a few feet away. It's the same in the classroom. In the gym, he won't play contact sports."

"But I thought he was loving basketball. Kyle was playing with him…"

"Something about that fire he set in the bathroom trash can changed things."

Her stomach cramped. Like someone was twisting his fist in it.

"Do you know what he wrote that he had to burn?"

Sara might not tell her what it was—Elliott had been told that he could tell the counselor things that would not be repeated to his mother—but Sara would tell her whether she knew.

"Not really. I've been able to make some educated guesses."

"He doesn't want me to know."

The woman's shoulder-length blond hair fell lightly against her blouse as she shook her head.

"So what do you think is going on?"

Sara had something to tell her. Faye knew her well enough to see that. She was just helping Faye catch up so that when it came, she'd have a better chance of dealing with it.

Two years in counseling taught a woman a thing or two about the process.

"Just another educated guess at this point, but I think Elliott's fears are turning inward."

"Meaning?"

"Maybe setting the fire scared him. About himself. It was such an in-your-face defiance of not only your rules but of the career you care about."

"So why did he do it?"

Sara shrugged. "The obvious. He wanted to destroy what he'd written—but why choose that means? I honestly don't know."

Faye heard the unspoken *yet* in the counselor's tone. Or at least hoped she did.

She told Sara about Wednesday night's sleepwalking. About her son's seemingly growing anger with her.

"I thought, when we talked about snitching on Monday on the way home, that he got it. That he understood why I told Reese I'd recognized Kyle at the scene. But he's been treating me more like an irritating stranger than a mom all week."

After a not-so-great weekend that had had nothing to do with her tattling on his friend.

But now her son was distancing himself from Kyle, too? They were going through all of this—the move to Santa Raquel, his time at The Lemonade Stand—so he could get better. Not worse.

Sara studied her in a way that made Faye want to be patient and wait. She didn't just like the woman—she trusted her. Implicitly.

Sara didn't talk about her personal life but Faye had heard that she was married to a bounty hunter who'd had a young daughter that Sara adopted. And that they had a year-old son together.

"I have a theory," Sara finally said. She sat up, both feet flat on the floor and faced Faye. "It's only a theory."

"I understand."

"I'd like to hear what you think about it."

Faye nodded, resisting the urge to twirl a piece of her long, dark ponytail around her finger like she used to do in school.

"I think it's quite possible that Elliott is starting to look at cause and effect as a means of trying to control a world that seems to be spinning out of control around him. Some of this is quite probably because of the move. A new home, new counselors, new schooling situation, new babysitter, you having a new job..."

"But..."

Sara put up a hand. Faye reminded herself to be patient.

"You were counseled to make this move. Everyone involved, myself included, told you Elliott's best shot was to be in a program like this one. I still believe that. But we also talked about the fact that there might be escalated acting-out at first, until he adapts and takes ownership of his new world."

Faye took a deep breath and nodded, letting Sara's peace creep into her again.

"You're here because Elliott is in behavioral

danger. We all knew that going in. And that's what we're dealing with here. I'm not sure this is anything new, just a continued manifestation of what was already there."

Feeling stiff, Faye said, "So the move gave him a sense of being out of control, but the way he's trying to gain control is by taking on the issues inside himself?"

"Basically. But keep in mind, his attempt to take control or deal with his issues—that's not something an eight-year-old mind is going to grasp. His choices are reactionary."

"You think maybe he doesn't even know why he set that fire?"

Sara's words scared her to death. How could they ever hope to fix this if her son's conscious actions were as unconscious as his sleepwalking ones?

"Just like someone suffering from grief goes through various stages, skipping some, getting stuck in others, Elliott is facing various ways of dealing with his past."

They were talking about her son. An eight-year-old boy, with a past he had to deal with. The facts cut her to the quick.

This was a part of her own process, she knew, but that knowledge didn't seem to help. Crying didn't help, either. So she just continued to listen.

"He knows why he set the fire. And I think

he knows why he's suddenly isolating himself. I just don't think he's doing anything as an effort to help himself through his issues. He's reacting *to* the issues."

Okay. She understood that. Felt like she had something to land on for the moment.

"I believe it's possible that Elliott is explaining his behaviors to himself, or maybe he's fearing, that they're the result of him being his father's son."

"He's afraid he's like Frank?"

She'd had the thought a time or two. Not maybe in the way that Elliott did, but...

"I've wondered if he treats me like he does because of hearing his father be so disrespectful to me."

Feared more than wondered. Had spoken to Sara and other counselors about it before, too.

"My suspicion is that Elliott has somehow become focused on a fear that he can't help but be like his father because he was made by him."

"Made by him?"

"A statement that he made to me. He'd been speaking in reference to something else, but all things seem to be leading back to that statement."

"As in, because he's biologically the son of Frank Walker, he will be like him even if he doesn't want to be?"

Sara's nod broke her heart. "And in order to protect others from him doing to them what his father did to you, he will distance himself from them."

"Tell me this is just a stage because he's so young…"

Sara's expression was serious. "Worst-case scenario, if he's not helped, he could become a recluse who develops dark thoughts that eventually consume more of his thinking than rational thoughts do."

It wasn't the first time she'd heard a potentially dire prediction where Elliott's future was concerned.

Faye said, "But he's getting help and there's every chance he'll grow up to be a perfectly healthy, happy husband and father."

Sara's caring smile was like sunshine in that room.

"That's our plan, Faye. You asked for the straight truth and I'm giving it to you."

She nodded. "I know." After living with Frank's lies for so many years, after ruining her life by believing them and acting upon them, she wanted the truth at all costs. And the reason she could trust Sara even more implicitly than she trusted herself was because the other woman had agreed to give her the stark truth. Every time.

But she had to ask, "Do you still think our chances are better than average that we'll get there?"

"I do."

Okay. She could do this then. She would do this. "Tell me what to do."

"First, tell me what you think about what I said. Do you notice anything about Elliott that would either support or disprove my theory?"

Psychology, after all, was not as exact a science as they'd all like it to be.

"I think, since I was already suspecting some of the same, you're probably right. I know it sure makes me feel better about him ignoring me this week if he's doing it out of some sense that he's protecting me. Though, at the same time, it breaks my heart that my eight-year-old son feels as though he has to protect anyone against himself."

"I'm not sure it's completely conscious at this point," Sara said. "I'm sensing that he doesn't want to be around others because he doesn't feel good about himself. I don't know that he's connected the other dots yet."

Head hurting, Faye tried to fight the thought that was assaulting her. She wasn't ready to deal with it yet. The third step of her plan. So far, things had fallen into place. But they had to have time for Elliott to get well before the next phase came to be.

Once the third step was complete, she'd have to leave. Clearly there was no way she could do that yet.

But, in her plan, the third step had only been periphery. Something that would have to wait until

Elliott was well. Until he could be exposed to something new without risk to his mental health.

The third step was something Faye had to do because it was the right thing to do.

But what if...

He could become a recluse who develops dark thoughts that eventually consume more of his thinking than rational thoughts do...

"Faye?" Sara's concerned tone pulled her back to the comforting room. To the fact that she wasn't handling the situation alone.

She had help.

Professional help.

"You've grown white. You're shaking. What's going on?"

She was scared to death. Not surprising the counselor had noticed.

"I'm trying to figure out whether or not I should tell you something."

"I'd think, at this point, the answer to that one should be obvious. I thought we'd already agreed that if we're going to help your son, you need to be completely up-front with me."

They had. Of course. Faye nodded but still didn't speak. Her son was not going to get well if they had to pick up and move again. Or if she did, without him.

By Sara's own admission, the most recent move was costing him.

"Step three was never about getting Elliott

well." She said the words aloud. Because they were all she had. She didn't know what to do. Was in over her head.

"Step three?"

Faye took a deep breath.

And plunged into a world that was going to take more trust than she had to give.

CHAPTER ELEVEN

WHY REESE PULLED into the cemetery Friday morning on his way back from a meeting with the mayor, he had no clear idea. He saw the turn coming up and it hit him that he should go in.

So he did.

He wasn't from Santa Raquel. The only person he knew who was buried there was Tabitha. She'd gone to high school in Santa Raquel.

He'd met her at college, but she'd always called Santa Raquel home. Burying her there had seemed like the thing she'd want. Applying for the job of Santa Raquel fire chief after her death had seemed like a way to honor her.

Too bad he hadn't spent as much time showing her that he cared while she was still alive.

It had been a while since he'd visited her grave. The flowers he paid to have on the site looked good. They were geraniums this time. He couldn't remember what had been there last time he'd been by. Something white, he thought.

He walked around the stone of the single grave. There was no married couple marker there with his name and birth next to hers with a dash waiting for his death date.

No plot purchased for him next to hers.

Which said pretty much what she'd said when she'd been alive. He wasn't "all in" when it came to their union.

He'd been faithful, though. From the moment he'd asked her to be exclusive with him.

The grass was cut. There were no weeds to pull.

He should go.

But he stood there thinking about a barely developing fetus. There'd been nothing to bury. Just a lab test to tell him the newly fertilized egg had been a boy.

His son.

Would he have made a good father? He'd thought so at one time. Not anymore. Nothing had turned out as he'd once thought it would. Including himself.

Not even his job. He was more dedicated to it, more drawn to it, than he ever thought he'd be. But he didn't love the work as much as he thought he would. He needed it. Was driven to do it.

It just didn't fill his house with happiness.

Neither had coming home to Tabitha.

He turned his back on the stone. Meant to walk away.

But he turned back.

"I'm sorry," he said.

The apology didn't do as much good as maybe

he'd thought it should have. It didn't do any good at all.

He still felt like shit.

"She's back," he said then. "I didn't know she was coming. I didn't ask her. I never would have hired her if I'd known. But she's back."

If there was a heaven, Tabitha would have made it in. And if angels looked down from their perch, she already knew what he was telling her.

She deserved to hear it from him.

He'd been her husband.

She'd been his second choice.

"I HAD MORE than one reason for coming to Santa Raquel." Still in Sara's office, Faye spoke slowly, choosing her words carefully, still not sure she wanted to expose the one secret she'd told no one. Ever.

She wasn't ready.

That was a given.

But if it would help get Elliott out of the personal hell she'd helped put him in...

"Or, for choosing The Lemonade Stand over the shelter in New Jersey," she corrected herself.

"It was best that you keep Elliott in California, in the warmer beach environment he's grown up in," Sara said, nodding.

She was probably trying to make this easier. Clearly she could tell that Faye was struggling.

But there was nothing Sara was going to do or say to make this any easier.

What if the whole thing blew up in her face? What if, ultimately, it hurt Elliott more than it helped? There was a very real chance that it could.

"Faye?" Sara didn't seem to be in any hurry. But she was clearly concerned.

Faye wasn't alone. She didn't have to shoulder her burdens alone. The idea, even after two years, still seemed brand-new.

"I'm going to tell you something, but that in no way gives the go-ahead for any action to be taken on it. Period." She was dead serious here. She knew her rights in terms of counseling confidentiality.

Sara nodded.

"I mean it. This goes nowhere besides you and me until I determine differently."

"Hey." Sara leaned forward, met Faye's gaze, took her hand. And held on. "This is me, Faye. You're safe here. You know that."

She was being counseled. Fine.

"Reese Bristow was not just someone I dated in college," she said. There was no question now where to start. The words were all there. "He was the love of my life."

Sara didn't seem shocked. But then she was trained to listen without judgment.

"We met in high school. In a suburb of San

Diego. Dated for two years and then through the first two years of college."

She could picture those days, but she wouldn't let herself travel back there. It hurt too much.

"I'd probably have jumped off a cliff for that man if he'd told me it was safe…"

She'd been so naive. So trusting. Had had no idea that people in real life used other people for their own cruel purposes. Not good, seemingly normal people.

Sara smiled but didn't interrupt. The compassion shining from the counselor's eyes encouraged her to continue.

"I had a scholarship to UCLA," she continued, filling in what seemed to be a necessary detail. "For nursing. And with the UCLA medical center right there, that was a big deal. There was only one school in the state that offered a bachelor's degree in fire science, which was Reese's choice, and that was Cal State. The campuses are only about fifteen miles apart so it didn't seem like a big deal that we'd be attending different schools."

For a second, she felt like her story would surely bore a woman who had much more important things to handle.

But for Elliott…

"About a week before UCLA's homecoming, he told me that he couldn't make it to a party that Friday night. He said he'd had some late drills that day or something." She knew exactly what he'd said. Verbatim. She couldn't get that close and not cry.

"A mutual friend of ours called me later that week…" She stopped. Thought. Rephrased. "What I thought was a friend of ours," she said. "Maybe he had a thing for me himself, or maybe he just had it in for Reese, but for whatever reason, he called to let me know that Reese wasn't coming to the party because he had a date with another girl. Someone named Susan Shepherd."

"Did he?" Sara's soft tone continued to keep her safe. Right when she'd been feeling like she *had* jumped off that proverbial cliff.

"I don't know. But I believe he did. After that phone call I asked him again to come to the party. I told him he could come as late as he needed. Whenever the night drills were through. He kept putting me off. Reese and I had been together a long time. I could tell that something wasn't right. And so I told him not to bother coming to Saturday's homecoming events, either. I don't know, maybe I was hoping he'd change his mind and come to the party with me. Or at least tell me the truth about what he was doing."

"Of course you did," Sara said. "It's a perfectly normal response."

Perfectly normal? Nothing about her memories of that time seemed normal.

"Whatever I'd hoped, he didn't come at all that weekend. I was planning to stay in the dorm and study. It wasn't like one missed homecoming was the end of the world. At all. But then my roommate's boyfriend shows up with his older brother in tow. Carrie, my roommate, had been looking forward to seeing her boyfriend for weeks. The guys had driven down from San Francisco and she'd begged me to hang out with them, to be a fourth for the brother so she and her boyfriend could have some time alone. She assured me that the older brother knew I was in a very committed relationship. And that I was going along as a friend."

Sara's expression darkened. Which, oddly, in that moment, gave Faye courage.

"It was my first time ever out drinking in campus bars without Reese, and I was picturing him out with this Susan I'd never even heard of, and I just started drinking like there was no tomorrow."

Funny how you sometimes manifested what you most feared. After that night there'd been no tomorrow. Not for her and Reese. Not for the life she'd planned for herself. Her marriage and family. Her nursing career. Her happiness. All of it wiped away with no hope of tomorrow.

Or so it had seemed.

It had all been her fault. Her little attempt at manipulation, basically giving Reese an ultimatum. Come Friday or don't come at all.

Her jealousy.

The drinking.

She'd made that choice. Consciously. And then, as the evening wore on and she was less able to make concrete decisions, she'd made them drunkenly.

Her escort, an older, more mature guy of twenty-three, had seemed really nice as he'd bought her more drinks. Seemed to understand that she was drowning her sorrows. Was willing to sit there all night and listen to her whine. He'd even put his arm around her and stabilized her so she could make it back to her dorm room safely.

And that was where she'd lost track of things.

"It's okay, Faye. You were a perfectly normal college girl with a broken heart."

Sara's words brought her out of hell. She'd gone so far back, she'd mostly forgotten that she was speaking aloud to another person, not just reliving the hell herself.

"I remember getting back to the room," she continued with the telling. "I remember being confused that Carrie and her boyfriend weren't there. I remember the guy trying to kiss me and me telling him no. I remember being scared when it seemed like he wasn't going to take no for an answer. I remember fighting him. Thinking of Reese. Starting to cry.

"And that's it. That's all I've ever been able to remember. Until early the next morning when I woke up alone in my dorm bed, partially dressed."

"Did you shower?"

"Of course I did. Immediately. I was so ashamed, I couldn't even look at myself. I hated what I'd done to myself, hated that I'd put myself in the situation to begin with."

She'd even gone through a time where she'd hated that she'd been so dependent on Reese, on their love, that she'd lost her mind when she'd thought he'd been cheating. Faye had learned that lesson well.

She would never, ever give a man that much power over her again. Would never believe in love that completely.

"Did you tell anyone?" Sara asked softly.

"No. All I could think about at that point was that I'd been unfaithful to Reese and the guilt was eating me alive.

"By that afternoon, I was shaking and sick to my stomach. I needed to talk to Reese but couldn't let him see me like that. I was afraid to call him. Afraid I'd start sobbing or he'd hear something different in my voice. And I kept thinking about him and Susan. What if he really had been on that date? What if he'd put going out with that other girl above my Friday night party invitation?

"But I was so scared and needed him so badly and I did a really dumb thing."

"You got drunk again?"

"What?" Faye blinked, back in the real world completely for a moment. "No! I've never done that again. Ever. No, I texted him and told him I thought we should break up. It was dumb. More of my stupid jealousy, trying to get a reaction out of him. I sat there shaking after I sent the text, waiting for him to text me back. Argue with me. Tell me how much I mean to him."

"He didn't," Sara said, still right there with her. Acting as though she had the rest of the day to be a friend to the mother of one of her patients.

"Nope. He just said, 'Okay.' And then asked why, as if he didn't already know. If he didn't care, I saw no point in telling him anything more."

"How long did it take before one of you broke down and talked about this?"

She looked at Sara. Kind of startled. "Why do you think we did?"

"You're here. Working for him."

And what woman would ever apply for a job with an ex with that kind of baggage still hanging between them?

Yeah, well...

"Maybe one of us would have, given time. I didn't have much of that. Less than a month later, I started to suspect I was pregnant. Reese and I hadn't slept together for a few weeks before homecoming so it was pretty clear whose baby I was carrying. What would have been the point of contacting Reese after that?"

"But you've talked now. He knows about all of this? That's how you can work so well together?"

Were they working well together? Reese was her boss. Practically a stranger.

She shook her head. And then so did Sara.

"I called the older brother as soon as I knew," she continued, because she had to get this out now or not at all. She wasn't coming back to this place in her life again. Not out loud. "Oddly enough, he was wonderful to me. He told me he hadn't been able to think of anyone but me since that night, but my roommate and his brother had broken up that weekend and he knew Reese and I were planning to marry...

"He tells me that the sex we had that night was the best he'd ever had. That, in the end, I begged him to take me and he just couldn't get that sound out of his mind. But the most erotic part was when I'd told him it was the best sex I'd ever had, too."

The best sex ever and she hadn't been able to remember a second of it.

"He asked me to marry him, and though I put off answering him for several months, in the end, I did. I had to quit school. While I could live with my father, he couldn't support me and the baby. He'd moved into a one-bedroom place. There was no one else to take me in, support me while I had a child. And how was I going to provide for my son? Besides, his father was head over heels in love with me and said he wanted his son..."

"Frank was the 'older brother'?" Sara's reaction

was...alarming. The shocked tone in her voice, the emotion simmering in her gaze.

She nodded.

"But that's not what I had to tell you. I mean, it's all part of it. None of this is to be repeated outside of you and me and these walls. Period."

Sara nodded. Gave her hand a squeeze. She'd actually forgotten that the woman was holding on to her. She grabbed hold this time, making sure that Sara didn't let her go.

"It gets worse," she warned.

"I know." Sara's soft tone had returned. "He was your abuser..."

Well, yes, that. But they didn't need to go into that. Faye had her own counseling avenues. This was about Elliott.

With a little shake of her head, she said, "Just before Elliott's sixth birthday, he had to have his tonsils out. Frank was working and couldn't make it for the surgery. He didn't come that evening, either. I spent that night in the hospital with Elliott. The next morning, Elliott was running a low-grade fever and they told me they might be keeping him a second day. I went home to shower and get some things to occupy him in case he had to stay in bed all day. As I came out of the shower, Frank was there. Naked. Ready..."

She had to swallow back bile. Even now.

"He said...he said before I could go back, I

owed him. My penance for being away from his bed all night."

She squeezed. Hard. Not realizing Sara's hand was beneath hers. And then she did. But not because the counselor had reacted. Sara was safety. An angel Faye didn't feel she deserved.

Maybe that was why Sara didn't say anything. Maybe she was sitting this one out.

But, no, she'd just let Faye squeeze the hell out of her hand.

Faye didn't have to handle this alone. She had support. Even physical support when she needed it.

"For once, I couldn't hide my disgust," she said. "We had a huge fight. It was bad." She didn't want to call up the details. It was enough to know they were there.

"And then he reached a point he'd never reached before. He looked me straight in the eye and told me I was nothing but a frigid bitch. Just like the first night. He said I was so tight and crying so hard he couldn't even get in me."

She wasn't crying. Shouldn't she be feeling more? Saying the words out loud for the first time?

They were there all the time, in her mind. But their release…she'd expected it to be…harder.

"Faye?"

Sara looked all business now.

"Are you telling me that you and Frank hadn't had sex yet when you found out you were pregnant?"

She started to shake. She felt cold and then hot. Thought she might pass out.

She breathed. Drank the water Sara handed her.

"He was there…" she said minutes later. "He was…his stuff touched there. But…" She looked at the counselor, just wanting to die. "I don't know. My periods weren't regular. What if there's a chance Elliott belongs to Reese? And I stole him from him? One stupid choice after another led me to ruin so many lives…"

"We'll talk about that, too," Sara said gently. "But first…"

Faye couldn't stop now. "Part three of the plan to come here, after getting the job and getting Elliott well, was telling Reese and giving him the chance to take a DNA test with Elliott if he wanted to. He's going to hate me even more than he already does. And I don't blame him. I've mostly made my peace with what's past and what I can't change. I just… I promised myself the day I left Frank to be with my son in the hospital that I would not take Elliott back to that house. And that I would spend the rest of my life making conscious choices. Planning everything. I will be a decent, good, hardworking person…"

She heard herself and stopped. Was embarrassed. Ashamed all over again. This wasn't about her. Period.

"Reese won't want me, but he might want Elliott. I'd made up my mind that if Elliott was well, and wanted to be with his father, I will let him go. But I can't do that yet. The last thing my son needs right now is his mother's desertion on top of everything else. He might not like me all that much, I might remind him of horrors from his past, but he knows I love him, and he needs that."

Sara smiled. Let go of her hand to pat it. And then sat back. "Slow down there, cowgirl," she said with a lighter tone. "You're right. Elliott needs you more now than ever. As a matter of fact, he needs you more than he needs anything else. Just trust me on that one, for now. No one is going to take that boy away from you.

"I've read your files, as you know, and aside from some remaining self-doubt, self-blame and one or two other things mixed in, you're a strong, healthy, capable woman. If you were asking to adopt a child, I'd recommend you for the job. You've been irrevocably hurt, Faye, but that doesn't make you any less valuable as a human being, a woman...or a mother."

Faye's eyes flooded. So much so that she couldn't even blink away the tears. Or see through them. She tried to hold back. To nod and get herself under control.

It took the next fifteen minutes to make that happen.

CHAPTER TWELVE

THE STATION WAS hopping from Friday afternoon on. Three crashes. Two fires. And a cat in a tree. Reese shook his head as he read over the paperwork on that one. As much as the world had changed, cats still ran up trees and people still called the local fire department to get them down.

There'd also been one elderly assist—a man who'd needed help lifting his wife off the floor after she'd fallen out of bed.

The fires had both been routine, if ever there was such a thing. A near miss from an illegal burn-off in a field. The farmer was going to be hit with charges on that one. A little more wind and they could have had the beginnings of a wildfire. California's worst nightmare.

Or at least Reese's.

The other had been an explosion in a nearby manufacturing plant. His crew had responded and had things under control in less than an hour.

By ten o'clock Saturday morning, the paperwork had all been signed. He had a pile of "to-dos" in his inbox. Grabbing his keys, he left them there.

He had a call to make, and didn't want to risk being overheard.

In his truck, he dialed before he was even out of the firehouse parking lot.

She picked up on the first ring. Like she knew his personal number. Or didn't and had no idea who she'd be talking to.

"Faye?"

"Yes, do you need me to come in? Elliott's already at the Stand for a computer thing he wanted to do. I've got a full grocery cart, but I'll just get the manager. He can have someone put everything back—"

"Faye." His tone was different this time. He'd like to think it was still completely professional but he needed her to listen. He knew this tone always worked when he was serious about something.

"Yeah?"

Seemed to still be working.

"I want to talk to Elliott…"

"He's not here right now."

She'd already told him that. Which meant that she was flustered. His first instinct was to take pleasure from that.

Because sometimes he was an ass.

"I'd like to stop by your house later today, if that would be okay. I want to talk to him at home."

"Why?"

Defensiveness was not what he'd expected.

Prevarication, maybe, but really he'd expected her to agree.

He was in the driver's seat here. She'd begged him for the job. "I've been thinking about Kyle at that scene. And Elliott having matches but not telling us where he got them."

That was his story and he was sticking to it. If the kid had called him as a cry for help, then it was Reese's job, as the Santa Raquel Fire Chief, to seek out explanations for unanswered questions.

"He's pissed at me for 'snitching' to you about Kyle. I'm not sure talking to him about that is a good idea."

"Thanks for the heads-up. I'd like to help with that, too, if I can. At this point, Kyle isn't in trouble. He's a witness to a scene. I've just got this persistent niggling about those matches…"

"He's going to be at the Stand until after lunchtime."

"Anytime is fine."

"He's had a bad week, Reese. I'm just…"

Was she afraid her son would say something she'd regret? Or act out in a way that would embarrass her?

She was a single mom of an eight-year-old at-risk kid. One would kind of expect some acting out.

"I'm not asking for a warm welcome, Faye. Or even a polite one. He called me. I'd like to follow up. And I prefer not to do it at The Lemonade Stand where our visit will be noticed."

It was a book of matches.

He had much bigger problems at his back, and he was supposed to be golfing with several members of the city council, including the mayor and the new chief of police. Why was he pushing this?

"Does it have to be at the house?"

She didn't want him there.

He understood. And still didn't like it.

"Where would you like it to be?"

"I promised him a trip to the beach this afternoon. He wore his swim trunks to the Stand."

Would it cause a behavioral problem for Elliott if she had to renege on her promise? He was only guessing. About all of it.

"I can meet you at the beach. Tell me which one and what time."

Was he nuts? In his golf shorts and shirt, he was ready for eighteen holes. Not a trip to the beach.

She named the beach, telling him where in the parking lot she'd be at two.

Reese couldn't help but wonder exactly what part of having him in her home scared Faye the most.

Wondered, too, why it bothered him so much.

FAYE HAD HAD a rough twenty-four hours. On the surface, she'd been a mom on her days off. Cooking. Cleaning. Grocery shopping. Watching a movie with her son. Coaxing him into a card game he didn't want to play, one he lost on purpose as quickly as he could.

He'd only played at all because she'd bribed him with a trip out for ice cream.

Just beneath the surface, she was flying out of her skin. She'd told.

Nothing else came with that.

Just…she'd told.

She'd had no idea how much safety had rested in her being the only one who knew.

She did, and maybe Frank. Probably Frank.

He had to know why she hadn't gone after him for child support. She hadn't wanted the truth to come out. Him keeping his mouth shut about it was why she hadn't charged him with domestic violence.

They were a pair, Elliott's "parents."

Partners in a game of keep-your-mouth-shut.

She'd told.

And now, a day later, Reese suddenly wanted an in-home meeting with her son.

She didn't think, even for a second, that Sara had betrayed her trust. Reese knew nothing about the conversation they'd had.

But karma had a way of getting you. Or something had a way of getting her.

She'd told.

Reese was instigating a conversation with Elliott. It was too much. More than she was ready to face.

Swamped with guilt—that's what she was. She knew it. Reese deserved to find out if he was a father.

He'd been number three in her plan. Right there all along.

"Maybe we'll see the friends you met last weekend at the beach," she said to Elliott as they sped away from The Lemonade Stand just before two o'clock. Regular parking filled up with tourists on warm weekend days like this, but town residents could buy passes to a couple of private lots. She had asked Reese to meet them at one of those.

"Nah."

Elliott shrugged one shoulder. He looked so cute in his green T-shirt and multi-colored fluorescent trunks that she got a little choked up. Elliott was small for his age. And tried to take the weight of a grown man on those thin shoulders.

"Why not?" she asked him. The rest of the news she had to impart hovered on the tip of her tongue, refusing to slide off.

He'd actually talked to her when she'd met him inside the Stand. Told her he'd had a good computer class. He was learning how to make a meme, he'd said.

"I don't know." He shrugged again. "It's more fun without those guys."

Sara's words from the day before rang far too loud. Elliott was isolating himself because he wanted to protect others from the "Frank" in him.

There might not be any Frank in him. Not genetically.

Environment played a part, too, of course. But he'd only spent the first six years of his life with the man. Sara seemed to think they could walk those back, at least enough for her son to be a normal, healthy kid.

During the years she'd been married to Frank, she'd hated how he ignored their son. Now she was beginning to see the silver lining there.

They were on the coastal road and their turnoff was coming up. She had no idea if Reese would already be there.

But her time was up.

"There's something we need to do before we head down to the water," she said, hesitant to have this blow up in her face with no time to fix it.

She should have told him as soon as she'd seen him. Before they left the Stand. But he'd been in such a good mood. She hated for others to see him at his worst. Even those trying to help him.

Especially those trying to help him.

For too long, she'd been the only one in control of Elliott's world. It was hard giving that up. Hard for her, as a mom, to see that her son wasn't completely well.

Harder still to know that, in part at least, she was to blame.

Elliott was looking at her, waiting for her to continue.

"Chief Bristow is going to meet us in the parking lot. He wants to talk to you."

"Am I in trouble?" The boy looked as though he might cry, but then quickly bore a hardened expression. Faye wanted to tuck him under her arm and run as fast and as far away as she could.

"No. You most definitely are not in trouble." She was not going to let Reese Bristow—fire chief or not, biological contributor or not—ruin her son's good mood.

Lord knew, Elliott had few enough hours when he could just be a little kid.

She pulled into the lot—slow enough to check for Reese's truck. To see him before he saw her.

"He's over there," Elliott said, craning forward.

Now that he knew he wasn't in trouble, Elliott seemed...perfectly fine. "I was hoping he'd be in a fire truck."

And just like that he was back to being a little boy.

"I'll bet if you ask him, he'd let you tour one of the trucks at the station," she said, her stomach cramping even as she made the offer. "You're old enough now."

With that one statement, she'd thrown Elliott and Reese together. She wanted to take it back.

But didn't. She'd promised herself that if she'd robbed Reese of his son, she'd rectify that in a way that was best for Elliott. Even if it meant shared custody. Or worse.

Her son was out of the car the second she put it in Park. Not waiting for her, he headed straight for the shorts-clad man heading in their direction.

Seeing them together—a first for her—just about did Faye in. Slowing, she figured that, since this was business, she'd leave them to it.

Mostly she knew that she couldn't approach the only two males she'd ever loved, other than her father. They'd see her crying.

And there didn't seem to be anything she could do to get rid of her tears.

CHAPTER THIRTEEN

REESE'S GOAL WAS to have his words with the boy in short enough order that he could still make tee time. He'd let his party know that if he wasn't at the course, they should leave without him. It was a friendly game, nothing resting on it. Wouldn't matter if they went out one player short.

He walked with Elliott, stopping at the edge of the sand, and climbed up to sit on a picnic table, his feet on the seat. It occurred to him too late that it probably wasn't a great example to set for a kid, sitting on a table with your feet on the seat.

"I talked to your friend Kyle," he started right in.

"Wha-um-what about?" There was that "um" again.

"He was a witness at a fire scene, didn't you know?"

He knew the boy knew. He'd heard that the kid had been hateful to his mother that week. With Faye's permission Lila was keeping him apprised due to the ongoing concern with two of the Stand's residents being recently involved in fires.

Elliott shrugged. Reese had been told to expect

the boy to clam up. Elliott didn't seem to confide in anyone. Which left those caring for him reading between the lines.

He was just a tiny, sandy-haired kid, sitting there next to him in those ridiculously colored trunks, his shoulders bony beneath his T-shirt.

"I need you to talk to me, Elliott. Man to man."

"Did Kyle?"

"Doesn't matter if Kyle did or not. This is between you and me."

Elliott's hands gripped the edge of the table on either side of his knees. He was staring down.

"You're the one who called me, remember?" Reese prompted.

The boy's nod wasn't much, but the way he raised his head, meeting Reese's gaze directly was more. Kind of took him aback.

"Do you know why Kyle was at that fire?"

"He was visiting his aunt."

"Why was he outside?"

"It was a fire!" Elliott's eyes grew wide as he stared at Reese. "He got to see the fire truck up close. And see the guys working it and all."

"He told you all about it?"

Elliott glanced down again. "Well, not really."

Instincts on alert, Reese leaned forward, his elbows on his knees. "What do you mean by that?"

"Well…um… I kinda overheard him telling some other kids."

"But not you."

"I was sittin'…you know…um…not with them."

Because he'd distanced himself. Reese knew that, too. But the boy had confirmed what Kyle had told him. And not because he was in Kyle's confidence.

"So…you think fire trucks are cool, too, huh?"

"'Course!" Elliott grinned, his legs swinging. "Mom said maybe I could…you know, ask you if I could, maybe…um…see one up close. You know, like, go on it or something when it's just… um, you know, parked or something."

Of course Reese could make that happen in a blink. But he wasn't ready to deliver his goods yet.

"I need to know where you got those matches, Elliott."

"I can't tell you."

"Why not?"

"Because it's the code. I swore. And if I break a swear, I'm a bad guy."

"Not if you're helping to stop someone from getting hurt."

"No one got hurt."

"But what about next time?"

"The matches are gone."

"But where they came from, maybe some more can come from there."

"Uh-uh. It was just that one pack. It was a special pack."

"You're sure about that?"

"Uh-huh. I'm sure." He looked Reese right in the eye again.

Elliott was not giving in on his matches source. Reese could have gotten a little more tough with the kid but didn't see that losing his trust was the best way to go at the moment.

"So then, if you're absolutely certain..."

"I am." Elliott didn't even break eye contact as he kept nodding.

"Then I have a deal to make with you."

"What kinda deal?" The boy looked a little leery.

"You swear to me, man to man, to call me if the need ever arises, then I'll give you a tour of a fire engine."

"Yeah!" Elliott's grin was matched by the enthusiasm in his tone.

"Wait," Reese said. He didn't want to scare the boy, but... "This isn't just for fun. This is a serious business deal. If you don't keep up your end of it, you will be held accountable."

"Yes, sir." Elliott was still looking him straight in the eye. It was kind of disconcerting—a kid being that...whatever it was. Confident, maybe. Or honest.

"And you haven't heard what 'need' means when I say you call if the need arises."

"It means that, like before, if I'm in trouble and don't want Mom to get in trouble, too, I call you."

"No."

"Oh." The expression fell, the boy's gaze didn't.

"Need means…if you ever even think about starting another fire, you call me instead."

Elliott nodded. "Yes." And then, frowning, added, "But that's not really fair to you pro'bly on that deal because I already know I'm not going to start another fire."

"It's my end of the deal. If I want it, then it's okay."

"Okay."

"And 'need' also means that if you ever hear anyone else even talking about fire, or liking fire, or how to start fires, you call me."

"Okay."

"I mean it, Elliott. That includes your friend Kyle. Anytime you hear him talking about fires, or fire trucks, anything to do with fires, you call me."

The boy nodded.

"Okay," Reese said, standing and giving the boy a hand down. Letting go of those small fingers, he put his hands in his pockets and turned toward Faye's car. She was leaning against it, looking out at the ocean.

For a second there, he needed to know her thoughts. Right then. Exactly.

The second passed.

"Shouldn't we make a handshake?" Elliott asked.

"Yes, of course we should." He took the boy's hand. Held it firmly. Shook it, man to man.

"We're agreed then," he said, meeting the boy's eyes. "You ever even think about wanting to start a fire…"

"I call you instead."

"And if you hear anyone else talk about fire, liking fire, wanting to start a fire…"

"I call you."

Elliott didn't blink, flinch or turn away. Reese believed he meant what he said with every fiber of his being.

He didn't like it that Faye's son wouldn't confide in him regarding the matches but he was satisfied enough with the outcome of their talk.

And he still had time for his golf game.

They headed back toward Faye's car. In a black mesh cover-up that hung halfway down her thighs, she'd taken towels out of the trunk. Had a soft-sided cooler slung over her shoulder, as well.

God, she looked good. As beautiful as any other woman on the beach. Maybe even more so. Her hair was down and those long legs…he remembered…

He was her boss. That was what he remembered.

She looked like a good mother. Well prepared. Capable, too. Except for the hand that quickly brushed tears away when she saw them coming.

Faye…crying?

At the beginning of a fun afternoon at the beach with her boy?

What was going on?

Not his business. He was her boss. Nothing more.

He had to do exactly what he'd do were he to come upon any of his employees standing in a beach parking lot with signs of emotional upset.

He'd make sure there was nothing he could do and then move on.

"Mom, guess what? Chief Bristow says I can come tour one of the fire engines," Elliott called to her before they'd reached the back of the car.

"Yeah!" Faye was turned away from them, ostensibly so she could reach into the trunk for the boogie board. She brushed her cheek one more time with her shoulder and then faced them with a cheerful smile. She adjusted the towels under her arm and the cooler strap slid off her shoulder.

"Let me get that for you." Reese had it on his shoulder before she could protest. He took the boogie board, too. And then the towels, handing them to Elliott.

"You're the man of the house, right?" he said to the boy.

"Right."

"Then you need to watch for things like this—men always help ladies where they can."

Nodding, Elliott tucked the towels under his arm.

"You know why that is?"

"Sure." Elliott shrugged. "It's a rule."

"No, it's because men have different muscular structures than women do. Inch for inch, they are genetically formed to be physically stronger. If you're given an ability, it's only right that you use it for good, right?"

He was making it all up as he went along. Would be berating himself shortly, he knew. A voice in the back of his mind was already trying to get through. But he had an employee in distress and no one seemed to have her back.

He'd do the same for any of his crew. Like he'd lent a hand when Brandt and his wife moved. And he'd stopped by the hospital to sit with Riley for a while when the man's wife had had surgery.

"Does this mean I gotta carry in all the groceries?" Elliott asked as they hit the sand and trudged between sunbathers and picnickers. Faye had stepped ahead of them, leading the way to find a spot and leaving Reese to get himself out of the hole he'd just dug.

"Don't you already carry groceries?"

"Sometimes," Elliott said. "When Mom makes me."

"The thing about being a nice guy is that you do stuff without being made to do it."

"So I gotta carry groceries." The boy kicked up sand with his sandals.

"What do you think? Because I think you should do what you think would be the best thing to do."

"Well…it sounds like I gotta carry groceries."

"Then, I guess, if it sounds that way to you, that's what you should do."

A few feet ahead of them, Faye stopped. Elliott dropped the towels at her feet.

"I'm going to the water now." He was already ridding himself of his sandals and didn't even look at his mom.

"Okay," Faye told him, tacking on a string of instructions obviously intended to keep the boy safe.

"I know!" he interrupted as he raced to the water's edge. He hadn't waited for her to complete her sentence.

Reese had to resist calling the boy back and demanding that he listen. Elliott obviously loved his mother. But he didn't seem to respect her much.

And Reese didn't like it.

THANK YOU FOR getting these for me." Faye hoped Reese heard the dismissal in her tone. He didn't have to stay. She didn't need him for anything. She'd been handling Elliott, and carrying his things, since the day he was born. A cooler and a boogie board were nothing compared to lugging a stroller, diaper bag and baby all at the same time.

Reese looked ready for a game of golf, but he wasn't leaving.

"What did he say about the matches?" she asked. If he had something to say, she'd help him get it out.

She needed him gone.

Needed some time on the beach with the sun's warmth on her skin and sounds of happy people having fun surrounding her. She need to relax and watch her son and pretend that they were as normal as any other family out there that day.

"Nothing. He won't say where he got them."

She wasn't surprised. When Elliott got it into his head that something was the right thing to do, there was no budging him. For whatever reason, keeping the source of his matches seemed like the right thing to him.

She just prayed that he wasn't keeping a secret that would hurt him. Or someone else.

Aside from the fact that he'd used them, a kid having a book of matches wasn't that big of a deal. Elliott's stubborn refusal to give up his source was more of a concern to her.

Reese wasn't leaving and she wasn't going to just stand there all day with her cover-up on over her black one-piece suit. Reaching for a towel, she spread first one and then the other, side by side. One for her and one for Elliott—keeping up appearances with Reese there, as though her son would actually sit with her—when he came running up to tell her he was starved and ask what she'd brought for a snack.

As though he'd plop down—right beside her—and stay there until he was full. She loved thinking that some day that might actually happen again.

What she didn't love was having Reese standing there, reminding her of the last time they'd been on a beach together. Not in her dream, but for real.

They'd gone home for the weekend. Reese had picked her up at her UCLA dorm and driven them both south to a suburb of San Diego where they'd gone to high school. His mother had just remarried and moved to Texas with her new rancher husband. Her father had gone on a fishing trip with some of his buddies and they'd had her house to themselves.

Reese had suggested going to the beach late one night and she'd loved it. Loved even more the way he'd made love to her that night. So tenderly, beneath the moonlight. And when the tide came in, he'd protected her from the waves. Telling her that he'd always be her shield…

A little girl next to her screamed with glee, and she landed back on the current beach with a mental thud that made her head hurt. One thing was for certain. She wasn't stripping off her cover-up in front of Reese.

So she dropped down onto her towel still dressed. And then, when she realized that Reese was now towering over her, wished she hadn't.

Shading her eyes, she looked up at him. "You got a golf game to get to?"

How did one dismiss one's boss when one had to kiss up to keep a job one desperately needed?

If she pretended hard enough, maybe she could convince herself that that was all there was left between her and Reese.

But something Sara had said the day before—after Faye had thrown up her past all over the kind therapist—if Reese was fully over what had happened, if he no longer had feelings for Faye, he wouldn't have cared that she came to work for him.

Her credentials would have been all that mattered.

Enough time had passed. They were no longer kids. They'd both been married. Moved on. Even Sara had expected that they'd had a conversation to put the past to rest and started anew.

"I've missed it," he said, and it took her a second of racking her brain to figure out what he'd missed.

Their lovemaking on the beach?

Being with her?

No. His golf game.

"I'd like to speak with you for a moment, if I may?"

"You aren't afraid someone will see us out here on the beach together and get the wrong idea?"

She was being…bitchy. Cantankerous at best. She hated to hear that tone come out of her mouth.

"I'm sorry," she said, almost immediately. "Please, have a seat."

If she wasn't going to get her downtime, then

so be it. She owed Reese more than an afternoon of her time.

She could possibly owe him a lifetime of Elliott's.

Not that she'd made up her mind yet, about pursuing that particular piece of information anytime soon.

Sara thought she should, as soon as possible. Had strongly encouraged it for Elliott's sake, but without telling Elliott until they knew results—and never, if he turned out to be Frank's son after all.

But to do that meant that she'd have to trust Reese to handle the information in a way that was best for Elliott.

Any kind of friction would not be good for Elliott. And how could a man find out he possibly had a son without friction?

Reese sat on Elliott's towel. Faye felt like she might start crying again.

It was just tension, she knew. A good cry, or a good night's sleep, either one, would take care of the weepiness.

The bone-deep pain might be more difficult to abolish. Parts of it, she'd been told, would be with her forever.

When Reese kicked off his sandals, a huge wave of desire slammed into her. More than she'd ever felt in the past.

Residual, she knew. Her psyche trying to get her back to her happy place.

Somehow she had to get through to the damned thing that going back only made things worse.

She was working on it. With Sara's help. And Dr. Bloom Larson's, too. Bloom, her personal counselor, was in private practice, but also knew Sara well.

"He's a good swimmer." Reese was watching Elliott as he swam out the couple of feet he was allowed so he could ride his boogie board to shore.

Faye had been watching for the brothers her son had met on the same beach the week before. Hadn't seen them yet.

There were other kids, though.

So far, Elliott was holding himself apart from them. One kid had already approached him. She hadn't been able to hear what the other boy said, but there'd been no missing the way Elliott had just shrugged and turned away.

"Aren't you going to take your cover off?" Reese asked next.

Definitely not a professional question.

"I'm just saying," he went on, "you need to get lotion on or you'll be paying for it tomorrow. I can't imagine a sunburn chafing inside a uniform will make for good performance."

Had he read her mind about the boss part?

She tried to ignore the fact that he'd remembered how easily she burned, clearly implying that they'd known each other in the past.

They could not open that door.

Period.

And if she ended up deciding that she had to ask him to give her a DNA sample?

She told the voice in her head to shut up.

"I'm surprised you didn't grease the kid down before you set him loose."

"I did. Before we left The Lemonade Stand. I usually do it at home before we come. He's too wiggly for me once we're near the water." She could have told him that Elliott didn't burn as easily as she did. Could have told him that he'd been blessed with his father's skin. But she was absolutely not opening up that door.

Neither Frank nor Reese burned as easily as she did.

As she sat there, trying not to look at Reese, trying to focus solely on her son, she couldn't help looking for resemblances between them, as she had from the second she'd seen them together.

It was nothing new, this need of hers to find Reese in her son. And then, when the regrets became too overwhelming, to convince herself that she saw Frank in him. She'd been comparing pictures—Elliott and Reese, Elliott and Frank—since the day her husband had told her they hadn't actually had sex that night in her dorm room.

Reese had been sitting with her a good five

minutes. He'd yet to tell her why he was on the beach with her.

Or what he had to talk about.

She wanted to push him.

But was having a particularly weak day.

Just sitting there with Reese, in whatever capacity, felt too damned good to not savor.

CHAPTER FOURTEEN

HE COULD HAVE made his golf date.

Should have made his golf date.

Reese wasn't happy with himself as he sat on the beach beside the woman he'd once thought was the love of his life.

A boss wouldn't sit in the sand with an employee.

She'd been crying. A boss would make sure she was okay. At least the kind of boss he aspired to be. The kind who did what he could and left as soon as he knew he wasn't needed.

His crew risked their lives every day they came to work. The level of trust and caring among fire people was extreme. Had to be.

Walking to the beach with her, in the company of her sensitive, troubled kid who was eager to get in the water, had seemed like the most expedient way to check up on her.

Once there, it had hardly been right for him to stand over her. Most particularly when he figured out that he could see down her cover-up and straight into the top of her suit. There'd been enough cleavage visible for him to fill in the blanks.

Who was he kidding? He'd been able to fill those in from the first time he'd seen Faye naked.

Going back to UCLA, in the backseat of his truck...

Was going to serve no good at all.

"You were crying."

"Just tired."

"You didn't used to cry when you were tired."

She looked over at him, took off her cover and smeared lotion on her skin. He'd have thought the move a come-on except that he knew that every second she sat there without lotion was danger waiting to happen with her fair skin. Her cover-up was lacy enough that the sun's rays could get through.

"I'm a different woman now," she said.

He would have liked to accept her statement and move forward. To get beyond the past. But the body she'd just revealed...his memory had been spot-on.

He knew it as well as he knew his own.

Better, in some ways.

He'd paid a whole lot more attention to hers.

That birthmark on her thigh—faint and small— he'd kissed it more times than he could count. Every time they made love.

It had been a physical signature of his love. From him to her.

Or something equally ridiculous.

As ridiculous as him thinking that she was the love of his life. That they'd be together forever.

"I've been doing some reading."

Yeah, this conversation should probably have taken place in his office, but there were windows out to the station there.

She was letting his reading comment lie. He hadn't used to be much of a reader.

"About domestic violence."

He felt her stiffen, so he hastened to assure her, "I'm not trying to impinge on your privacy or personal life."

Her head turned as Elliott ran down the beach a couple of steps.

"I just want you to know that I'm more aware now than I was during our first interview."

She turned back to him. Either because Elliott had run back or because he'd shocked her, he didn't know. Wasn't about to ask.

She continued to watch her son.

"I'm sorry for the hard line I took that first day." He didn't have a problem apologizing when he was wrong.

Giving an inch to Faye felt like ten miles—in spite of the fact that she didn't seem interested in anything from him at all.

"I'm not going to pry. I just want you to know that if you ever need anything, if you ever have a… situation…we…the crew and I…have your back."

Her chin trembled.

Though she was facing the ocean, he could see tears in her eyes.

"Thank you," she said, sounding almost normal.

He nodded.

His job there was done.

Picking up his shoes, he stood, took one last look at her, told her to have a good rest of the day and headed back up the beach.

THERE WAS ANOTHER gasoline fire. It happened Sunday night. Faye wasn't on call, but she heard about it when she got in Monday morning.

It had been set on private property near an animal pen not far off the beach. Two chickens were dead. Reese had been up a good part of the night processing the scene and was planning to spend his day off in LA again.

Faye hated that the fires were happening at all. That they seemed to be escalating. But she was relieved to know that Reese would be out of town for the day.

Sara had met her at the door of The Lemonade Stand when she'd dropped Elliott off that morning, wanting to know what she'd decided. The woman wasn't going to force the issue of the DNA test, but she'd made her opinion clear.

Faye told her she wanted to wait until after she met with Bloom later in the week. And so there she was, caught between two choices. Not too late to go back. Or she could go forward.

She played out different what-ifs. Ran through different scenarios.

And knew two things.

First, there were no easy or right answers.

Second, there would be consequences either way. Good and bad.

The question was, then, which way was best for Elliott?

Some days it was keeping Frank as his father because it was a world he knew. He'd be secure with his mother and he was already getting counseling for the rest.

Some days it was having Reese as a father. Elliott could rid himself of the feeling that he was in some way damaged because he was Frank's son. He and Reese would bond. He'd have a positive male role model in his biological father. But it would change his whole world once again. And even good change was a stressor.

Though kids generally acclimated quickly to good change, Sara had assured her.

But the kicker…he could be made to live with Reese half of the time. If Reese pushed for shared parenting.

The Reese she'd known probably would do that. He'd wanted a family even more than he'd wanted to fight fires.

She'd heard about his wife being killed in a car

accident. Knew that she'd been pregnant with their unborn child. Everyone knew about it because Tabitha was from Santa Raquel and he was in the first responder business.

He'd lost his unborn child. And Faye had robbed him of his firstborn.

Potentially.

If he was the father.

Around and around she went over the next few days, until she thought she might go crazy.

She'd screwed up so badly in the past. How could she trust herself to get this one right?

Some moments, she wanted to find out the truth without Reese being any the wiser.

"I thought about grabbing a soda can or something he drinks from out of the station house," she confessed in her weekly counseling session with Bloom Larson. Married just a year to Detective Sam Larson of the Santa Raquel Police Department, Bloom had been a victim of her psychology professor husband and Sam had been the detective who'd put her husband away.

Everyone in town knew the gist of what had happened. Bloom had told Faye more of the details because she'd struggled, as Faye was, with her ability to trust her own judgment. If anyone was going to understand, it would be Bloom. She'd waited until Thursday, her usual day off, for her therapy meeting with Bloom. She didn't want any special favors, like someone covering for her. Didn't need favors or questions about why she needed them. She would pull her weight and hold her tiny family together at the same time.

Bloom smiled at her. "How many times have you thought about stealing his DNA?" she asked.

When she put it like that…

"I've lost count," Faye said, grinning. It was a really dumb idea.

But… "In some ways, it seems like the best choice," she continued. In a blue cotton sundress and sandals, she sat across from the professionally suited psychiatrist in her office. She loved it there. Everything was colorful. Bold. Particularly the paintings all over the walls. "If Reese isn't Elliott's father, then we know, no one is hurt and everything goes along status quo."

It was the only choice she liked. *Stealing* Reese's DNA for the test.

"And if he is Elliott's father, how do you explain waiting eight years to tell him? How do you explain passing his son off as another man's child? Or do you just admit to stealing his DNA?"

Like she would have stolen his son?

She heard what Bloom wasn't telling her.

This wasn't necessarily a matter of legalities or of right and wrong. It was a matter of integrity.

If Reese turned out to be Elliott's father, the two of them were going to need to be able to work together for their son's sake. To trust each other.

Her only hope of Reese ever trusting her, or

even halfway respecting her, would be to be up-front with him from the beginning.

"It would mean telling him everything," she said aloud. About the phone call she'd had about Susan. Her jealousy. Her drunkenness. And what came after.

"It would also mean being able to ask him anything," Bloom said. Different from Sara in that she was more analytical, more...scholarly...in her delivery, Bloom was also more to the point. Maybe because she was hardened by abuse, too. She'd traveled the road. Had scars that would never go away.

As only a woman who'd been there would truly know.

"Ask him what?" Faye was certain her therapist expected her to connect dots that she wasn't seeing.

"What would you ask him if you could ask him anything?"

"Whether or not he went out with Susan."

Bloom nodded, and things started to fall into place for Faye. The picture was scary. So much was at stake.

But...

"If I knew that he really did have a date...if he really had turned me down because he was being unfaithful..."

It wouldn't change everything.

But it would change a lot.

"Maybe you'll find some peace within yourself in the midst of all of this." Bloom's tone was almost as soft as Sara's. Yet her words had the impact of an oncoming train.

"If he was really two-timing me, then my choices...it wouldn't just be about me being jealous, but about acting from a truly broken heart."

"You told me, the first time you mentioned Reese, that when you talked to him after you'd received that phone call, you sensed something different about him. Yet I've never heard you give any real credence to the fact that you might not have been the only one at fault in this whole thing. Frank aside, of course. I'm speaking purely about you and Reese now. You act as though he's the only wronged party. That you're the only one who did something wrong."

"But if he really did go out with her..."

"You thought so at the time."

"But I also thought Frank was telling me the truth when he said I'd loved having sex with him."

"Your trust had been broken, Faye. By Reese. Everything that came after...you were injured, working through broken trust."

"If you're trying to convince me that I did nothing wrong, that this is all Reese's fault..."

Bloom's quick shake of the head stopped her words. "You made choices—I'm speaking of after that night you went out. Your choice not to tell Reese what had happened. Your choice to marry

Frank. What happened before that, the things that Frank did—those were in no way your fault. Period. And for the rest of your choices, you've taken ownership. You're being accountable. But maybe too much so."

Her choices were her own. No matter how many times she'd been told differently, she still felt like being too comatose to protect herself that night in the dorm room was her fault. But Frank's behavior hadn't been.

Two years of counseling had helped her see that much, at least.

"Maybe if you find out that your instincts were right, that Reese had been seeing someone else, you'll start to forgive yourself for what you see as the mistakes you made afterward. Or at least give yourself credit for knowing that something was wrong. And look at what came later with a little more compassion for yourself."

Give herself credit.

Wow. The effect of those words on her was huge. She felt it in her stomach. In the shakiness in her knees.

She'd always been afraid that Reese had gone out with the other girl. That he'd stood her up for the other girl. But she'd also always had doubts. What if he hadn't and she'd ruined her life out of gossip and immature jealousy?

Sometimes she'd hated Reese for being unfaithful. And then others she'd hated herself for believing someone else, not trusting him and then acting so foolishly upon that assumption.

But what if instead she'd acted straight from the heart? What if she'd believed because her heart had been telling her so all along? What if she hadn't been acting out of wrongful jealousy, but from truth?

It wouldn't change the things that had come after.

But knowing would change her.

And a healthier her would help her son.

"I have to ask him," she said, looking Dr. Larson right in the eye. "Because if I find out I was right, it'll restore some of my trust in myself, which will spread to Elliott. How can I help my son trust himself—and me—when I don't practice self-trust? Kids learn most by example."

The therapist smiled. "Exactly," she said.

And just like that Faye knew what she had to do.

CHAPTER FIFTEEN

REESE COULD HARDLY refuse to meet with Faye on her home turf—citing the non-professional location as a reason—when he'd been the first one to request a meeting at her home.

She'd left a message on his office phone, which he'd received when he'd settled at his desk with a cup of coffee Friday morning.

"I need to speak with you at your earliest convenience, during one of my days off, at my home if at all possible."

He listened to her message again. She was setting the stage for something big. The tell was not only in the odd note of…something not good… in her voice but also the extent to which she was controlling the details.

In sweats and a T-shirt, he'd been planning to spend the first part of the morning in the fitness center. And then out in the house, helping with equipment care. Maybe not the usual routine of a fire chief but Reese was, and always had been, a firefighter first. He didn't want to lose that edge in the midst of administrative duties.

And that was just what he was going to do.
But he returned the call first.

HE WORE JEANS, a white polo shirt and boots to the meeting. Regulation boots. They were a conscious choice, part of his working arsenal, to remind him that the meeting was between boss and employee.

Not jilted man and ex-lover.

So she'd been unfaithful to him. That reflected on her, not on him. He'd been receiving offers ever since. From beautiful, intelligent, successful women. Had even married one of them. He was alone by choice.

The house was impressive, one of the antebellum mansions that faced the ocean. His truck was dwarfed in the long, circular drive.

With an eye on the front steps leading up to a porch with white wicker furniture, he exited the vehicle.

If nothing else, the porch looked inviting and in good repair. He took that as a good sign.

The sun was shining. He'd just finished a delicious lunch at the house with his crew. And it was Friday. A quick meeting with his paramedic and he'd be on his way to see a buddy from college to go over the series of gasoline fires that he was no closer to solving. A fleck of white paint. A size-ten shoe. And now two dead chickens.

Gasoline in a circular format—always—with a small pile of ashes in the center.

Someone had to be buying the gas. He'd been to every station in the city and outskirts, asking if anyone remembered someone filling up a gas can. His perp could just as easily be using various stations, or siphoning from cars anyplace between there and LA. It was what he would do if he wanted to escape notice.

"Reese?"

Almost to the front steps, he turned at the sound of Faye's voice off to the left.

She'd come around the side of the house—what was it with her and the sides of houses? She'd dive-bombed him in his own driveway after her son had confessed to setting the fire in the bathroom at The Lemonade Stand.

"I'm out back," she told him. "It's private. Suzie and Elliott are at the Stand so we won't be interrupted."

She wasn't having him in. Another boundary. He welcomed it.

More curious now than anything—hoping he'd be able to resolve whatever issue she had with ease, keeping things nice and clean—he followed her through a six-foot-high, heavy, wrought-iron gate.

Even the backyard grabbed his attention with its charm. Though the entire space was obviously closed in by the wrought-iron fencing, all he could see were perfectly manicured eight-foot shrubs around the perimeter of the luscious green grass.

In the center was a fountain with seats around it. Interlocking pavers surrounded the fountain, and beyond them were flower beds that rivaled the botanical garden he'd visited the previous summer in LA.

Faye led him farther into the yard, to a small gazebo. Taking a seat at a glass-topped, wrought-iron table, she motioned him to another chair.

Pouring him some ice tea from a pitcher on a silver tray, she added two slices of lemon from a small glass bowl.

"It's already sweetened," she told him, sliding the drink his way.

They'd both preferred sweet tea and she used to make sun tea on the roof of her dorm. At home, she'd made it on the run-down back stoop of the house she and her father had shared.

He'd always loved her dad, though maybe he was embellishing his memories. A man without a father—especially one whose father had run out on him and his mother—tended to glom on to other father figures.

He wondered again what had happened to Len.

"Thank you for coming," she said, ignoring her own tea.

If she didn't want tea, she'd made it for another reason. Faye's control of the situation, as though she'd made a list and was following it, was nothing like the woman he'd known.

Even her ponytail looked completely controlled. Like not even one hair dared to not follow protocol.

Her expression was serene, calm. Blank.

And he tried to go no further down than that. His trip to the beach the previous Saturday, the cleavage he'd glimpsed in real time, not just in memory, had given him several nights of unrestful sleep.

He knew she was in a sundress, though. The soft blue, white and pink cotton hugged her slender waist and curved out over deliciously perfect hips...

He was a man, after all. And had followed her to the backyard, with that butt right in front of him the whole time.

"I need to speak with you about something very specific without my peers being able to see through the window of your office," Faye said.

He didn't like the sound of that.

Still somewhat at ease, he understood. Helped by the fact that he'd reached the same conclusion the week before.

Spreading his hands wide, he scooted further down in the chair, getting comfortable. A boss move to put her at ease. "I told you at the beach that the team and I are here for you. Anything you need. You've already proven that you're an asset to us. When you join the Santa Raquel Fire Department, you join a family."

Professional family.

No way were he and Faye personal family.

He glanced at the old house where she was living. The white paint on the surface of the structure, the rain gutters, the shingle roof, all appeared to be in as pristine condition as the backyard.

But those bars on the windows...

"I assume those bars have a release latch," he said, looking at them. She'd said she and her son rented out the apartment on the top floor. Three stories up. Too far to jump. "And that there's an emergency fold-down ladder in every room..." They hung on the windowsill, allowing occupants to exit quickly and safely in case of fire.

He felt her movement, her agitation, but didn't turn from his view of the house.

"There's no latch," she told him. "They open with a key."

"And the key's in the lock in each room?"

"No. I have them all. The whole point of living here is because I can sleep at night knowing my son can't get out."

She'd told him about the nightmares. Had mentioned bars. But...

He looked her right in the eye. "Faye, these old houses, they were built before code and while there's a lot you can do to make them fire-safe, you're still more at risk. On the top floor...you and Elliott would be trapped...you have to have a quick exit..."

She stared at him, those big blue eyes seeming to see too much. She didn't say anything. Just nodded.

Frustrated by her lack of immediate attention to this very real danger—one never had warning when a faulty hundred-year-old electrical wire would burst into flame—he tried to figure out what the nod meant. In the old days, it would have meant acquiescence. He had a feeling that had changed.

"Suzie had a sprinkler system put in when she had the wiring redone," she said after a long moment of silence.

Rapping his fingers on the table, he decided to leave the matter alone for the moment. Sprinkler systems were expensive but effective. The "new wiring" comment appeased him, as well. He was pretty sure she'd chosen the statement deliberately.

"Sometimes there are no easy answers and you have to weigh all sides of a situation," she said, looking toward the house. "In those cases, I find that you have to determine which avenue is the least dangerous, given the circumstances, and take that road."

Avenues and roads. He preferred it when she didn't speak in metaphors.

"In this case, the chance of my son throwing himself out a window while sleepwalking is far higher than that the house will catch fire. I have the keys to the bars in easy reach for me, not him, in every room."

She'd told him about one episode. Maybe she'd alluded to others, but… "How often does he sleepwalk?"

He'd thought the activity to be an anomaly, not the norm.

"Lately, once or twice a week."

And then he remembered more… "You said a lot of times he meets some ordinary physiological need and goes right back to bed."

"Correct."

"How do you know he's not just awake and needing a trip to the bathroom?"

Back when they were together, he'd have asked her how she knew her son didn't just wake up needing to pee. They'd been able to talk openly about everything back then. Her period or cramps. The time he'd had diarrhea for three days and had preferred death.

"You know," she said. "You can stand right in front of him and he doesn't react. He doesn't see you. If you stand directly in his path, he'll walk right into you."

"But he doesn't walk into walls?"

"Sometimes. A lot when we first moved here. But he knows the apartment now. I guess his brain remembers."

He was studying her now, house and yard forgotten. Trying to get inside her head, where he'd once been welcome. To do that, he had to be able to envision the life she led.

"Do you make certain that the floors are cleared of anything that might have been put down or left during the day, just in case?"

"Yeah." Her gaze softened. It was the first time he'd seen that look since before they'd broken up. He'd kissed her, long and hard, before she'd left his car to return to her dorm room. He'd had no idea that was going to be the last time he saw her.

A sharp jab of pain brought him back to his senses.

What in the hell was he doing?

That was when he remembered, he had no reason to get back inside her mind, her world. A quick self-check confirmed that he didn't want to be there, after all.

He took a sip of his tea and pulled his ankle up to rest on his knee, avoiding her eyes.

He was there for business.

The End.

CHAPTER SIXTEEN

FAYE HAD LEARNED the source of her strength the moment she'd held her newborn son in her arms for the first time.

Elliott was it.

She could do anything if it was in his best interests. If it was for his good.

She'd thought she was bearing Frank's atrocities because it was best for their son that they remain a family. Because Frank didn't beat her, or even belittle her in front of the boy.

She'd thought that part of her life was completely separate from her son. Elliott had never said a word to the contrary.

Not until the day he'd understood that he never had to see his father again.

She'd talked to a counselor before breaking the news to the then six-year-old boy. She'd been prepared for many eventualities: his anger, his fear, his refusal to go with her, his blame. They hadn't prepared her for his one-word response.

"Good."

She'd promised herself, after she'd left Frank, that she'd never go into a situation unprepared again. The promise had been comforting. She'd wanted to keep it.

But it was unrealistic. She could control many things but not everything.

Just as she'd been unable to predict Elliott's re-action the day she'd told him about the divorce, she could not possibly know how the next moments in her life were going to play out.

And now, two years later, she couldn't predict how Reese was going to react to the questions she had to ask. She felt like she might throw up, though.

He was in the middle of a work day. He wasn't going to sit around wasting his time.

And she wasn't sure she could work herself up to this a second time. She'd been awake far more than she'd dozed the night before, playing everything out in her mind.

The time. The surroundings. Where everyone would be. The tea. That last touch had been that morning as she'd stood in her bathroom and opted for light makeup. She sure as hell didn't want him to think she was coming on to him. Which was why she'd worn her "old lady" dress, as Elliott described it. It embarrassed him when she wore it. She was planning to change before picking him up from the Stand.

Her palms were wet so she touched the tea glass, letting glass sweat and nerves mingle.

Look him straight in the eye. That was next on her list.

Deliver rehearsed line one, came after. There was much she couldn't predict, words she'd have to come up with on the spot. But she'd already planned out—actually had written it out that morning after dropping Elliott off—all that she knew going in.

Reese's dark eyes were slightly hooded. He wasn't sure of her. Wasn't completely comfortable. But she didn't think he seemed all that worried, either.

He was not going to be happy.

"I have something to tell you. And then to ask you."

Line one had looked good on paper, had sounded better in her head.

Too late to change course. She had a plan and sticking to it was the way to keep herself healthiest.

"But before I get to that, I have a question to ask you."

His answer wouldn't affect Elliott's paternity—but it mattered to her self-trust, and thus her son's ability to trust himself.

Reese's warm hand was so close to hers on the table. If she moved slightly, her knee would be touching his. She wanted to. So badly. More than she'd ever imagined.

She hadn't planned to feel like this.

Panic pulsed through every vein in her body. Painfully. Taking her air.

For a second she sat suspended in a space where only throwing herself in Reese's arms would bring her breath. Life.

He'd been her everything. There was a level, deep down, where they had met and everything was all right.

It had been there from the very beginning.

She needed to meet him there. Immediately.

"Ask away." He'd turned his head, still looking at her but not quite head-on. This man didn't trust her.

And without trust, there was no deeper world. Or, at least, no access to it.

She didn't trust him, either. Because of a phone call that may or may not have been truth, their world had been obliterated. Fact.

If Reese had been unfaithful to her, they'd both been responsible for the demise of their relationship. That didn't change things. But it mattered.

"I asked you to a party the Friday night before homecoming," she said, just as she'd rehearsed. No accusation. No emotion or drama. "You had night drills."

He actually jerked. She felt it in the brush of his calf against hers.

"I know this is not a current-business question, Reese, but I'm asking you to believe that it's taking me straight to what I've brought you here to tell you."

"And this thing you have to tell me…the thing after a different question other than the one you're currently asking…this thing is current business?"

Not fire business. But… "Very much so."

He nodded and sat up straight, his legs farther away, his elbows on the arms of his chair. "I remember the night you're referring to," he said.

"Did you go out with Susan Shepherd that night?"

His eyes narrowed. And she knew. He didn't have to answer. She just knew.

"This is important why?" he asked, sounding less professional, and less friendly, by the second.

There was no script for that. So she went with the truth, just as she'd planned.

"It's important to my mental and emotional health."

He studied her, as though looking for the lie in her story. Looking for how she was trying to get something from him. At least that was how his reaction seemed to her.

She found herself doing something she'd warned herself, over and over again, not to do. She was getting defensive.

Her tongue started moving before she could stop it.

"I knew, Reese." How could the betrayal feel

fresh all over again? "Joey Moore called. He told me you'd turned me down because you were going out with Susan."

Shifting in his chair, Reese leaned forward. And then back.

How could a man look so incredibly good to her as he sat there with guilt written all over him?

"That's why I told you not to come to home-coming at all," she said. "Because I knew."

She could see the movement in his jaw as his muscles tensed.

"I wanted you to break the date. To come to my Friday night party. To prove to me that I meant more to you than she did."

"You didn't think about just…I don't know… asking…"

Later, she had.

When it was too late.

"After that weekend, I…" No, wait. She had to follow her script. "By the end of the weekend, I'd convinced myself that I'd been wrong. And that I'd done you a huge disservice. I'd tried to manip-ulate you into doing what I wanted, and I'd acted out of jealousy without ever giving you a chance to explain."

He nodded. That was all. Just a nod.

She couldn't leave it at that.

"But if I was right, Reese, if my sense that what Joey said really was true, then I've spent nine years erroneously mistrusting myself. Nine years when I needed to be able to trust myself more than anything else in the world."

Damn the tears that came to her eyes. She'd promised…

He bit his lower lip. Jutted his chin some more.

"Did you go out with Susan Shepherd that night?" She had a plan. Couldn't move on without an answer.

He looked her straight in the eye. "Yes."

THERE WAS MORE Reese could say. So much more.

He could tell Faye how he'd been observing a fire scene earlier that week. He'd watched a burning beam fall on a fireman, hitting him across the back of his shoulders, knocking him unconscious.

He could tell her how he'd kept the incident to himself because he hadn't wanted to scare her or give her a reason to doubt his career choice. The accident had made him look at his life differently, had messed with his brain. For a few days there, he'd been consumed with fear.

So he'd asked Susan out just to be sure that he wasn't making a mistake, spending his entire life with one woman. He'd gone out with Susan to make certain that Faye was the one.

And to run from the truth that had come home

to him. If he married Faye, he could also be asking her to sign on to early widowhood.

If they had a family, he might leave his kids fatherless.

As Reese sat in that charming backyard, sipping sweet tea with two lemons, it all came rushing back to him. With more clarity than he'd seen in…ever.

He could have shared the clarity with Faye.

But this was her meeting. Her business.

He was her boss.

The kid he'd been had gone on a group date with Susan as his companion. He'd never touched her. He'd been in his own bed, alone, by midnight.

Faye eventually married the other man she'd dated that same weekend. Married him and had his son.

She'd broken up with him in a text message. Because she'd known about Susan.

He didn't want to dredge up the past any more. He'd worked too long and too hard to get his present just the way he wanted it.

HE'D BEEN UNFAITHFUL to her. He'd blown her off to go out with another girl. The news should have been catastrophic. Should have hit her like bricks to the head.

Instead, while her heart bled a bit, Faye was overwhelmed with the knowledge that she'd been right. She'd known. She grieved. Had been grieving for nine long years.

Now, along with the pain came a sense of relief. Like she'd been holding something so tightly for so long that she quivered with its release.

She'd known.

Had been trying to tell herself.

Finally, she was capable of hearing.

She wanted Reese to go, but she wasn't done.

Elliott deserved the chance to not be Frank Walker's son.

The first time Frank had abused her, within a month of their son's birth, she'd discovered a place inside herself. A safe place. A little "room" she could go to deep in her mind. It blocked out the physical pain—mostly. If she could concentrate hard enough on the room, on being there, on what she was doing there, on which imaginary person was there with her, she could endure whatever else was happening to her.

For a moment, sitting in the garden with Reese, she tried to access that place in her mind. To find peace, and the numbness that would allow her to get through the rest of the interview.

Interview—that was a good word. Impersonal.

She was *interviewing* Reese.

That was all.

CHAPTER SEVENTEEN

"I HAVE A STORY to tell you."

Sweating, ready to lift dumbbells twice his weight and then toss them across the street, Reese welcomed Faye's words.

Because a story in the present left the past behind.

And got to the point of a visit he was deeply regretting.

He hadn't touched Susan—hadn't been able to get Faye out of his mind long enough to even relax with the other girl. Couldn't even picture her features clearly anymore.

Faye had known?

Joey's face, not looking so good, flashed before his mind's eye, and he knew he had to get back to work.

The past was done.

He couldn't change any of it.

Not Susan. Not Faye. And not Tabitha, either.

"Before I start, I need your word that you will let me finish without interruption," Faye was saying now.

What was it with the woman and all her rules? Her need for control?

Had being abused given her some kind of obsessive compulsive disorder?

"I won't interrupt." He gave her what she asked for with one purpose in mind. Getting out of there as quickly as possible.

Her nod seemed like a good sign. And then she bit her lip.

If she started to cry again, he wasn't sure he could stop himself from taking her in his arms and begging her to forgive him for Susan.

But his date with another girl hadn't been the only problem between them. With clarity came truth. Faye had needed more from him than he'd been able to give.

As much as he'd loved her, the college boy he'd been, and the man he'd grown into, hadn't believed enough in the bone-deep kind of love she'd needed.

They might have had a lifetime together, maybe. If they'd worked hard and were lucky.

If they could make it through the differences of opinion that would be inevitable.

But their love hadn't been strong enough to make it through one...

Enough. No more going back.

She was taking a sip of tea. Seemed to have collected herself.

Thank God.

If he had to see a therapist because of this meeting, he was billing her.

The thought was beneath him. But satisfied something in him, too.

Until she opened her mouth and started to speak. Telling him about Carrie's boyfriend, the brother that had driven down from San Francisco. About agreeing to go out with them, to keep the brother company so Carrie and her boyfriend could dance and have some time alone together.

By the time he got that she was explaining something he didn't want to know, he was already in too deep. It wasn't his promise that kept him from interrupting.

It was his inability to speak at all.

She'd spent the evening drinking to shut up the pictures in her head of him with another woman. Had talked about him all night.

The idea of it made his heart pound.

This didn't sound like a woman who'd break up in a text message. Not even because of Susan.

She'd been so drunk she'd been unable to walk by herself?

Stunned, he couldn't even picture Faye in that state.

Even with all that, nothing prepared him for the next part of her story. She told it in a calm tone. As though speaking about someone she didn't know.

Like a man watching a train wreck he knew

was going to happen but couldn't prevent it, he listened as she spoke about the next morning.

Blood surged through his veins. His teeth were gritting together so hard he had half a thought that they might break.

"You were raped."

It had never occurred to him. Not once. Not even in his craziest, darkest moments. Faye had been raped?

She was one of the college statistics? The unconscious girl raped after having had too much to drink and trusting her companions?

One of the girls who didn't come forward.

Reese heard roaring in his ears.

Closed his eyes against the rage.

He'd hated her for so long…

Hadn't been able to forgive…

And now he knew…

He knew why she'd sent that text message.

Reese had promised her he wouldn't interrupt. He hadn't promised he wouldn't leave.

Half-aware of the chair falling backward behind him, he left the table. Headed toward the gate.

She didn't call out to him.

But he felt her back there. Sitting alone.

He turned around. Saw her there. Shoulders straight. Watching him without a shred of emotion on her face.

This was what that bastard had done to her.

Stripped her of the open, nurturing heart that Reese had cherished.

But he hadn't cherished her. He knew that now.

Reese wasn't sure who he hated more in that moment—the brother. Or himself. Truth was, he was a bit angry with her, too, for going out at all.

And that made him hate himself more.

Bitterness became acid on his tongue.

He wanted it there. Wanted anything that would take away awareness of the gaping hole deep inside him.

He strode back to the table. Looked her right in the eye. Meant to say something decent. But couldn't get his mouth open.

He just kept staring into those beautiful blue eyes.

And felt his own grow moist.

God, what had he done?

ELLIOTT. SHE HAD to think of Elliott.

Reese was going to have questions. He was going to want to know how she came to be married to Frank after that disastrous homecoming night.

She had to give him the truth. To paint the picture exactly as it was. It was the only way to help him trust her.

And he had to trust her. If any of them were going to get through this and find happiness on the other side.

She'd cried her tears. Would be crying them for the rest of her life. This pain she could handle. Most of the time. She'd learned how to manage.

But Reese...

In all of the years she'd known him, she'd never seen him cry, or even express any deeply intense emotion. Other than passion.

"It's okay, Reese," she said. And then did the unthinkable. She took his hand. "Please sit back down."

He did. But she wasn't sure he'd be staying long.

"I'm so..." He hadn't let go of her hand. Started to pull her toward him.

The way her free hand came up to stop him wasn't planned. She didn't know who was more surprised, him or her.

If he'd been any other male, she'd have understood and expected the reaction. But this was Reese. And she'd recently discovered that he was the one man her psyche would let near her.

She'd been making love with him in her sleep for weeks. Waking up turned on as hell.

"You said you wouldn't interrupt." The words came because they'd been rehearsed. He had no idea what Frank had done to her over the years.

And she wasn't about to tell him.

The conversation wasn't about details, or her current sexual inabilities.

She'd cry about that again later, when she was

alone and could hug herself. Hide her wounds. Let herself nourish the damaged woman inside.

As quickly as she could, she told Reese about finding out she was pregnant a month later. About calling the brother. She told him what he'd told her about that night, how he'd said they both agreed it was the best sex they'd ever had.

Reese stood up again. "That's it. That's enough. I get that you must have a need to be cruel to me, Faye. That you blame me for what happened. And if it makes you feel any better, I blame myself now, okay? But I'm not going to sit here and listen to you telling me in detail how sex with another man was far better than…"

She was afraid he was really going to go. He couldn't. Not until they were done here.

She got up, too. Stepped right up to him, face-to-face, until they were almost touching.

How could a man still smell the same after so many years?

How could she remember the scent?

And how could she, so damaged by Frank's abuse, get wet from just a whiff of that scent?

She'd ask Sara or Bloom. She'd think about it later. She couldn't get distracted. She'd almost made it through.

She wasn't going to let Elliott down now.

As always, thoughts of her son gave her strength.

She put one hand on his chest.

He stepped back.

"Please, Reese. I asked you to trust that there would be reason for telling you this. I'm not saying what I'm saying to be cruel. I need you to understand…"

"I have no need to understand that you enjoyed…"

I didn't! The words screamed from inside her. They didn't make it past her throat.

"If I don't tell you this part, you aren't going to understand the next…"

Whether it was her tone of voice, a look in her eye or some need he had to hear the rest, she didn't know, but she was glad when Reese sat back down.

She did, too, keeping her knees close to him. Allowing herself that comfort.

She told him how the other man adored her. How he wanted to make a home, a life, for her and their son. She told him about her hope that Reese would argue with her about breaking up with him. That he'd call. Come to get her.

And how, when he didn't, she knew she had no choice. She trusted that she'd loved being with the other man because she couldn't trust anything she'd felt with Reese. Because she couldn't trust Reese.

She knew when his eyes narrowed again that he'd figured it out.

"Frank." He bit out the word. "The brother was Frank. You married the man who raped you."

That he had used that word again felt like a gift. A lift to her soul.

And, maybe, a paving stone to the question she had yet to ask him.

CHAPTER EIGHTEEN

HE HAD TO GO. Reese couldn't stand looking at Faye.

Couldn't stand being close to her.

He couldn't stand himself, either.

Shaking his head, he was at a loss, almost numb, unable to process everything.

He was her boss.

The idea sat well with him suddenly. Became almost a godsend. He'd dealt with inescapable, almost unbelievable tragedy during the course of his work.

He knew how to do that.

When he was working, he had to focus on the facts and determine how he could best help.

The facts.

Had Frank Walker raped Faye? Or had she enjoyed the sex as he'd told her?

It was possible she had. Reese had been her first lover.

He'd been pretty much as green as she'd been when they'd started out.

But he'd never been inside a woman before. Never even touched a naked woman before Faye.

An older, more experienced man might have done better.

But she'd woken up in tears. Devastated.

Even hungover and with no memory of the night before, a woman would surely hold on to any residual pleasure, right? Subconsciously at least?

He needed facts.

To help where he best could.

And move on to the next item on his to-do list.

At the moment he couldn't remember what that was.

The meeting with Kellogg, his buddy. Someone he'd known a long time. But not as long as he'd known Faye. New family.

New history.

She was watching him. With a lack of employee distance. While he assessed his schedule, she seemed to be assessing him.

Maybe she just knew him well enough to know that he needed a minute.

He'd changed over the years. But not nearly as much as she had. He'd grown more into himself. She'd grown into someone else.

And yet, when he met her gaze, he felt…something. Recognition. The woman he'd known… parts of her still existed.

He just wasn't sure how they fell into the rest of her.

And didn't want to know.

"You said you had a question." He assumed the storytelling was over.

Had he really been there less than an hour?

Seemed like days.

"I need a sample of your DNA."

Reese's jaw dropped.

FAYE COULDN'T BREATHE. Sitting in the chair, she felt herself getting light-headed. She tried to calm herself, muscle by muscle.

She'd done it.

She'd made it through the presentation. The next part, part four, his answer, was completely out of her control.

She had no idea what to do while she waited.

The man across from her sat there, completely frozen. She wanted to lay her head against his chest, a chest she could picture naked.

Slowly, deliberately, as though being programmed, he bent to pick a piece of lint off his foot.

He was going to leave without doing his part, without answering her. He wasn't even going to give her a chance…

Panic flared inside her.

"Elliott had a tonsillectomy a couple of years ago." She blurted the words. She'd said them to Bloom Larson, who had understood.

Hadn't she? Or was that Sara?

"When I got home from the hospital Frank…

was abusive." Reese was leaning forward like he was going to stand. She rushed ahead. "For the first time I didn't comply—" *Doesn't matter why. Just keep going.* "—I showed my disgust. And he unleashed like never before…"

She had no plan for this, no rehearsed words, but Reese was watching her. And she knew for certain that she had his full attention.

"He told me I was frigid." Because he'd made her that way. She knew that now. Just as she knew the condition might very well be permanent.

That was very definitely not Reese material.

"Just like that night in your dorm room, he said." She tripped over her tongue in her hurry. "His semen touched me, but he couldn't penetrate. I was too tight…"

Even in her drunkenness she hadn't welcomed another man.

Not that it mattered anymore…

"Elliott's been getting worse," she hurried on, pulling out every card she had and throwing them on the table. "Not his grades, he's doing well there. But his sleepwalking. His disrespect for me and…he's isolating himself. Sara Havens, his counselor at the Stand, believes it's because he's trying to protect everyone from the Frank inside him. Some little-boy way of fighting back against what he heard between his father and me, that he can't handle."

With head bent, Reese looked at her. She'd

never seen this expression before. It was old. And tired. "You asked for my DNA."

She met his gaze head-on. "I didn't sleep with Frank again—or at all, I know now—until after Elliott was born. There's still a chance he's Elliott's father, but from what I'm told, there's an equally good and possibly better chance that you are."

His lower lip thinned. His chin puckered. He stared at her.

"And if you are, then the news could greatly affect the next years of his life.

"If what Sara believes is true, the news could completely turn him around. Eventually." She had to be completely honest with him.

About Elliott.

And ignore the fact that she was sitting with the love of her life, discussing the possibility that they had a child together.

She'd thought life had already exacted all of its most painful moments on her. She was discovering that there was no end to them.

"There would be another period of adjustment. Change, even good change, is seen as a negative thing to a lot of kids. In Elliott's case, more so, because he already struggles with a sense of insecurity. Most kids adapt to change more quickly than adults, but with Elliott, having so much change…"

He was going to hate her if Elliott was his son.

For so many reasons.

Not least of which was the fact that Faye hadn't kept him any safer than she'd kept herself. She'd exposed him to something so hellacious that he had to take his schooling at a secure shelter with daily counseling.

Reese nodded. He stood. Turned to leave.

"Reese?"

She wanted to go after him. To cling to his arm and beg if she had to. Nothing was beneath her anymore, it seemed. Not where Elliott was concerned. But she was shaking so badly her knees gave out on her.

He was opening the gate before she got out of her chair.

She stumbled after him.

"Reese."

"I need you to leave me alone now, Faye," he said.

He wasn't going to give her the DNA sample. He was walking out of her life for the final time.

And he was probably going to fire her.

She saw it all coming like a big black freight train racing down the track.

"Please, Reese."

He shook his head, opened the door of his truck. "I need to think."

He was gone before she could move again.

But the tears pouring down her cheeks weren't all filled with sorrow. Reese was going away to consider her request.

There was some part of him that was still the man she loved. And some part of her knew that.

They might have eradicated their sacred, shared space—if it had ever existed—but as with all things, a piece of what they'd been remained. Maybe just a little piece, but it was there.

The idea of it comforted her.

HE MISSED HIS MEETING. Didn't even call to excuse himself. Sometime after four o'clock, he received an inquiring text.

To which he didn't reply.

He was, bottom line, a fireman. Emergencies were common. And didn't always allow time for niceties like adjusting social calendars. Kellogg would understand the missed meeting.

Reese wasn't sure anyone would ever be able to make sense of the thoughts spiraling through his mind.

He wanted a drink. A strong one.

He thought of Faye…so drunk she couldn't walk home alone.

He went to the woods instead.

To climb as high as he could get on the tallest peak of the mountain closest to Santa Raquel. It took him until dark. And then he sat there, atop the cliff, and breathed.

Brandt was on duty. Reese had already signed himself out before he'd left after lunch, figuring he'd be spending the rest of the day with Kellogg.

He hadn't thought of that until he sat there alone in the dark, though.

Hadn't given a thought to the station. To the lives that depended on him. The town that expected him to be mindful of their care.

As he'd climbed, he'd tried to eradicate the pictures in his head, scenes concocted by Faye's words and real scenes from his past with her.

He thought about Tabitha.

About the son she'd tried to give him—about the fact that she hadn't even felt loved enough to tell him she was carrying the child.

And about a little boy who was isolating himself from the people and friends and love he needed most because he feared he was evil like the man who'd made him.

Reese had no choice here.

He knew that.

Just as he knew that once they opened this Pandora's box, if it turned out that Elliott was not Frank Walker's son, life was going to get real hard in a lot of ways.

Reese wasn't father material. He knew that now. Risking his life was an everyday thing for him. He thrived on the adrenaline of knowing he was challenging nature to save lives.

And he wasn't what Faye needed, either.

Not that she was asking him to be. Not anymore. That ship had clearly sailed.

For both of them.

And yet…

The pictures would not let up. Then and now. Faye's eyes, trusting and then empty. Her voice, filled with laughter, emotion, passion. And then… empty.

And her arms.

At one time, they'd opened for him even across the city. She'd always welcomed him. Whether they were having a spat or ready to make love, he'd open his arms and she'd walk into them and hang on tight. That woman had had a grip that…

Today, he'd tried to pull her closer and she'd stopped him. With a hand up that had delivered a very clear and serious message.

Any farther and he was moving against her will.

A crime in his book.

He hadn't abused her. Not physically. But he'd abused her trust. Been unfaithful to their love. He'd lied to her.

And she'd married her rapist.

He couldn't wrap his mind around any of it. Didn't even want to.

He wanted it to go away.

Wanted himself to go away. Right over the mountain, to a new town, a new start. To fight fires he understood.

And then, in his mind's eye, he saw Elliott. The serious look in those blue eyes—his eyes? But Faye's were blue, too—and heard again the solemn oath the little boy had made, exchanging a phone call for a fire-truck tour.

The kid had called the fire chief to confess to a fire in a boy's bathroom trash can. He'd been prepared to go to jail.

He walked in his sleep and got violent sometimes when he did it.

He loved his mother but was also hateful to her.

It was that last thought that got him.

On his feet, Reese headed down the mountain. He was well trained. Knew how to move in the darkness. And he took his time.

Out of nowhere came a replay of Elliott's grocery bag conversation on the beach.

Of a doctor telling him that he'd lost a son.

Of Tabitha's desperate emptiness because he couldn't give her what she needed.

He was probably going to start looking for another job, preferably farther north.

But not until he'd done what he could to be the most help.

Not until he'd done what he could to teach one little boy—his or not—that a man didn't disrespect his mother. Ever.

CHAPTER NINETEEN

FAYE WASN'T SURPRISED when she didn't hear from Reese over the weekend. She'd given him a lot to process. In some ways she was glad for the reprieve. She purposely left her phone at home when she took Elliott to the beach on Saturday, but she spent the afternoon looking over her shoulder, worried that Reese would come find her there. Made sense that he would, if he had something to say. It was where they'd talked the week before.

Elliott was being his usual surly self. Wouldn't sit at the same table with her when she took him to get hamburgers so she'd asked for a takeout bag and taken him home. He ate at the table. She didn't eat.

It was almost a relief to be called into work Saturday night. Her work generally meant a life was in danger and she never wanted that to be the case. But to have the chance to save a life...

The crash was a single car wrapped around a tree. It was filled with teenagers. As she approached, she heard moaning, crying and screaming.

The call had said there were at least three.

One male, two female based on her first impression.

The front end of the car was smashed in to the steering wheel. Front seats were where the back should be, somewhat on top of them. A team member was already prying open the trunk. Faye didn't stop to see who.

Rushing to the passenger side where the door was partially open, she pulled with every ounce of force she had, then shined her light inside. Looking for eyes staring back at her. For trapped bodies, freed bodies and signs of bleeding.

She was going to have to choose who she helped first. There was no time for emotion. Her decision was based on her chances of saving a life. Of saving the most lives.

A pair of blue eyes stared back at her. Male. Young. Fifteen to seventeen. Her heart lurched. The boy had a mother at home completely unaware...

A girl was there, too. Screaming. While it was horrible to hear, it was also a good sound.

"Shhhh," she said, dropping her bag and bending to the girl first. Same approximate age as the boy. No visible bleeding. Pupils dilated but not dangerously so. "Save your energy," she told her.

"Get me a gurney!" Faye cried as loud as she could. Then she continued to talk to the girl. "Watch my face," she said. "Just concentrate on my face." The girl's arm was so badly broken that the bone was showing through her skin. She had some lacerations but otherwise seemed okay. "You're going to be fine, but we have to get you out of here to get to your friend, here. It's going to hurt. Try to moan, not scream." The last was just to give the teenager something to concentrate on as she taped the girl's arm to her stomach.

Hardly hearing the screams at that point, she helped Brandt get the girl onto the gurney, and then, as Brandt whisked her toward a waiting ambulance, she went to work on the boy.

Riley had the trunk open and another EMT was working on the person in the back. She turned to the boy whose eyes she'd first seen.

He'd lost consciousness. A blessing. He probably wasn't going to make it.

The driver, she'd already ascertained. He'd been belted in. The windshield had pierced through him, just below his rib cage. His arm hung nearly severed.

Right side. She felt for a pulse. If by some miracle the glass had missed vital organs...

The pulse was strong. She could save him!

The next twenty minutes were a blur of activity, of focus without conscious thought, without emotion as Faye used all her training to slow bleeding, to do what she could to try to prevent full-on shock and get the young man out of the car and onto a stretcher.

Brandt was back. He assisted where he could.

But it was Faye who lifted the teenager out of the car. She'd been the one who could get farthest in, could get a grip on that mangled body, knowing what to support and how. She didn't contemplate. She worked.

She saw him to the stretcher. Ran with it to the waiting ambulance. Climbed in back with him. Rode with him to the hospital. She stayed long enough to hear that he was in surgery and still alive.

And then, in blood-stained clothes, she went home to shower and lie down on the couch in her son's room. Elliott could hate her if he needed to.

And she'd love him.

Because that was what she had to do. What she would do. With every breath she took. Every day. For the rest of her life.

Her son was safe at home. In his bed.

Suddenly nothing else mattered.

REESE HEARD THE call come in. A one-car accident. He waited for a call. When it didn't come, he willed himself back to sleep.

And when that didn't work, he got himself a beer and sat in his home office. He went over his notes, over the copies of evidence he'd brought home pertaining to their serial arsonist. They were about to get through a Saturday night without a fire.

Because Kyle was on notice?

Reese wanted it to be that simple. But he didn't think so.

The choice of whether or not to give his DNA to Faye for a paternity test should be simple, too. If it was the right thing to do. His answer was either yes or no.

Just that clear.

And not clear at all.

He'd given up on being a father. Wasn't father material.

If he didn't do the test, Elliott's world wouldn't be further upset. The kid could go on with the status quo.

And what if that status quo ultimately did more harm than good?

What good would it do him to find out he had a father, one who wasn't going to be a father to him?

Or to be split between homes? His and Faye's?

How cruel was fate that the one thing Reese had wanted, the one big dream he'd had—a family with Faye—would arrive nine years too late and in such a twisted, agonizing fashion?

It wasn't like they could go back.

Elliott was eight years old and troubled. Two hours and three beers later, Reese went back to his bedroom. He lay down and stared at the ceiling.

Cursing fate.

SURPRISINGLY, FAYE SLEPT relatively well for the couple of hours she got before rising to go to her own bed. She left before Elliott awoke and found her there.

She'd needed the sleep and needed it even more on Sunday as her son deliberately challenged every order she gave him—from bringing her his laundry to brushing his teeth.

More like refused to do anything she asked.

The one thing he'd done was carry in the groceries when they got back from a tense trip to the store. If she picked up ham, he wanted bologna. When she got the creamy peanut butter he liked, he exchanged it for crunchy. He wouldn't eat crunchy, but she left it in the cart.

When he announced that he was going to eat donuts for breakfast that week, she told him that he was not and took them back out of the cart.

"You aren't the boss of my stomach," he informed her so loudly that the older woman shopping in the same aisle looked up. Faye ignored the disapproving look on her face.

She couldn't give in. But she was so tired of the constant fight.

When they got home and Elliott insisted on carrying up all of the groceries, she started to breathe easier. When he wasn't exploding with anger at the world, Elliott was kind and funny. He'd always been so helpful.

She might not get many hours with that boy anymore, but the thought of even having a couple of them that weekend brought tears to her eyes. She quickly brushed them away before he saw them.

And was rewarded by his refusal to put the water bottles on the bottom shelf of the refrigerator. He had to use the restroom, he'd said.

And didn't come back.

Something was going to have to change. She knew that. With Reese's help or without, they couldn't go on like this.

And the thought of hearing from her ex-lover, of moving forward, made it hard to breathe. Made her yearn for sleep.

About a year's worth.

While she desperately wanted to stop time, to put off the inevitable next step—either way it went—she was resigned to the inevitable when she got a text from him Sunday night.

He wanted to meet her in his office first thing the next morning. Asked her to come straight in after dropping off Elliott.

Will do, she texted back. She always went straight from the Stand to work.

The waiting was over. The wondering would soon be over. There was a measure of peace to be found in that.

She would have felt a whole lot better if he'd asked to meet her someplace outside of work. His choice of meeting spot told her his answer: business, not personal. He was going to turn her down. And ask her to resign.

It had been a chance she'd had to take.

In the morning, after it was done, she'd panic. And then do what she had to do. She'd get out of her lease. She and Elliott could move into the Stand until she found another job and a cheaper apartment. All things that could be dealt with in the morning.

That night Faye lay down in her bed, covered up and cried.

SHE WAS ARMED with internal fortitude—anything for Elliott—and ready in blue jeans and her dressy white top, with her hair pulled back and makeup applied well.

She knocked on Reese's office door the next morning. She'd almost worn sandals instead of her work boots but had changed her mind when she heard her son call out to her from the kitchen to tell her they were out of milk. If he hadn't had two bowls of cereal during the night, they wouldn't have been. She'd given him a pastry for breakfast and put on her boots.

She didn't want Elliott to notice them missing from her feet and ask why. Not until she'd had the day to make plans. To give him a done deal so that he'd know that he was going to be taken care of.

"Come in," Reese called from his office, further evidence that she was leaving as of that day. He could have opened the door to her.

Or even left it open as a sign of welcome.

Seeing him in a white shirt and tie behind his desk put another nail in the coffin. And that was fine.

She'd had to try. And now she'd move on. She'd find a way.

Maybe moving Elliott across the country *was* the answer. Taking him away from what was familiar meant ridding him of a sense of living as Frank's son. Maybe distance would help the memories fade...

It didn't jibe with what Sara said about keeping a semblance of sameness in Elliott's world, but it made sense. It was the best she'd been able to come up with in the middle of the night, exhausted as she sat at the kitchen table and watched her sleeping son eat cereal.

That and the fact that at least she wouldn't be pulling Elliott away from new friends. New closeness. Her son had already done that by himself.

"Have a seat," Reese said, giving her a brief glance before returning his gaze to an open file folder.

His actions bordered on rudeness.

Still, she couldn't blame him. At least not totally. She'd screwed up. Made incredibly foolish and immature choices—trying to jealously manipulate him rather than just ask him outright what was going on. Getting foolishly drunk. Waiting over two years to come to him with the knowledge that he might be a father—the first six years she hadn't even known it was a possibility. She'd had a period after sleeping with Reese the last time. It had been really light. But hers had always been erratic, so, for her, light for a month wasn't unusual.

According to her doctor, when she'd asked after Frank's revelation, that light period could have been normal for her, but she also could have been newly pregnant and spotting.

Still, Reese wasn't blameless, either. He'd gone out with Susan.

All weekend long her feelings about that had vacillated. She'd been comforted beyond measure by the fact that her heart had been right when it had told her that Reese was being unfaithful to her. And devastated, even after all this time, to find out that he really had been.

If making her wait now was some kind of power play, she hoped it did something for him. She was beyond being intimidated.

When he put the folder down, she almost stood, just to be ready to walk out.

For all she knew, the information in that folder was hers—maybe he was reading over the resignation letter he'd typed up, ready for her to sign.

"I'm sorry to make you wait," he said, his hands on the folder. "You're a couple of minutes early and I'm a bit late. We had a call at five this morning. A heart attack…"

He was talking about work. It calmed her.

Gave the moment some normalcy. She stayed put and listened.

"I meant to have this all read before you got here but couldn't proceed with our meeting until I got through it…" He motioned to the folder.

So she'd been right. It contained her file.

"I won't keep you in suspense," he said, his brown-eyed gaze calm but distant. "I've reached a decision. And I have…non-negotiable demands that go along with it."

He sounded like a chief. Not like a potential father of her child.

She nodded.

He was telling her not to beg again. He had no worries there. She'd made the last request of him she was ever going to make.

"I not only agree to submit to paternity DNA testing, I insist upon doing so. If you were to change your mind at this point, I would take you to court for the right to do so."

Faye stared, caught up on the word *agree*. Court. Rights. That was all way beyond her ability to comprehend in that moment.

"In addition, I insist that Elliott not be told until the results are in."

He paused, so she nodded. No-brainer there; she had already decided that.

"I insist that if I am his father, I be involved in the process of telling him. I want to be included in the meetings between you and his therapist and be involved in the decision making that determines how, when and where he'll be told."

Another pause. Another nod. She was going to have to start breathing soon or she wasn't going to be conscious for some of this meeting. She tried to take in more than short, staccato wisps of air.

"If the test is positive, I will be involved in decisions regarding his life, most particularly about educational choices and financial support."

She wanted to nod that time. It was taking everything she had to remain professional.

And she suddenly understood his choice of meeting place. He wasn't going to accept any emotion between them. This was all business.

"And I want it understood that we are not and are never going to be a family."

He raised his brows at her lack of response.

"I understand." She found words because she'd been over this part a million times in the past two years. She hadn't quite processed that they were here, at this point, that it was really happening, but she'd played it over so many times in her imagination that she knew her part. "I'm fully prepared to give you full visitation, shared custody even, with the only caveat being that it's within Elliott's best interests. The only time I will step in, from here on out, is if my son is being further damaged by choices we've made."

He studied her for too long. She was about to crack.

But she wouldn't do it in front of him.

He hadn't mentioned her job. But it could soon become impossible for them to work together. To continue on as though they had nothing in common. Most particularly if it came out that they shared a son.

"What about my working here? What will we tell the others?"

"Your job is secure as long as you do it well. As for the rest, we'll discuss that once we know more."

That was what she couldn't do. Just leave things to chance.

"Reese, don't you think we should have a plan? DNA tests only take a couple of days now. When the results come back, it'll be go time. We need to plan for either eventuality."

He shrugged. "If they come back negative, nothing changes. No need to plan for that eventuality. If it comes back positive, we meet with Sara and go from there."

He made it all sound so simple.

Doable, even.

It wasn't going to be that easy. Maybe in terms of Elliott's best interests, it would be easy to decide some things. But even there, they had to factor in her son's emotional reaction. While ultimately it had to be better for Elliott to have Reese for a father, his immediate reaction could go either way.

"Sara will guide us through Elliott's part of this, Reese, but what about us? We have emotions, too."

He leaned forward and lowered his voice. "You and I are not an 'us.' We are just two people dealing with a critical situation."

He didn't fool her that time. Reese was hiding. No way the man she'd known was that dead.

"You will feel things, Reese, either way," she told him softly. "All of this thought and energy spent, the waiting, the wondering, you'll feel something if you find out he's not yours. But even more, if he is, it's going to change your whole life. Even if you chose to ignore the news and move away, it's going to change everything. But being here, being a part of his life—"

"I see I need to make something else clear," Reese interrupted. His tone had changed, but it hadn't grown any warmer, or more personal.

"I have no intention of being a hands-on father, with talk of shared custody, et cetera. I've learned some things about myself in the years we've been apart. Things you'd have no way of knowing. I am not a man who believes in deep, abiding, forever love. I feel the feelings, but I know that they are transient. I've been thinking about why I went out with Susan and I've realized that this is part of it. You needed more than I could give you, Faye. I let you down. And my wife, too, for that matter. If that boy is mine, I've made up my mind that I will not give him false expectation as I gave both of you. Right up front, it needs to be understood that I can be relied upon for some things but not for others."

He'd gone and done it. He'd opened the floodgate. Right there in his office. She'd been teetering on the brink, had been so close to getting out of there intact.

"What did I ever need that you didn't give me? Except, in the end, fidelity. You make me sound like some clingy, needy woman," she said. "I've never been that. Growing up alone with my father, having to take care of the house... I've always been self-sufficient." She would not be told, ever again, that she was something she was not.

Her years with Frank had solidified that one.

His bowed head didn't bode well. She bit her lip. This wasn't about her. Couldn't be about her. If she'd just screwed up Elliott's best chance...

Still, she wanted to ask him what false expectations he'd given his wife. Why his shoulders had dropped. As though, in telling her who he was, some life had drained out of him.

She wanted to but didn't. And wouldn't. He was not her business. He was firmly outside her circle of control...

He threw out a hand haphazardly. As though he didn't know what to do with it. "I just need it understood that there are to be no expectations other than the ones we delineate."

Good luck with that one. She couldn't afford not to give him everything he required. But…

"Reese, I think you need to understand something here. Elliott is an at-risk child with a mind of his own. You can set down whatever laws you want for him, but you can't dictate what he does with them. With his mind. Or with his heart. We can discuss all of this with Sara, but I can already tell you, just knowing my son, if he finds out you're his father, he will definitely have expectations. And something else I've learned, you might as well forget about living up to them. It's impossible."

Chin jutting—she was beginning to hate it when he did that—he rocked his head from side to side. Not nodding. Nothing with that much commitment attached.

"I work in a dangerous field. If I'm faced with risking my life to save another life, I do so. And will continue to do so. The boy will have to accept that, at the very least. That is as far as I can compromise on that one."

What was wrong with him? This wasn't the man she'd known. It was barely a semblance of him. She wanted to ask about his wife's death. Had he loved her so much that losing her had killed a part of him?

But he'd said he'd let his wife down, too. She'd died in a car accident. Surely he didn't think he could have prevented that?

So how did he think he'd let her down?

And how was she going to agree to his stipulations when she knew they were impossible? There was no way he could be involved in any capacity without some expectations being formed.

"No one is asking you to give up your job," she said. As far as she knew, anyway. Unless…had his wife wanted him to quit fire work? But he'd said that Faye had expected too much, too. "If you remember, Reese, I encouraged you to follow your call to work with fire. When we found out that it meant going to different colleges, I still encouraged you to go. I helped you get settled in your dorm. I was proud of your career choice, not afraid of it."

His jaw clenched. She'd overstepped. Gone too far.

Fine.

"You said that you were willing to take part in counseling as we proceed with this," she said. "Sara will tell us how to help Elliott understand." It was the best she could give him.

She wasn't going to lie to him. Or compromise her integrity with him.

He picked up the folder. "I've typed up my stipulations, along with my consent to the testing," he said. Picking up a pen, he signed the top page, then handed the folder and pen to her. "As soon as you sign, we can discuss details for the testing."

The news was beginning to sink in.

She was finally going to know if Reese was her son's father. Irrationally, inexplicably, uncontrollably, she wanted that more than she wanted to live out the rest of her natural life.

CHAPTER TWENTY

ONCE THE DEAL had been signed, Reese couldn't get the testing done soon enough. What Faye had said about the outcome changing his life forever wasn't sitting well with him. He tried to ignore her words.

But they nagged at him. Like a pesky gnat he could barely see but that kept making him itch.

His first thought had been to get samples from Elliott and Faye—tests were more conclusive if the lab also had the mother's DNA for comparison—immediately and take them to his friendly LA lab, have his own sample taken, and have them processed immediately.

Faye thought it better for Sara to determine how best to secure Elliott's sample so as not to raise his suspicions, and to have a local lab run the test.

There was no valid, professional or mature reason to disagree.

By noon on Monday, he'd already been swabbed and dismissed. When he'd pressed, the technician had told him he could know as early as Wednesday, depending on how soon the other two samples came in.

With the rest of the day off, Reese threw in a load of laundry. Went hiking. Did another load of laundry and headed to LA to look again at the serial gasoline fire evidence. That was what should occupy his thoughts. That was what should keep him up at night.

He'd done every test he could think of on the white paint. It was interior paint generally used on household walls. Which meant that whatever the perp had burned in that particular fire had most likely come from inside a house.

The escalation told him the arsonist was angry.

Dead chickens…he didn't know if those were accidental or on purpose. The gasoline hadn't gone all the way to the pen, but dried brush had caught fire, which was how the chickens died. It was the only thing different about that particular crime scene. Other than the fact that the fire had been set closer to human habitation.

Each one was getting closer.

His arsonist could be getting more careless. Or perhaps the fire truck had taken longer than he'd expected to arrive on scene. The arsonist needed whatever was in the middle of that circle to burn off before the truck arrived, but then needed the truck there quickly to avoid notable damages.

Was the perp testing Reese? It wasn't the first time the question had occurred to him. Was it someone who had a beef with him? Trying to find out if his crew—and he as investigator—could keep Santa Raquel safe?

The police department was working any and all leads. They'd already cleared anyone else connected with the fire chief position when it had been open. Anyone who'd interviewed, expressed interest, and any family members of the same.

The perp was meticulous enough to leave no trace. Maybe that was why he kept the scenes small. Contained by circular gas, and only enough to burn for so long.

Had that last fire just been a miscalculation of how close and how dry the brush had been?

His instincts said not.

The way the crime scenes and damages were escalating, if he didn't uncover the arsonist soon, he could find himself at a scene that included household damage and loss of human life. He was not going to let that happen.

Certainly not because he'd given a sample of his DNA to a lab technician.

He was far more professional than that.

ON MONDAY NIGHT Faye had to ask Suzie to sit with Elliott. There was a fire and she was on call. Brandt had told her it was another gasoline fire when he'd called her in.

What she didn't know was that the fire was within blocks of the Santa Raquel hospital. It was set in a dirt parking lot, in a larger radius than ever before.

No one was hurt, including the crew putting out the blaze.

Less chance of brush catching fire there, but the gasoline circle ended just feet from a gas line. There could have been an explosion.

"Do you think he knew about the gas line?" Brandt asked Reese as the crew surveyed the damage. They'd had to use water to extinguish the fire. Reese's crime scene was fairly well washed out.

"If he did, he deliberately stopped before he got to it" was all Reese would commit to.

While he and Brandt went over the scene, Faye stood back. Watching the man who'd once been her whole life.

Was he also the father of her son?

They wouldn't know until Wednesday.

Would it hurt him if he found out that he wasn't? Deep down? In that place he was trying so desperately to hide from her?

He had good reasons. She wasn't going to occupy it. She had no business going there.

And yet...

Watching him at work, knowing that if there had been a danger of explosion, Reese would have been the one on the front line, she could no longer pretend that she didn't care.

No longer pretend she didn't want him.

Right up until the part where he actually touched her, that was.

Remembering how she'd instinctively pushed Reese back when he'd tried to pull her closer, she turned away from watching him. She had no right even thinking about him like that when she knew that she couldn't deliver.

He'd talked about not setting false expectations. She'd dismissed that as unrealistic for a possible future with Elliott.

But perhaps Reese had had the right idea.

Perhaps she needed to listen more to what he said. And to the things he didn't say.

If she'd done so in the past, perhaps she'd have known they had a problem before he'd stood her up to ask out another girl.

Duly noted. Faye went to the truck to wait for her ride back to the station.

WHEN REESE SAW the call come through to his private line at the station from The Lemonade Stand the next day, he answered immediately.

Only a non-911 emergency would bring forth such a call.

"Chief Bristow?" The childish voice set him back in his seat.

An emergency...or the child to whom he'd given that private number.

"Elliott? Is that you?"

Could the boy somehow know that Reese had

spent the past twenty-four hours bonding with him in spite of himself? Mentally becoming a father overnight even though he might never be one?

It was the curse Faye put on him. He knew that. She'd planted the seed that he was going to change. That he had more going on than a test, even if it turned out Elliott wasn't his.

Damn her for saying so.

He'd never be having these thoughts otherwise.

"You said that I could have a tour of a fire engine, sir."

The boy's tone sounded more assertive than questioning.

"I did. Yes."

"I'd like it today," he said. And then, in a softer voice added, "Please." And then, "Sir."

"Elliott, does anyone know you're making this call?"

"No, sir. You told me I could just call this number and talk to you and no one would have to know." Another small pause. "Sir."

Stop with the "sirs" already. He held his tongue on what he'd have said naturally. Trying to figure out what to do. He *had* told the boy he could call in complete confidence, but he'd been referring to Elliott calling about those matches. Or anything he might have heard about a fire.

"Have you talked to your mother about the engine tour?"

"You said I could have it, not her."

"But she has to be willing to bring you here."

"She will."

"We haven't set up a time yet."

"But can we?"

"How do you know she won't already have something planned?"

"She don't do nothing except work and take me places."

He wanted to talk to Elliott about that. About the way the boy talked about Faye as though she owed him. This conversation was *not* the time.

"Please, sir. We…um…had a deal."

The "um" had him sitting up straight. The first time Elliott had called, he'd said it a lot. But that day on the beach, he hadn't said it as much. Only when he was uncomfortable.

Something the boy did when he was nervous? Or afraid?

Or was Reese overanalyzing because he thought he might be a parent? Could he take that chance?

"Do you have something to tell me, Elliott?"

"You told me you'd give me a tour of the fire engine."

Was this a test? A kid who felt the need to check up on the adults in his life? A natural inclination toward doubt?

Did he need to know that Reese would keep his word? Or did he just want a fire engine tour?

He went with the latter because it made the most sense.

"Your mom is working today. I'll arrange something with her," he said, and then, in spite of himself, added, "Because, Elliott, your mother's time and her opinion come first. You got that?"

"I guess so."

He thought not.

FAYE WAS JUST helping herself to a Crock-Pot sloppy joe when Reese came into the kitchen. It was the first time either of them had entered the room upon seeing the other already there.

It wasn't like the crew all sat around one big happy table together. Sometimes everyone on shift ate at once but not often. There were jobs to do, schedules to keep and a lot of guys went home for lunch.

When Reese came in, she was the only one there. She knew he'd already eaten because she'd seen him sitting at the table when she'd come for lunch half an hour earlier.

"I was looking for you," Reese said, easily enough.

He didn't have results. She knew that, though it was the first thought that ran through her mind. She was the one who'd get the call, as they'd prearranged.

And he seemed too...open.

There was no doubt in her mind, no matter how the results came back, that Reese was going to shut down upon hearing them.

"What do you need?" she asked, licking her finger after setting her bun on the paper plate.

Reese wasn't answering so she looked up at him. Saw him staring at her tongue on her hand. And got instantly turned on.

For a second there the idea of making love with him on the table flashed through her mind.

And then she grew up.

And cooled down. Opening the refrigerator door, she got a bottle of water to drink with lunch.

"I was wondering if we could schedule Elliott's fire engine tour this afternoon."

Whatever she'd been expecting, it hadn't been that.

"I guess," she said. She didn't want to see him and Elliott together yet, but she didn't have a legitimate reason to say no. "I can bring him here instead of taking him home when I go pick him up, but then I'll need another break to take him home."

She usually split her lunch hour to do the twice-a-day run to the Stand and home. Suzie had offered to take Elliott back and forth, but she thought it important that she do it herself—to stay in touch with Elliott's moods. To know if he was scared or upset before or after school. To be sure that he knew that she loved him first and foremost.

"Fine. What time is that?"

"Three today." Other days it was four. She

could leave him there as long as she needed to if she was out on a call.

"I'll be ready." He turned and walked out.

Faye tossed her sandwich into the trash and went to work out.

CHAPTER TWENTY-ONE

WEDNESDAY MORNING ARRIVED. Up before his alarm, as usual, Reese showered, put on pants and a polo shirt, and ate his cereal.

Faye might get a call from the lab that day. She might not.

Either way, his life wasn't going to change.

He'd get up every morning before his alarm. He'd shower. And he'd choose between peanut butter toast and cereal for breakfast.

There'd been no big revelation with Elliott's visit to the station the day before. He'd had Mark do the tour because Mark was the equipment manager and knew everything in the truck as well as anyone. Everyone joked that the trucks were Mark's.

Faye had gone to the video room to watch a training video and then mark off a minor continuing education requirement with some reading and a quiz online.

Reese had just been…available. In case Elliott had had some ulterior motive for arranging the tour for himself.

But he'd been right after all. The boy just wanted to see the fire truck.

There'd been no psychic bonding. No heartstrings. Just a kid who had a thing for fire trucks.

He got that.

Accepted it.

Liked it, even.

It made Elliott a normal kid, and it let Reese off the hook.

He wasn't at the station ten minutes on Wednesday when his private line rang. His heart sank, then started a rapid tattoo. It was a little early for the lab to have called but not impossible.

He assumed Faye would use his private line rather than come into his office. They were both working Wednesday, though he didn't think she'd arrived yet.

Staring at that ringing phone, he knew he didn't want to talk to Faye in person. If he didn't answer, she might come in…

"Chief Bristow."

"Sir?" He recognized the child's voice immediately.

"Where are you, Elliott?"

"At…um…the phone by the cafeteria. The one where you dial 9 before you can call."

He was at The Lemonade Stand. Which was, to Reese's knowledge, just where he should be.

"Are you okay?"

Of course he was. He was at a shelter where people were paid to keep him safe. A lot of people.

"Yes. Sara's over there watching me. I asked her could I use the phone and she brought me here. I told her it was private and she went over there."

He felt relief for Sara's help, and then stopped himself. He was acting like he had some kind of personal connection to the boy's care.

He didn't. Not even if he had a biological connection.

"Do you have something you need to tell me?" he asked, summoning his fire chief voice.

"Yes."

He sat forward. Picked up a pen but didn't reach for anything to write on. He'd had a hunch the day before…

"Is that why you called me to get a tour of the engine yesterday?"

"You said a deal is a deal."

And if there was no deal, then that just made Elliott a snitch. Suddenly he understood.

He'd have thought the same thing. Sometimes a guy had to do things he wasn't proud of in one sense so he found a way to do it and still be okay with himself.

"That's right," Reese said now. "So if you know something, you have to tell me. You've had your tour."

"I know, sir. So I asked Sara could I call you."

"You did the right thing, my man." Reese shook

his head, told himself to reel it in. He was not going to change.

Sure as hell wasn't going to become some kind of sap.

It was a DNA test. Biology. His life was not going to change either way.

Frank Walker was probably Elliott's father. And Reese was still the fire chief the kid had called because they had a deal.

"You going to tell me what you know?" he asked when the boy didn't say anything more.

"I know something about that fire that happened by the hospital. But I can't tell you what. You just said I had to call and tell you if I know something, so I did. Bye."

The phone went dead.

Reese dropped his pen.

FAYE WASN'T EVEN at the station yet when Reese's name came up on her smartphone. Loving how eager he was to hear if there was any news, she answered immediately.

"I haven't heard anything yet."

"What? Oh, that. I'm not calling about lab tests, Faye. I need your permission to go to the Stand and speak with Elliott."

Her heart sank.

"He knows something about the serial arsonist."

"How do you know that?"

"I can't tell you right now. I gave my word I

wouldn't say anything. But I need to speak with him. Now."

"Do you think he's in any danger?"

"Not while he's at the Stand."

He sounded so…businesslike. And he was scaring her. Thinking of the fire Elliott had set in the boy's bathroom trash can, she got more agitated.

"You don't think…there's no way Elliott has anything to do with those fires, Reese. He's been home in bed every single time one was set. Or at least home in his pajamas."

"I'm not accusing him of anything, Faye. I just need to talk to him."

"I don't like it. He sets a fire and now you're talking to him…"

"He knows something. The longer I spend talking to you instead of getting to him, the longer it will be before we'll have some answers."

We'll have some answers.

She hated the weak moment but loved that she wasn't rushing back to the Stand to deal with this one herself. She reminded herself that she didn't have to carry the whole world alone.

"Please, by all means, speak with him. I'll call right now and let Lila know you'll need to have him taken out of class…"

"He's with Sara right now. I'm hoping to get to him while they are still in session. I have a hunch it might be better if none of the other kids know he's talking to me."

Right. She'd known Elliott had his regular weekly session with Sara that morning. She was just off her game. Waiting.

Wondering...

Sara had been planning to talk to Elliott about his father—Frank, for now. To see if she could get Elliott to open up more about his feelings about his father—and how they reflected on him. It was natural Elliott would love his dad. And considering what he knew of his father, that love could make him feel like there was something wrong with him.

Because as far as Elliott knew he was Frank's son.

That he loved a bad man because he was that bad man's son and therefore like him.

"Fine. I'll let Lila know. They can keep him in Sara's office until you get there," she said, feeling a headache coming on.

There were so many possibilities. So many theories. About everything.

She needed facts.

And plans.

And then life would settle into something she could live with.

REESE GOT BUBKES.

So much for his life changing. So much for any wayward thoughts he might have entertained during the night about his ability to get through to a troubled kid.

Half an hour with Elliott and the kid had told him nothing.

He'd said he'd call and say if he knew something and he had. He wasn't saying where he got his matches. Wasn't saying what he knew about the fire.

Or even who he knew it about.

On a hunch, Reese checked up on Kyle's activities over the past couple of days but the kid hadn't left the Stand at all in almost a week.

He and his mother had had one visitor, a family member.

Kyle got good grades, followed the rules, helped out with the younger kids whenever he could, even did dishes after every meal and helped his mother with the laundry.

The kid had also talked Elliott into playing basketball again.

He was still so disgusted with his unproductive afternoon as he did code inspections, that he didn't give a thought to his phone ringing.

Until he saw Faye's number come up.

After the uncomfortable edge he'd experienced when his phone had rung first thing that morning, he'd determined that he'd best not be in the office for the rest of the day.

He wasn't going to be a sitting duck when he heard whether or not he was going to be a father.

A biological father, he amended, thinking of his bubkes.

Sitting in his truck outside the construction site he'd just visited, he let the phone ring. Thought about not answering.

The news wasn't going to change whether he heard it then or later.

Hands shaking and sweaty, he stared at her name on his caller ID.

Faye.

He couldn't not answer her.

"Reese?" She sounded upset.

And he knew. "It's Elliott," he said. "Something's happened to Elliott." He should have pressed harder. Taken some action that would make the kid to talk to him…

"He's just been blessed with a new father, Reese." Her sniffle distracted him. Faye was crying.

That meant…

"I'm his father?" Oh, God. Something was wrong with him. His hands were trembling like a girl's.

"Yes. They said the test was unequivocal. A match on all markers."

"I'm his father." Coherency wasn't an option. Reese didn't have a coherent thought in his head.

Faye's sniffle brought him back enough to know he was still on the phone with her. And that the news affected more than just him.

"Have you told Frank?" First things first. Get the abusive man out of their lives. Which meant…

"We have to visit San Diego county records and get his name off the birth certificate," he said. The man had hurt Elliott enough. There was no way he'd ever have access to the boy again.

Yes. That was right. Take action. Do what he could to be of the most help in the situation.

"Okay."

Good. The woman hadn't argued for once.

No, that wasn't fair. Faye had always been pretty agreeable.

"Where are you?"

"At the station. Sitting out in my car."

He nodded. She was on shift. Of course she was at the station.

"I'm his father." Wow. He felt kind of sick to his stomach.

And a tad bit like a superhero, too. But that would fade. As soon as he processed…

"Yeah."

"So…now what?" He didn't want to hang up yet.

"I haven't been in touch with Frank since the divorce. I don't even know where he is, nor do I want to know. I'll contact my attorney, who will notify him. And I'll call to see what changing his birth certificate entails. I hadn't thought of that and it's a great idea. Absolutely necessary."

Fine. They had a plan.

"But in the meantime… I guess this means we need to schedule a meeting with Sara Havens ASAP."

ASAP. Because he was a father.

Reese had to call his mother. She'd want to fly home to meet the boy.

Best wait on that one.

"Fine."

"When is good for you?"

It dawned on him. Faye was the mother of his child.

Closing his eyes, he leaned his head back against the headrest.

"What happened to Len?"

"Sorry?"

He was tired. So tired, yet pulsating in every fiber of his being.

"Len would have been around Elliott, he would have been helping you…what happened to him?"

Len Browning was his son's grandfather. He needed to know.

"He was killed, Reese." He heard pain more than words.

"Killed how?" He should have been there. He'd let them both down.

"Muggers. He was out late one night, walking his dog. They jumped him. He refused to give up his wallet and they shoved him. He hit his head against a tree. They took his wallet and ran. He was dead the next morning when someone in the neighborhood found him. It was seven years ago."

Anger boiled. Burned. Left him with a hole deep inside. "I'm sorry." He should have been there.

He'd never liked the neighborhood where Faye had grown up. But Len...he'd been the greatest dad.

His son would have been so lucky to grow up knowing him.

"So Elliott doesn't remember him?"

They had business to take care of. He just needed a few details out of the way. Then he'd be fine.

"They never met." She sniffled again.

He wasn't being fair to her. This was a hugely emotional day for her, too. To find out that her boss was her son's father. That he...Reese...had fathered her only child.

He still couldn't wrap his mind around that.

"They never met? I don't understand." He focused on what he could.

"Dad...didn't understand why I was suddenly marrying Frank...instead of you. Of course there was no way I could tell him why. He didn't approve. He wanted me to wait. Frank knew that and took an instant dislike to him, as well. He banned my father from our home. Forbade me to see him…"

Eyes popping open wide, Reese straightened. "He forbade you?"

"I know." He could feel her sigh through the phone and was certain she'd just shuddered.

He had to let this one go. It wasn't his business.

And she'd gotten the help she needed on that score. But…

"I'm sorry. About your dad."

He was livid about the rest of it. But he'd climb a mountain or ten. He'd work through the anger that seemed to be building up inside of him over a lot of things. Faye's past was not his to fix. He couldn't do her any good.

And he always stuck to where he could do the most good.

She sniffled again and he knew he'd made her cry.

"About the meeting with Sara, I'll make myself available anytime. Just let me know when." He tried to instill calm in the storm raging between them.

Just like he used water to douse flames.

"I'll talk to her before I pick up Elliott," Faye said.

Relieved that she'd be seeing the counselor fairly soon, he nodded. She was in good hands.

So why was he still worried about her?

"I can't believe I'm his father." He didn't know why he chose then to remind her.

"I'm so glad you are, Reese. You have no idea how glad. No matter what else happens, what's to come, I'm thankful beyond measure that you're his father."

"Even though it means you married him when you didn't have to?"

"I don't know. I don't think like that. I can't."

How could she not?

Or maybe those kinds of thoughts were just off-limits to him. In another hour or so, he'd be good with that.

"I gotta go, Reese."

"I know, me too."

"I'll call as soon as I talk to Sara."

He nodded. "Thank you."

He wanted to say more. Knew more needed to be said but before he could figure out what it was, she hung up.

Leaving him alone in his truck, just a fire inspector outside a construction site. No. Not just a fire inspector. Fire chief.

Even that didn't do it for him.

He looked at the trees. The gravel. The sky. The seats of his truck.

Nothing seemed familiar.

Not even him.

She was right.
He'd changed.
He was Elliott's father.

CHAPTER TWENTY-TWO

SARA WAS ABLE to meet with them that evening. Her husband, Michael, was a bounty hunter. He was trying to track down a pedophile who'd jumped bail so Michael's eight-year-old daughter and Michael and Sara's toddler son were both at the Stand with her that day.

Faye took Elliott home as usual. She was finishing up her third shift in a row. She'd be at the station until ten and then on call for the rest of the night.

As her boss, Reese told her she could take the time from station duties for her meeting at the Stand.

He told her by phone. He hadn't been in.

She'd yet to see him since he'd found out he was Elliott's father. But because she was working, couldn't get to Sara's office as early as she'd have liked.

As she'd expected, Reese had gotten there first. He and Sara were chatting with the door open as she approached.

In golf shorts and a polo shirt, he was sitting on one end of the couch, his face in shadows. That was the end where Faye usually sat. Sara was in the armchair across from him, a lamp lit on the table beside her. The corner of the room where her desk sat was dark.

He was her son's father—that oh-so-hot man sitting there, discussing weather patterns on the ocean and how they affected wildfires.

He barely glanced at her as she sat on the opposite end of the couch before returning his attention to the therapist.

"So…" Sara sat forward, looking between the two of them.

Faye tried to catch Reese's eye, but he was paying intent attention to Sara.

"I understand that we are only here to discuss today's revelation in terms of Elliott," Sara said.

Reese must have given her to understand that. Faye had not.

She'd rather hoped they would talk about how the two of them were going to cope with this wonderful yet painful turn of events. How were they going to treat each other as parents of the same child? Living as strangers.

"In today's world, many people who have completely separate lives have a child in common," Sara continued. "There's no reason why Elliott can't be made to feel comfortable with the situation, given time. The way your son will cope with this is largely up to the two of you."

Sara looked at Reese. So Faye did, too. He was nodding in Sara's direction.

Suddenly, sitting there so close to him—and yet so far away—she couldn't bear to see him. Finding out they had a son together should have returned some measure of closeness between them.

Instead, the chasm seemed to have deepened. He was acting more distant than even an employer would. He was acting as though she didn't exist, like she wasn't even in the room.

She understood. She couldn't blame him. He was a man who'd always wanted a family—in spite of his bunk about not living up to expectations—and she'd kept him from the first years of his son's life. Added to that injury was the fact that, largely because of her choices, his son had significant emotional issues.

He had to be furious with her.

Sara interrupted her thoughts. "In my recent conversation with Elliott regarding his father, he revealed that he is struggling with the idea of being the son of a 'bad man.' His words. I don't know that he's rationalized it all.

"But his answers to my questions certainly indicated there's an issue there. I think this new turn of events couldn't have come at a more critical time and depending on how things are handled in the next little bit, you could very well see vast improvement in him more rapidly than we'd hoped.

"There are no guarantees, of course. There are

never guarantees. But today's news could potentially be a lifesaver for your son."

Your son. Heretofore those words had only referred to her. Frank had never, not once, been present for any meeting regarding Elliott, or even attended school functions.

Elliott wasn't Frank's son!

That was going to take some getting used to. But even with Reese's distance, with his probable anger, even with the regrets that were eating her alive, she was still utterly and completely thankful.

She hadn't given her child Frank as a father. She'd given him Reese.

She'd gotten that one thing completely right…

"Do either of you have ideas as to how you'd like to break the news to Elliott?"

Faye looked to Reese, who shook his head, his eyes still on Sara.

"I was hoping you'd have some direction for me…us," Faye said. She was getting what she wanted. She had to buck up here.

There were just so many things she'd missed. The little things.

Not *me.*

Us.

Our son now meant her and Reese.

Nice to think about not having to make all of the decisions on her own. But she also had to remember that she didn't have the right to make decisions alone, either. She had to think about no longer having the exclusive right to make happen what she wanted for Elliott.

Sara took a moment and assessed the two of them.

Faye could only imagine what she was thinking. How were two people who couldn't even acknowledge each other in a room manage to raise an insecure, emotionally needy child together?

"What I'd suggest is that you, Faye—" Sara nodded in her direction "—and I talk to Elliott together. Here. At The Lemonade Stand. All around, it seems best to me. I feel that it's a given that Reese should not be there. Elliott only knows him as the fire chief, and that very briefly. We need him open, comfortable, as secure as possible when he hears this news. We don't want him to feel the least bit intimidated."

"Agreed," Faye said.

"Agreed." Reese spoke to Sara, but he sounded… congenial. Like he wasn't there under duress, but because he'd chosen to be there.

I'm his father. Reese's repeated words from earlier that day came back to her. He had to be in shock. She had no business judging him, period, but especially not right then.

"I think it's important to do this here for two reasons," Sara said.

"Because he doesn't get as defensive and argumentative with you." Faye had to put it out there herself, before the counselor told Reese how little her son respected her.

"Here he doesn't push his boundaries," Sara agreed. "He doesn't trust us enough to express the full brunt of his anger. Which means that here, he'll be more amenable to taking in, rather than deflecting, what we tell him."

She liked the way Sara put it better.

"I also think it will be good for him to have someone with a sense of authority break the news," Sara said. "The less emotional it is when he hears it, the better he'll be able to allow himself to accept it. At least on a surface level. He'll be dealing only with his own emotions, not the giver's, as well."

Stealing another glance at Reese, she wanted to smile. And cry.

He seemed to be soaking in every breath the counselor took. Talk about absorbing. As though he couldn't get enough, fast enough. He might not want to be a real father but he sure as heck seemed to be trying to get his new role right.

Because he was a good man.

She'd known that in high school, when the man in him had still been emerging.

Sara continued sharing her thoughts with them, predicting possible reactions, behaviors Elliott could feasibly exhibit over the next days and weeks. Things they could expect. Basically, preparing them to help their son.

"So, we need to decide when we're going to

do this." Sara looked at Reese. "The biggest burden here, in some ways, is going to fall on you. If Elliott senses that this news is not positive for you, he'll most likely blame himself for ruining your life. And probably find himself unworthy, unlovable, because his biological father doesn't want him."

"Have I given an indication that it's not positive?"

Sara smiled. "No."

"Okay, good, then I guess we're good there."

"Do you need some time to absorb the ramifications of all this?"

He shook his head. "I don't think so. It sounds to me like the boy is the critical matter here. I'm an adult. I'm not the one who's relying on others to look out for me."

Exactly. Faye couldn't agree more. With regard to herself and Elliott. She and Frank had never agreed on anything where Elliott was concerned.

Now she knew why. He'd known all along that Elliott probably wasn't his son. The *bastard*.

Even after all this time, Frank's abuse continued to infiltrate her life. But she was free of him. Never had to see him again.

She and Elliott had new lives and...

"So, is tomorrow good, then?" Sara asked. "You're off, right?" She looked at Faye. "I can clear my schedule for the morning. We can give Elliott all the time he needs."

She looked at Reese. He was nodding at the counselor. "Fine with me," he said.

And just like that, it seemed to be set.

"Do either of you have any questions or concerns?" Sara asked, seemingly in no hurry to end her work day.

"One," Reese said.

Faye could only see his expression in profile, but he seemed to be...a lot more calm than she was. There was no emotion, not even anger emanating from him.

Possibly because he was pretending she wasn't there?

"Is there any particular manner I should use when I do address the boy? After he's told, when the two of you decide it's time for me to see him. I don't want to cause further damage."

"Just be yourself, Reese," Sara said. "Elliott's a smart kid. One of the things we know he values is honesty. Don't try to pretend to be something you're not. That will hurt him more than just about anything at this point. That's why it's paramount that you are okay with this. If you aren't and try to pretend otherwise, he'll know."

"The struggles I'm facing have nothing to do with Elliott," Reese said. "As far as he is concerned, I'm eager to do what I can to help. Under the guidelines you and I have already discussed," he added. "You've assured me that as long I speak openly with Elliott about what he can and cannot expect from me, I should be able to be a positive male role model in his life."

Faye's heart jumped. He'd met with Sara early. Without her. That whole thing about expectations…he was totally serious about that.

He really thought he couldn't meet expectations?

The idea didn't meld at all with the man she'd known.

He was already taking ownership of his part in their son's life. He wasn't going to let Elliott down. He was being responsible, doing more in half a day than Frank had done in eight years.

Those were the only things that could matter to her now.

She had to keep her wits about her and her emotions in check. Just as Reese was doing. For their son. Elliott was going to need her now more than ever.

In the morning, their entire world was going to change once again.

REESE HAD ONE thing on his mind. Preparing himself to fight the battle of his life. For the war against the damage that had been done to his boy.

He'd spoken to the counselor. He'd spent the afternoon on the internet, reading forums as well as scholarly articles regarding troubled boys under age ten.

"Okay, before we go, we need to get a few things straight between you two."

Sara's words pulled him up short and gave him the first burst of powerful emotion he'd had since he'd stepped into that office.

He stared at his son's therapist. He'd thought he'd made it very clear that this meeting was to be only about Elliott.

"This is strictly in regard to your son," Sara said, her tone firm.

Reese settled back. He liked the woman. Found her competent and comfortable to talk to.

"First, Reese, the entire time you've been here you haven't once acknowledged Faye."

Of course he hadn't. One thing at a time. Right now that was Elliott. He and Faye…they were going to have to wait.

"How do you think Elliott is going to react if you two aren't able to treat each other well? He's already witnessed that kind of relationship between his mother and Frank. It's the last thing he needs to see between the two of you."

Point taken. He looked at Faye. Felt a tightness in his throat. Thought of the boy.

"You and I are going to be fine, aren't we?" he asked. "We have a good working relationship. No reason we can't carry that over to caring for Elliott, is there?"

"I see no reason why not." Faye didn't sound like herself. But then, he imagined, neither did he.

He looked back at Sara. "Faye and I respect each other," he told her. "I suspect that that was a major missing key regarding her previous relationship."

The therapist looked at Faye. "You're okay?"

Throwing up her hands, Faye glanced at him. He tried, with a glance, to tell her everything would be fine. She turned back to Sara. "I mean… I'm…this is all a lot to take in. But as you already know, today's outcome was…a godsend to me. Reese and I—" her gaze came his way again "—we'll be fine. It's just…we need some time to feel our way, is all. And I don't think we can do that until Elliott is in the mix and we can determine what he's going to need from us. Individually and together."

Right. He nodded in agreement.

"It's kind of like being new parents," she continued. "We have no real idea what we're getting into. But we're determined to be there for Elliott, we're equally dedicated to putting him first."

Exactly. She put into words just what he'd needed to hear.

Probably because she'd been at this a whole lot longer than he had.

"Good." Sara stood.

With Faye next to him, he was up and holding out his hand to Elliott's counselor, ready to be on his way, before it hit him.

This was it.

No more talking about it. No more just considering. He'd heard. He'd understood.

He'd signed on.

Literally.

By morning, he was going to be a father.

CHAPTER TWENTY-THREE

REESE WAS GOING to need some things. Walking through his house later that night, he tried to see it through the eyes of an eight-year-old boy. The place was okay. Nice. His salary had allowed him to buy a bungalow on the beach.

It wasn't big but it had three bedrooms. Plenty for one guy living alone. And it had private beach access.

He used the second bedroom as his computer room. He'd never gotten around to furnishing the third bedroom. He'd used it to store boxes when he first moved in. He'd slowly emptied them one by one through the ensuing months. When he'd finished with the last box, he'd been done with the room.

Staring at it just before ten o'clock that night, he was filled with a restlessness he didn't like. One that drove him to get rid of it.

He picked up the phone.

She'd already invented the wheel. It served no purpose to do it twice.

She picked up on the second ring. "Reese?"

"You still at work?"

"Just leaving."

Good. He wasn't ready to have his crew know yet. "We didn't talk about work specifically today," he said. "It's my wish that for now we remain as we are at work. No one there needs to know, yet, that I have a son. Or that he's also your son."

"You can't ask an eight-year-old boy not to tell people who his father is, Reese. What happens when people see you together?"

Right. He'd been too busy thinking about beds. And the California Department of Public Health, the purveyors of birth certificates.

"I'll hold a meeting in the morning. Let everyone know I have a son. Just in case something comes up. But I'm not going to say who he is. Or even that he lives here. Not unless I have to."

"I'm meeting with Sara in the morning."

"I know." He didn't want her at the station when he held this particular meeting. Didn't want everyone looking at the two of them and getting ideas. "When we're at work, and Elliott's needs aren't an issue, we will continue there just as we have been. We don't seek each other out. We do our jobs."

"Okay."

She didn't sound happy about that.

He'd like her to be happy but he couldn't change things. He needed distance. And she needed the job.

No good looking at other things he couldn't change. No purpose to be served there.

"California Department of Public Health has the birth certificate," he said next. Since he had her on the phone, he might as well get it all taken care of at once. "Removing a parental notation and adding another takes a superior court order. I've contacted an attorney and he is making a motion on our behalf. We'll both have to be present, show the lab results and sign some kind of acknowledgment."

"Does Frank have to be there, too?"

"Absolutely not." Because they had the lab results. "He'll be notified." He wanted to tell her not to worry, that she never had to set eyes on the bastard again.

But it wasn't his place. He'd given himself a place and that's where he had to remain.

He would man the front line. Apply himself one hundred percent where he could do the most good.

"Thank you."

It occurred to him then that he might have just stepped in it. "I should have checked with you before contacting the attorney."

"In the future, it will be required. But this time…no, Reese, I'm glad you took care of it. The sooner, the better. Seriously. I…it was nice. Makes me feel good that someone…you…did that for me."

Good. Fine. Moving on.

"As I've said, I have no intention of requiring

any kind of custody…or even visiting arrangements, in a live-in sense. His home is with you."

"What if he wants to spend the weekend with his father? Elliott's a boy, getting older by the second. He's going to want guy time."

"I know. And that's why I called. I have no intention of requesting or implementing my own visitation rights. But if the boy wants to stay over here sometimes, I'm going to need a place for him."

There. Putting it out there hadn't been as hard as he'd expected. He wasn't building a home. Just setting up a room for Elliott to stay in sometimes.

"That's why you called?"

"Yes."

"Are you asking for help?"

"I just figured…you know him. You know what he likes. He needs consistency. Security. I have no idea how to implement that in terms of him staying over."

"I'm happy to come take a look and see what we can do, if you'd like."

Yeah, he'd like that. A lot. Because it would be good for Elliott.

"Tomorrow?" It was her day off. "Assuming things go well in the morning with your meeting with Sara, and Elliott spends his normal day at the Stand."

"Are you going to move the staff meeting tomorrow morning so you can be at the Stand when we tell him?"

Before they'd left the therapist's office earlier that evening, Sara had said that it might be a good idea if Reese was around the next morning. Just in case Elliott asked for him.

But out of sight, in case he didn't.

"Of course," Reese said now. "I'll call the meeting for seven. You'll get the message. You just don't need to show up."

"I'm glad. That you'll be there. At the Stand when we tell him."

A flood of warmth hit him. Inside. All over.

For a second, he reveled in it.

Then he got real.

"I'll see you in the morning," he said. And hung up before she could blindside him again.

ALL NIGHT LONG, in between restless bouts of sleep, Faye played out scenarios in her mind. How Sara would look when she talked to Elliott. The expression on her face. Where the woman would be sitting. Where Faye would sit. She played it out with Elliott close to her. And far away. She had to be prepared for any and every eventuality. The meeting was critical.

She would not let her son down again.

And she wouldn't think about Reese, either. Her heart was so confused where he was concerned.

She loved him. She'd always loved him. She'd

given him a part of her heart and it had been for keeps. That wasn't up for debate.

Never had been.

But that didn't mean she still had to be in love with him. Or that she could, or would ever want to, have a relationship with him in any sense other than co-parenting.

She could dream about him that way. Apparently she was going to spend the rest of her life looking at him and getting turned on—if the past weeks were anything to go by.

But that was where she stopped.

Frank had made sure of that.

When thoughts of her ex-husband intruded, she turned over in bed and started again, picturing Sara, Elliott, words, differing reactions.

Her son...excited. Baffled. Angry and then excited. Happy. Nonchalant. She went through them all.

And still, when she arrived with him at the Stand the next morning and Sara met them as they were coming in, nothing happened in any way as she'd imagined it would.

Just in case the excited/happy scenario played out—which was the reaction she hoped for, given the father Elliott was trading in for the one he was getting—she'd had him wear his favorite blue shorts and the blue shirt with the pocket on the front so he'd be ready for pictures.

For herself, she'd chosen a blue polo-shirt dress

that hung a few inches above her knees. And the sandals that matched. So she'd look good next to him and Reese in those pictures she was hoping to get. Her hair was down. Her makeup to her satisfaction. No mascara or eyeliner, just in case of tears.

Her phone was set to flash. The soft lighting in Sara's office was comforting but, she imagined, not that great for pictures.

But Sara walked them outside.

Glancing around as they crossed a grassy lawn with bungalows set along a winding, flower-graced sidewalk, Faye searched for Reese. Sara had said he should be close by but out of sight. How could that possibly happen now?

They ended up in the Garden of Renewal. Beautifully landscaped with a waterfall, trees, shade, benches and gorgeous colorful blooms everywhere, the garden had been designed by the husband of the Stand's resident nurse. The couple lived on-site with their children and his mentally challenged brother and sister-in-law, as well as their child. Faye had met them all—and wished she could know them better.

"Are we on a nature hunt?" Elliott was asking as they entered the garden. "Adam says he went on a nature hunt with you and it was fun."

Faye once again looked around for Reese. They

had the garden to themselves. Faye figured there was no mistake about that.

"We're not on a nature hunt" was all Sara said. "We're here to talk." Taking Elliott's hand, she led him to a bench. She sat on one end, indicated that Faye should take the other end and patted the middle for Elliott.

The boy stood in front of them. "Am I in trouble?"

"Nope. And if you'd rather not sit, that's fine. Your Mom and I just have something to tell you."

"It's bad, isn't it?" He looked at Faye. "You're not going to die, are you?"

"No!" She wanted to reach for him, pull him down next to her. But taking her cue from Sara, she didn't. Things weren't going as she'd imagined them. They weren't in Sara's office. She couldn't see the expression on the other's woman's face. Elliott wouldn't sit where he was told. He had thoughts about her dying? He saw that as a bad thing?

And there was no Reese.

"It's not bad, either," Sara said, her tone soft, yet filled with authority. "At least, I hope you don't think so. But it's big. And, I think, if you want, it will be a lot of fun, too."

"Do I gotta move?"

"Nope."

"Do I gotta quit going to school here?"

"Nope."

Elliott shrugged. Kicked at the dirt with the toe of his tennis shoe. "So what?"

"You remember when we talked about your dad?"

The boy's face fell. He didn't say a word.

"Well, I kind of got the feeling that you felt like you and he are different. A lot different."

Elliott shrugged.

"So it made me think about some things your mom had told me that you didn't know about. Things kids your age don't really care about, but things grown-ups do care about."

Elliott glanced at Faye then, his face twisted. Half-filled with accusation. Like whatever was coming was her fault. Again. Like she was constantly messing up his life.

It was an expression reminiscent of Frank.

But in his eyes she saw a pleading look. Like he wanted her to get him out of whatever was to come.

"I talked to your mom and we did some checking…"

Her stomach tripped. Every muscle inside her tensed. Growing tighter. Squeezing against her chest.

"The man your mom thought was your dad, Frank Walker, he didn't just hurt her, he lied to her…"

"Yeah. I know." Elliott was not impressed, so far.

"He lied to her about being your dad."

The tennis shoe in the dirt quit moving. If it was possible for leaves on trees and bees on flowers to freeze in place, Faye was pretty certain they just had.

She didn't think Elliott knew how babies were made. He hadn't yet asked about sex. She hadn't told him.

She'd been living on borrowed time.

She and Sara had determined that it was best to help Elliott deal with his troubles before he learned about sex or associated Frank's twisted abuse with healthy sex.

"Did he tell you he lied?" Elliott asked Sara. "Did you talk to him?" The boy looked around.

"He told your mom."

He looked at Faye, clearly not having any of it. "Why didn't you tell me?"

"There are things a person has to do by law, Elliott," Sara said, before Faye had a chance to reply. "Things to keep grown-ups from breaking the law and hurting kids. Your mom had to follow the law before she could tell you."

He looked from Sara to her. Seemed to be assessing. With no sign of angst.

Good. That had been part of her best-case scenario.

"Do you know who my dad is?"

The question came. Sara knew her stuff.

Biting her lower lip, trying desperately to keep the tears from her eyes, Faye heard Sara say, "Yes, we do. That's what we came here to tell you. That's the big news."

"Who is he?"

"Reese Bristow."

Faye held her breath.

Elliott's nose scrunched up. He shook his head. "I don't know who that is."

"Chief Bristow," Sara clarified.

Mouth hanging open, Elliott stared at them. His gaze widened.

Faye could feel his agitation. Saw his arms start to swing. His feet shuffled. She was ready to take him in her arms, to hold him while he…she didn't know what…

She was shocked when he got the meanest look in his eye she'd ever seen from him.

"You lie!" He said it so intensely his voice broke. "You lie! You lie! You lie!" With that he turned and ran from them into the woods, repeating the accusation over and over again.

Faye jumped up to follow him, but Sara held her back.

"Let him go. He's safe here. There are walls surrounding the entire property, remember? Security and every other staff member are on alert. And Reese is standing just on the other side of those trees."

Faye started to cry. Let the counselor sit her back down and rub her shoulder as she sobbed.

It was too much.

She'd been alone for so long. Knew her job. Her purpose. She'd had things manageable.

And now it was all changing.

Her entire life was flying out of control and she didn't seem to be in charge of anything.

CHAPTER TWENTY-FOUR

REESE HAD PACED in worse places. With his phone in his hand, ready for a call or a text letting him know whether he was needed, Reese tried not to get caught up in the drama of the moment.

Kids found birth parents. Birth parents found kids. This wasn't rocket science. Or even a miracle. It was life.

He thought about his own father. How he'd have felt if the old man had shown up when he was a kid. A simple "I'm sorry" would have probably done it for the young Reese.

Not so his mother. And not for him anymore.

But Elliott was still at the kid stage. From what Reese remembered of his own childhood, he hadn't cared all that much about what was going on around him when he was Elliott's age.

He'd cared about baseball. Being liked. And firehouses. He'd been fascinated by the engines and the people who worked on them his entire life.

His mom told the story of how, as a two-year-old living across the street from a house fire, he had watched as the fire was put out. She had tried to pull him away, but he ran back to the window over and over again, climbing on the couch so he could see.

He had no recollection of that.

To take his mind off his own childhood as well as Elliott, Reese thought about his serial arsonist.

He was convinced he was dealing with a young male. Roughly 88 percent of arsonists were male. The pathology of the serial arsonist had four major categories.

The first, and most obvious to him, was financial gain: someone wanting to collect insurance money. Certainly not the case here.

Second, pyromania: the need to see fire destroy things. He'd thought maybe that was the case, but then why set the majority of fires just far enough away to prevent any real destruction? So far?

Third, and also completely unlikely, was to destroy evidence of other crimes. Set a fire to cover something up. Like murder.

Which left Reese with the fourth category: retaliation for some perceived or real persecution. This type of arson was most often caused by a youth.

And he was right back where he'd been. A kid, old enough to wear a size-ten shoe, was setting fires. He was angry. Getting angrier. And bolder.

A rustling in the trees distracted him. Wondering about the wildlife in the private refuge, he turned.

And saw the blur of a child running willy-nilly

through the woods. Branches scratched him as he pushed past. Brush tangled around his feet but didn't slow him down. He was mumbling but Reese couldn't make out the words. Another second passed and he was able to make out the child.

Elliott.

His son.

Talk about trial by fire...

The thought hit him as Reese took chase. Right or wrong, he had no idea, but he couldn't let the kid just...hurt himself like that.

Elliott was fast. Faster than Reese remembered being at that age. But Reese's legs were longer and he had the added advantage of clear thinking. Circling to the right, he landed right in the boy's path. Managed to grab his arm as he slowed to change course.

"Whoa, there," he said, careful to use enough force to stop the boy but not hurt or scare him. "What's going on here?"

Elliott had been crying.

"I'm fairly certain that you aren't supposed to be out here running in the woods on a school day."

If Elliott didn't want to deal with him as a dad, that was fine. But then they needed to get him cleaned up and back to class. It wasn't good for a boy to live like an animal. Chasing through the trees to deal with life.

Elliott wasn't trying to get away but Reese still

didn't let go. He switched his hold to a hand on the thin shoulder.

And remembered his own recent trek up a mountain.

"Sometimes it helps, just being out in nature. But if you're going to be out here, you have to be smart about it. This—" he pointed to Elliott's arms "—isn't smart. You've got scratches all up and down your arms. And your legs, too."

"I don't care."

"Well, you should care. You only get one body. You need to take care of it."

Sara had told him to be honest. Other than that, he had no idea what he was doing. Had no father/son relationship to draw from. But looking at the state the boy was in, he figured he couldn't do much worse than Faye and Sara had done.

Not that he was pointing any fingers. They were dealing with a disturbed kid here.

Leaving the reprimand for the moment, he started to walk. A guy needed movement to work off stress.

And time to process, too, without everyone picking at him.

He had no idea how far the conversation with Sara had progressed. What had been said. Figured he ought not bring up anything. Who knew what the catalyst of the run had been? He didn't want to set Elliott off again.

He didn't even know the boy's triggers.

Other than snitching. That was no good. He had that one down pat.

Five minutes into the walk, he was rethinking the validity of his choice. Considering other options. Coming up pretty much empty, other than to return Elliott to the people who knew him and who were trained to help him.

"They say you're my dad." Elliott's voice fell quietly in the woods.

Hand remaining on the boy's shoulder but without the comforting squeeze he felt driven to give, Reese said, "Yeah, that's what they told me, too."

"I don't believe 'em."

"You don't want me to be your father?"

The boy shrugged. "I just don't believe 'em is all."

"How come?"

Those blue eyes—so like Faye's—gazed up at him. "I'm not that dumb."

"What dumb?"

"You met me a couple a times. They need a new dad. You get picked."

He could see how it might look that way. In an eight-year-old mind.

"I gotta tell you, I found it kinda hard to believe, too. But they aren't lying to you, Elliott." *I'm your dad.* The words wouldn't come.

The boy scoffed. Kicked up a stick with his shoe. Kept walking. "They tricked you is all. But they aren't tricking me."

"No one's trying to trick you."

"Uh-huh."

"So…even if you think they would, why would I go along with it?"

"You like my mom. Kyle says that when a guy likes my mom enough, I'll get a new dad."

Oh, boy.

He and Faye hadn't talked about some really important things. Like sex. Had Elliott heard the sex talk yet?

Eight was a bit young, in his perspective, but kids grew up a lot quicker these days. Still…

"What did they tell you?"

Elliott grabbed a dead branch off a tree. Swung it in front of them. "That they did some checking and it turns out you're my dad."

Feeling his way as though he was treading in a minefield instead of a safe wood, he asked, "What kind of checking, did they say?"

Elliott looked at him, his eyes narrowed. "Don't you know?"

Truth. Be honest. "Yeah, I know."

"So why you asking me?"

"Because I don't know how much you know."

"Well, I know plenty. I know they're lying to me."

Reese stopped, pulling the boy to a halt in front of him and kneeling down. Some things had to be said man to man. Face-to-face.

"Elliott, they are not lying to you. You might

not like the news. You might not ever want to get to know me. No one's telling you that you have to. But what they're telling you is the truth."

With a harrumph, Elliott shook his head. But he was still standing there, and had dropped his stick.

"Do you know what DNA is?"

"It's on TV and stuff."

"It's something that every single person has inside their blood or their spit. It stays there, always, and doesn't ever go away."

"What if you bleed? Blood goes away then."

Okay. He could do this.

"The DNA doesn't go. It stays. Your DNA is like your body's name tag. Scientists can take a sample of things from people and do tests in a lab and find out who the person's parents are. But only if the parents also give their DNA—they do a comparison and see if the two match."

"Like a pair of shoes."

Sure. Like a pair of shoes. He nodded.

"Except that with shoes there are like a million pairs all made in the same factory at the same time and they all look alike," Reese said. "But a pair of shoes that only one person has worn, and has worn both shoes always together, now those would be more like the kind of match I'm talking about."

Elliott stared at the ground, giving Reese the impression the boy was under-impressed.

"So your mom and I went to the lab and gave our samples."

"I didn't."

It got a little tricky here. "No, but someone got a sample of your DNA when you didn't know."

"Who?"

He shook his head, almost smiling at how good it felt to know an answer. "No way, buddy. I'm not snitching."

But he made a decision.

"Here's the thing, Elliott. I knew your mom before you were born. We were boyfriend and girlfriend. I loved her and she loved me. And that's when you came along.

"But we didn't know it yet. Before we found out, I did something really stupid. I asked out another girl and your mom found out. Then she met Frank. And right after that, she discovered she was going to have you.

"Frank told her that you were his and she believed him. He told her that he loved her very much. And that he loved you, too, even though you weren't born yet. That's why she married him. Because she loved you so much and wanted you to be loved as much as Frank said he loved you."

"He didn't."

"I know. Because he knew he'd lied and that's what lying does to you. It makes you mean."

When those blue eyes, just inches from his own, looked straight at him, Reese died. Went to heaven. And thumped back to earth. Good Lord, what had he gotten himself into?

"If you're lying to me, it'll make you mean."

"That's right. Which is why I won't lie to you, ever."

"My dad…Frank…was really mean to my mom."

"I know."

"Did she tell you?"

"Yes."

Elliott nodded. Then asked, "But you like her again?"

"I never stopped liking her, Elliott. Not for one second."

"Do you love her?"

He'd just said he'd never lie to the boy. Tripped up in the first hour of parenthood. Didn't bode well for him.

At all.

"Yeah, I do."

Trying to prepare himself for the next question— *are you going to marry her?*—Reese scrambled for the right way to explain things.

But Elliott didn't ask. After seconds of silence, he nodded again.

"Am I in trouble?"

"For what?"

"Running off and yelling at my mom."

"I don't know, maybe. We should probably go back and find out." He held out a hand, not sure if

Elliott would take it. When Elliott grabbed hold, his heart took another dive.

"You sure that test can't make a mistake?" Elliott asked as they headed toward the grassy acreage between the woods and the rest of The Lemonade Stand's campus.

With no idea where Faye and Sara were, Reese figured he could always call or text when they made it back.

"I'm positive."

"And they got my right DNA?"

"Every bit of DNA inside you is exactly the same."

When he noticed Elliott half running beside him to keep up, he considered the smaller legs and slowed his pace a bit.

"So...what do I call you?" the boy asked.

In all of his dealing with the situation, he hadn't thought of that. "Dad, I guess. Unless you got another idea."

"No, Dad's fine."

Dad's fine. No, Dad was anything but fine.

Dad might never be fine again.

But he swore to himself that his son would never, ever know that.

CHAPTER TWENTY-FIVE

FAYE NEEDED A good cry. The sun was shining. Humidity was low and the air was warm without being hot. Life was progressing just as she'd planned. Maybe even better than she'd planned. She shouldn't have to cry.

Wow. Hard to believe that it was all working out. Finally.

It was almost anticlimactic. Not that she was complaining.

Driving along the coastal road that bordered Santa Raquel, half an hour early for her meeting at Reese's house to help him create an environment where Elliott would feel at home, she could hardly believe how the morning had transpired.

Her son had run off into the trees screaming at her.

And he'd come walking out of them hand in hand with Reese.

Tears blurred her vision and she pulled over. She was a paramedic. She knew what happened when people drove without clear vision.

The vision of Reese's big hand surrounding Elliott's smaller one would be imprinted on her mind forever. Sitting in her car in a scenic lay-by, she stared out at the ocean, wondering if she'd ever understand life. Or herself.

Just when she thought she was getting it right, overcoming the hurdle that was keeping her from happiness, she found another in her path.

She should be elated. She thought she'd played out every happy scenario the night before. But not one had been as good as seeing Reese and their son walking hand in hand.

She hadn't even dared dream of something that miraculous.

And then, when Elliott had walked up to her, hugged her and apologized for running off, she'd barely been able to contain herself.

She had. For his sake. She'd held him tight but not too tight. Or too long. She'd told him that while running off had not been okay, she understood why he'd done it.

He'd asked if he was in trouble.

She'd told him he wasn't.

He'd asked if he could go to class. They were making a vinegar and baking soda volcano that morning and he didn't want to miss it.

She'd looked to Sara, who'd nodded, and that had been that.

Oh…and the "See ya later, Dad" that had been his parting remark.

Just like that…Reese had become a father.

She was elated.

So why was she sitting in her car alone, staring at the ocean, sobbing her heart out? What in hell was the matter with her? Sucking in air, Faye hiccuped and another fresh wave of grief washed over her. She had to stop.

She was due at Reese's in twenty minutes.

Now was not the time to fall apart.

Now was the time to start enjoying life. Enjoying being a mother. It was a time to be positive and strong. Her son had had a huge boon in his life that day. A healing one. Sara had said there were no guarantees.

And Faye didn't kid herself that there wouldn't be setbacks. There was still hard work ahead of them. This was only the beginning of getting her son on the right track. But she knew that Reese's arrival in Elliott's life was a healing step.

And so, with a firm shake of her head and another deep, albeit shaky, breath, Faye wiped her eyes, blew her nose and put her car in gear. To go to Reese's house.

For Elliott.

THERE WAS NO reason for Reese to be cleaning toilets and vacuuming. The remotes on the coffee table and the work boots by his seat at the kitchen table didn't have to be put away. Didn't matter what Faye thought of his sloppiness. Leaving a few things where they were convenient didn't make him a bad example to Elliott.

But he took care of it all, anyway. Put the boots in the laundry room and the remotes in the end table drawer.

He tried to see his house through her eyes. As she assessed it for her son's sake.

Their son's sake.

The thought made his stomach roll but he didn't let it slow him down. He'd done pretty much what he could by the time he saw her car pull into his drive.

Shoving the vacuum back into the hall closet, he contemplated the decor in his foyer. It was a gift from the crew he'd left when he'd taken the Santa Raquel fire chief position. A pair of boots sticking out of a pair of jeans that bunched just right so a guy could step in, pull up the pants and be out the door. The whole thing was shellacked.

Probably not anything a woman would want inside the front door of her home.

But this wasn't a woman's home. This was his.

Stepping outside, he met her in the drive.

"Let's go around back first," he said, suddenly a little uneasy. Probably best to wow her first. Then show her the rest of the place.

His backyard was small, just a patch of grass with paver edging. But beyond that, and visible from the table and chairs on his patio, was a half wall, four steps, pristine beach and waves lapping against the shore. You could see all the way to the horizon.

"Wow, Reese, this is fabulous. You could sit out here and watch ships on the ocean!"

He nodded. Figured it was best to let the place speak for itself. She'd see what she was going to see.

She looked up at him. This was the first time they'd been alone together since he'd found out he was a father.

To her son.

He and Faye Browning had made a baby together.

As many times as he played those words through his mind, they still weren't sinking in.

Probably because they weren't meant to. Faye wasn't a Browning anymore. The people they'd been…had been left in the past.

Because they were meant to stay there.

"Do you ever?"

For a second he panicked. Did he ever what? What had he missed? Tabitha used to tell him he never listened to her…

"What?" he had to ask.

"Sit out here and watch the ships on the ocean."

He glanced at the table. At the barbecue.

"I sit out here and drink beer while I grill whatever it is I'm going to have for dinner." He wasn't getting into any ship-on-the-ocean conversations with her.

Because he'd brought her to the steps, making sure she got a good look at the beach, there was only so much room to stand. Their shoulders were practically touching.

Bad move on his part. He needed to walk away. But had a strong urge to put his arm around her. Keeping his hands firmly in his pockets, he gave her a minute to enjoy the view.

"What happened to you, Reese?" The voice was familiar, from long ago. Filled with caring. No hint of intrusion.

"What do you mean?"

"What happened to make you so closed off? You used to be the guy who wasn't afraid to go deep. To discuss things that matter more than work. You had soul."

Words from the past. The exact words she'd always used to describe him when she was telling him why she loved him so much.

"I have a soul."

"Of course you do. I'm not saying you don't. But you didn't just grow up, you've changed almost beyond recognition. Don't get me wrong. I'm not judging. I've changed, too. It's just…we both know what happened to me. There are clinical files on the reasons for my shutdown. But you… I mean, I understand how devastating it had to be to lose your wife, and your child. It was a terrible tragedy. I understand the grief. Even not being able to get over it. But you…it's like you've given up. I never imagined you'd do that."

Reese stood completely still.

He hadn't seen that coming.

From the old Faye, maybe. But not now.

They'd set boundaries. She'd respected them.

If she thought that just because Elliott was his son it meant she was going to waltz back inside his mind...picking at his thoughts...analyzing things that were none of her business...

"I'm sorry, Reese. I shouldn't have said that. I don't know what's the matter with me today. I guess it's just the aftermath...so much tension. Whew." She smiled and backed up, then turned toward the house.

"She died because of me."

He didn't like what was happening to him. Would not let it go too far. But he couldn't just let her walk away thinking she'd done something wrong.

They had to get along so they could parent together for Elliott's sake.

Elliott had asked if Reese still loved his mother. Reese had told the truth but the boy was bound to have more questions. They had to deal with this.

"I heard she was killed in a car accident."

She was back. Standing beside him on the top step leading to the ocean. Hands at her sides. He didn't look but he could feel her there. Could almost feel her heartbeat. He could damn sure feel his own.

"I could never quite get it right with her," he said now. Because Faye was right. He knew about what she was dealing with and how it affected their son. Elliott was on the brink of disaster—or recovery—and it depended largely on him and Faye. If they screwed up now, they might not get another chance with him. They had to get it right this time.

He could watch Faye's back, in terms of Elliott's exposure to her issues. He needed her to be able to watch his, too. In terms of how his own shortcomings might affect the boy.

How far back did he go?

"I cared about her. I liked her. Liked spending time with her. I honestly wanted to make a life with her..." A more realistic-looking one than the one he'd envisioned with Faye. He'd grown up after she left him.

"She knew going in I wasn't what she called the 'mushy' type."

Faye shifted. He knew how difficult listening could be. He'd been there, that one afternoon in her backyard. There was no way to make it any easier. But their son needed them to get themselves, and keep themselves, healthy.

He needed this, not just for himself, for his job, but for a father/son relationship. He had no idea what that looked like, so he went with his gut.

"I thought we'd reached an understanding, but I just couldn't seem to make her happy. She wanted 'all in,' as she called it. She wanted us to be that couple in the song, where one goes to heaven and the one left behind begs the heaven-bound to wait for him."

Too late, he remembered a long-ago night, lying in bed with Faye naked in his arms, and her asking if he believed in heaven. If he believed they could be together, even there.

He'd promised her that he wouldn't go to heaven if he couldn't be with her there.

Like he had any control over the afterlife. He hadn't even managed to stay with her in this one.

She wasn't saying a word. The old Faye wouldn't have stayed silent, but this did make it easier for him to continue.

Neither of them wanted to go back. Neither of them could. Understanding that made this whole co-parenting thing possible.

"She'd come to me that day and asked some question about the future. Wanting me to tell her what I saw it looking like. In terms of us. I don't remember what I said. What I remember is wondering why, after three years of marriage, she was still bugging me about such things. I'd just come in from a fire. I was tired, dirty, wanted a shower and then bed."

"Had you eaten?"

Her question seemed to come out of the blue but then there they were again, flying back to the past. Reese had a thing about going to bed hungry, and he tended to get grouchy when he needed to eat. Faye had always made sure they didn't forget to eat. Seemed so…simple back then.

So ridiculous now.

"Yeah. I'd grabbed a burger on the way home," he said, trying to remember if he'd told Tabitha he'd eaten. If she'd asked.

"I manage that better now, by the way," he added. So she'd know. For Elliott's sake. "Protein bars are a godsend…"

She wrapped her arms around herself.

And he got back to the business at hand.

"It wasn't the first time she'd come at me like that. Looking for reassurance, I guess. Wasn't even the hundredth. But that particular day, she didn't let up. I got impatient, hurt her feelings. I tried to make it better, she thought I was appeasing her. Which I was. Which made it worse. I asked her if we could please do this another time. She burst into tears and ran out."

That was the gist of it, anyway. She'd screamed at him. He'd raised his voice back. They'd both obviously reached their limits.

"When I heard her car start, I ran out, tried to stop her. And then jumped into my truck. I followed her. She sped up. I could see she was still crying. I didn't know if it was better to let her go off like that or keep trying to stop her. I figured if I was behind her at least she'd know I cared. In the end, it didn't matter what choice I was going to make. I never got the chance. She pulled out in front of an oncoming truck and that was that."

"You saw the crash?"

"I was the first responder." She'd know what that meant…he'd been the one who'd seen the damage up close. The one who'd tried to save his wife's life.

"I'm sorry, Reese."

Yeah, so was he. Over and over and over again.

And not just for Tabitha.

"I later found out, from a friend of hers, that she'd been waiting for me to get home to tell me that she was pregnant."

Her head turned.

So did his.

And he and Faye met again.

CHAPTER TWENTY-SIX

SHE COULDN'T DO THIS. Tearing her gaze from Reese, Faye took a step back into the yard. Still close, but back enough to take a breath.

She'd almost kissed him.

Had wanted to kiss him.

He'd just told her about his wife's tragic death and two seconds later her entire body was on fire for him. What the hell was the matter with her?

Psyche regressing, needing to heal or not, this was too much.

"We should get the house business done so you can get on with your day." Walking past her, Reese led the way into the house. He didn't give her a lot of time to take things in as he hurried her through a kitchen that was clean but cluttered with things on the counters. Vitamins, artificial coffee creamer, fish food to name a few.

An immaculate, lighted fish tank took up most of one wall in the dining room. The colors of fish, the underwater plants, the peacefulness of it, reminded her of Bloom's office. A sucker fish attached to the front glass stared at her as she walked past.

It was like the thing knew she was lusting inappropriately after his feeder.

"Elliott will love that tank," she said, reminding herself why she was there. The only reason Reese had invited her to his home.

His furniture was big. Dark leather. He had things lying around in the living room, too. Not dirty, just...convenient.

He'd apparently been looking at his tablet while sitting on his couch. A couple of books and some pamphlets on domestic violence were on the coffee table. Oddly, she didn't see any remote controls.

While she'd have added some kind of art to the bare walls, window treatments to go with the shades, overall, she loved the place. It felt comfortable.

It felt like Reese.

It felt like she wanted him to take her hand, lead her back to his bedroom and slowly strip her of her clothes, one piece at a time. "Kissing her naked," he used to call it.

"The other rooms are back here." Reese didn't seem to be at all affected by her being in his space. His tone was even, his stride confident.

"This is the computer room." He stopped in the first doorway along a hall off the living room. Other than a big L-shaped desk, a nice leather office chair and electronics, the room was bare.

"Here's the bathroom." It had toilet paper on

the roll. A brown towel a little crooked on one bar. Nothing else.

"That's my room." He pointed to a closed door at the end of the hall.

A door closed to her. Her mind got the message. Her body did not.

"My bathroom is there, too," he added.

And then he took her to the only other door off the hall. "This is where I thought I should have a bed for Elliott. Just in case."

Expecting to see a room filled with clutter, odds and ends that didn't go anywhere else, stuff that didn't have a home, Faye was saddened to see… nothing. The room was completely empty. As though someone had moved out.

Or hadn't moved in yet.

And suddenly she had a purpose. Something she could *do*.

For the next twenty minutes, she talked to him about twin beds, a dresser with deep drawers, a computer desk. She talked to him about beige paint, fire engine wallpaper border for the top of the walls, about a night table that would hold a lamp for soft light and reading, she hoped. About a red shelving unit for books or toys.

His eagerness, his approval of her every word, egged her on and she was to the point of discussing an area rug to cover the nondescript carpet when she realized what she was doing. She was helping Reese give Elliott the room she'd always wanted to give him. Frank had forbidden the expenditure, and after Frank, giving Elliott a healthy home had been her biggest concern.

Tears threatened again. She'd thought she'd cried them all out, earlier. Apparently not.

Reese must have seen something in her expression. He reached toward her and she backed up.

More than anything she wanted to be in his arms. To lose herself in the comfort she used to take from him as a matter of course. But she couldn't.

Not only because he was no longer giving it but because she couldn't be that weak again. She had to rely on herself. It was a lesson she'd learned first when her mother had died and left a nine-year-old girl to learn how to cook and make sure the laundry got done.

Taking another step back, she knew she had to make it to the hallway. And then the front door.

They were through here. She'd given him plenty to get started. He could call if he had questions…

"Faye." His voice stopped her flight before she'd even made it out of the room. "Don't go."

She turned around but wouldn't get any closer to him.

"It's been a crazy day. A tough day. We're both…feeling our way here. We've just found out we're parents. Together. There are bound to be surges of…emotion." He didn't try to get any closer. "But we're going to be okay. We're going to make this work."

She wanted to believe him. Nodded. But had no plan. Couldn't find one for their situation.

"I know I got close to blowing things back there, at the beach. I don't know…standing so close to you, I just… I'm sure you've done it, too. You know, remembering back to the days before Elliott was conceived. It's natural. Given the suddenness of this situation…"

He was right, of course. Though the situation wasn't as sudden for her as it was for him. The only thing sudden for her was the certainty of his part in it.

"Anyway, I just want you to know…you don't have to worry. Or be nervous of me. I'm not going to take advantage or compromise our situation by allowing things to get…physical…between us."

A jolt of elation speared through her—having to disallow physical relations intimated that he wanted her!—but she was back to earth in a second.

"That's the third time you've either pushed away or stepped back from me and it's…worrying, Faye. You don't need to be afraid…"

It was the second time he'd told her that. But it wasn't the words that got to her. She heard the hurt in his voice that she'd be afraid of him or even concerned.

She waited while she choked back tears. Nodded while she calmed herself, finding her emotional shield. Her emotional and physical issues were hurting Reese, which could be detrimental to their co-parenting effort.

She couldn't help her reaction, but she could help him understand.

"It's not you, Reese." She heard the cliché and wanted to cringe. "It's any man who gets close to me."

She'd never talked about this outside of counseling. Felt dirty doing so now, as though she needed to shower, then cover herself with a blanket and a pair of sunglasses.

But she was committed to enduring whatever she must to help her son be well. Which meant helping his father understand what they were dealing with.

She'd known, when she'd opened the door to Reese's possible fatherhood, that she'd have to tell him what had happened. He had to know what their son was fighting. What he'd overheard.

Ironic how things worked, the way fate gave you a push when you weren't moving fast enough to suit it. Reese bringing up their mutual sexual hunger was no mistake. But him thinking he had to apologize...

"I'm thinking that you're going to be able to help Elliott in more ways than you know," she said. Of course she'd had this conversation, mentally rehearsed it, many times. But she hadn't planned on it happening that day. Not yet.

She had about five seconds to replan.

Sliding his hands in his pockets, he stood there filling up that empty room—filling her life just as he'd always done—and she was about to change the way he looked at her forever.

"Elliott needs a positive sexual male role model," she told him.

He shrugged. "A father. All boys need that."

She bit her lip. Wanted to be back in her car overlooking the ocean. "No, Reese, a positive *sexual* role model." She repeated herself. Didn't know how else to say it. "As opposed to a negative one." She hoped the clarification would help.

Chin raised, he seemed to clue in to the fact that she was trying to tell him something. That they were no longer having a conversation about her rejection of closeness between them. For a second, she wished he could see her dreams, the ones she'd been having about him lately...

"I don't want to hear this, do I?" It was the old Reese, looking her in the eye, trusting her to know him well enough to read his mind. To *know* what he did and did not want. Or need.

"No."

"But I need to."

"For Elliott's sake, yes."

He nodded.

"You'd be hearing it from Sara soon enough,"

she said, knowing that he wouldn't let her back out on this then, not even if she tried. Counting on it.

"I'd rather hear whatever it is from you. First-hand."

She'd known that, too.

"A month after Elliott was born, Frank demanded that I resume sexual relations with him." No. Wait. She'd jumped too far ahead.

"Prior to that, other than that night in my dorm room, he hadn't touched me. I'd refused to have sex with him until after the baby was born. I had a rough pregnancy, was sick a lot, and thought my aversion to sex was due to all of that. All those months, I thought it was a product of his feelings for me—that he agreed to honor my wishes on the matter. I thought it was a sign that he really cared as much as he said he did. I can't tell you why he agreed. But I can guess. He didn't want to touch me because my pregnancy was a huge turnoff to him. He knew I probably wasn't carrying his child."

She couldn't look at Reese. Couldn't bear to see the distaste on his face. Or the pain.

No matter what they didn't mean to each other now, they'd once been close. They'd been each other's first lovers.

Her stomach started to cramp, and she took a few more steps behind her until she felt the solid wall at her back. She let it take her weight, as she bore the weight of the burdens she'd brought on herself.

One night of drunken stupor had changed the course of her entire universe.

And her son's, as well.

Reese didn't seem to move. She knew he was waiting. She had a crazy wish that he'd save her from the next moments. And from so many in the past.

When would she ever learn that no one was going to save her from anything? Her counselors could help her learn how to ease the weight of her burdens but no one could carry them for her.

She thought of things she'd been told over the past couple of years. Tools she'd been given. Visit the past when you must, if moving forward requires it, but don't linger. Don't glom on to it. Get right back out again.

Stay grounded.

She felt the wall at her back.

"Frank had a need to dominate. As time passed, he grew increasingly aggressive."

Flashes of memory attacked. She refused to linger on them. The flashes came more rapidly. Lined in red.

A leather strap against her hand. Against her naked backside.

No!

She'd promised herself she didn't ever have to go back.

"Elliott…"

Fingers on her arms. Male hands. She was back there, feeling them gripping her firmly. She was that woman. The one who didn't fight.

But there was no pain now. These hands were warm and eased her gently down to the floor. She sat, head down, until Reese's weight was there beside her, his arm around her, his hand guiding her head to his chest.

"Tell me."

CHAPTER TWENTY-SEVEN

IN HIS LINE of work, Reese had seen a lot of horrific things. He'd trained how to distance himself from them so that he could do his job. He'd mastered the art of compartmentalizing.

He told himself he was only working—doing the most he could to help Elliott—as he sat with the mother of his son and listened.

Understanding that he had to know what Elliott knew.

"…leather straps…" He heard Faye's voice. Swallowed back bile.

He wasn't there to slay Faye's demons. Or to take on any more of his own. He was there to find out what gave his son nightmares, made him angry and kept him locked up inside.

He was there to gain the knowledge that he needed to do his job.

"He liked it when I cried. At first I tried not to, so he wouldn't like being with me. I quickly learned that the faster I cried, the sooner it was over…"

She was trying not to cry right then. He could

hear the tears in her voice. He could hear her strength, too.

It almost undid him. The way she was trying so hard to be just fine. To take care of everything. To make the world right no matter what.

That inner determination of hers had been one of the first things that had drawn him to her. The way she didn't cry over spilled milk but rather wiped it up, moved on and found a way to do without milk.

In all the years he'd known her, she'd never once complained about having to be housekeeper, cook and high-school student. Never heard her rail at a world that had left her motherless. Or feel sorry for herself because she wore clothes from yard sales and thrift shops.

She'd found ways to make them look good on her, with ties and dyes and whatever else she'd done...

"When he was turned on enough, he'd start having sex on me..."

He'd once gone into a burning house and found a child no one had known was there. The boy had been about twelve, a runaway. He'd still been alive when Reese had grabbed him up and raced out. But a good bit of his skin had been gone.

He'd thought he'd never deal with anything worse than that.

He'd been wrong.

But he sat there, fighting the instinct to pull her

fully into him. To take her pain inside himself. To share it so she wouldn't have to feel it alone. He knew he couldn't do it, didn't have that kind of place in her life anymore. Knew that if he tried, he risked having her push him away completely.

Risked having to hear all this from a stranger.

As bad as it was, he needed to hear it from Faye. Needed to hear her.

"The whole time, every time, he'd tell me I liked what he was doing to me. He'd make me tell him I did..."

He pushed back against all emotion. He pushed back hard.

"If I didn't say it, he'd get rougher. And when I did say it, he'd tell me to speak up. To say it louder. He'd lean down and growl the command in my ear..."

She shook her head. And then looked at him.

The jolt that hit Reese would be with him forever. He'd expected to see tears in her eyes. And a plea for help.

The self-recrimination...the eerie emptiness behind those eyes...

He swallowed.

"I did it, Reese. I had to make him stop. It hurt so bad..."

Her voice broke. He thought he saw a glimpse of the old Faye in her eyes.

"So I did it. I told him I liked it. *Yes, yes, just*

like that. I like it." Her voice took on a mimicking note.

"He'd tell me to say it louder. And…God help me…I did."

He got it. Like a lead bolt in the head. That was what Elliott had heard. That was the demon they were fighting. A mother being raped. Repeatedly. Night after night. And her young son having to hear her say how much she liked it.

May Frank Walker rot in hell.

He couldn't think beyond that. Faye…Elliott… they'd have been his family if he hadn't asked Susan out…if he hadn't panicked after seeing a veteran firefighter go down beneath that beam… if he'd done as Faye asked and gone to her Friday night homecoming party…

She'd already been pregnant then.

Reese didn't know what to do. To say. He just sat there. Half holding the woman he'd once loved so fiercely and swallowing back tears.

"I'm sorry." The words seemed so menial, but Faye couldn't find any others. Nothing was ever going to erase the past. Nothing could change it. She knew that.

But she didn't blame Reese for his silence.

She'd robbed him of his son. Given the boy emotional issues that could ruin his life.

Frank's sick desires were not her fault. She'd had no way of knowing he'd lied to her about the night they'd met. His brother vouched for him. Even after the abuse had started, his brother—who'd long since broken up with Carrie—would hear no wrong about Frank.

She couldn't be held responsible for Frank's treatment of her, either.

She knew that. Not just because she'd been told that thousands of times over the past couple of years, but because it was true. What Frank had done was on Frank.

Just as it was true that she hadn't known her son could hear them. He'd been a sound sleeper. She'd put him as far away from the master bedroom as she could get him. Had a white noise machine play soothing sounds in his room at night. Had checked on him every evening after Frank went to sleep.

He'd never given any indication that he'd been awake. Most nights, he probably hadn't been.

Unlike most men, Frank hadn't been one to just fall asleep afterward. He'd want to hold her and talk about how great it had been. To tell her how great she was. To watch sitcoms on the television in their bedroom.

As though they were one of those perennially perfect TV families.

G-rated.

The times Elliott had still been awake when she'd checked on him—as she'd later found out—he'd feigned sleep.

Fear, his counselors had told her. He'd been afraid he'd be in trouble if she discovered he knew about her "other" self. Or maybe he'd been afraid of her. The counselors hadn't said so but she'd wondered.

"I'm so sorry," she said again, sitting up. She stared at the opposite wall. At the tips of Reese's shoes on the carpet in front of them. She was sorrier than he'd ever know. Because while Frank's sins were not her own, hers were.

"So sorry, Reese. I never would have knowingly endangered our son. I wouldn't have hurt him for the world. I thought I was protecting him. As long as I satisfied Frank, he was a good provider. I thought he was Elliott's father. And when I thought about how hard your father's desertion was on you—how badly I'd needed a mother growing up—I thought it would be wrong to rob Elliott of the man who gave him a good home. Frank was never short with Elliott. Never cantankerous with him. He just…ignored him. I thought it was because he was a little guy. That once he grew up they'd start sharing interests…"

She was babbling. Justifying? This wasn't about her, or why she'd done what she had.

This was about the state their son was currently in.

"Reese?" She finally looked at him.

The moisture in his eyes wasn't spilling over. But it cracked the hard place inside of her.

"If I hadn't gone out with Susan…"

The words hit her hard. Knocked her senseless. She stared at him.

Saw the pain on his face, knew only a small portion of it was showing, and laid her head back against his chest. Not for real. Or for keeps.

Just for the moment.

"Why did you?"

Reese wanted to ask what Faye meant when she broke a more-than-ten-minute silence. He knew they had to move, had to deal with life. He'd just been loath to shift her. Loath to stand and face her and know that they had to move forward.

They couldn't fix the past.

But he owed her the truth.

So he told her about the fire. About the beam falling on a man he was there to learn from, to someday emulate.

"I thought I was fine, at first," he told her. "And then I just…wasn't my normal self."

"I knew something was different about you that week. I thought it was because you were two-timing me."

The word *two-timing* stung. Because it was true.

"No, that was a result of me being different."

"So you see a guy almost die and that makes you unfaithful?"

Feeling trapped—between the urge to let the

warmth of her linger against him a little longer and to push her away and get the job done—Reese resisted the urge to lose his fingers in her hair.

"It made me want to be certain that I wasn't missing out on something in life." He told her the bald truth. The easiest one of the two.

The other truth, that as a firefighter he'd risk widowing Faye and any future family they had every single day when he left for work, he kept to himself. No point in going there. He'd already discussed his limitations with her.

He'd already established that there would be no expectation of family or pretense of forever. He was a father. He would do all he could to help his son.

Expectation ended there.

The thought hiccuped in his mind. He pushed past it.

"What did you find out?" she asked.

"About what?"

"About missing out. Were you?"

She was focusing on things that no longer mattered. Things they couldn't change. Things that weren't going to change.

When he didn't answer, Faye pushed herself away from him. He missed her.

"It is what it is, Reese. You found something better, that's fine. I'd just like to know. I've spent a lot of time coming to terms with the past so

I don't continue to stumble over it all through my future."

"I didn't find anything better." And he felt like he'd just lost the last bit of warmth he was ever going to know.

"So it was all for nothing?"

He stood up. Held a hand out to help her up. She stood on her own.

He'd thought that night with Susan had been for everything, not nothing. It had proven to him once and for all that in Faye, he'd had all he was ever going to need. He'd found out too late. By the time he'd heard from her again, she'd been done with him.

She'd already been living her Frank nightmare.

There was no point in doing this anymore. They had their answers. And they were going to have to live with their regrets.

He did that by focusing on his work. On the good he could do.

How she did it was up to her.

Lord knew, he hadn't been much help in that department.

CHAPTER TWENTY-EIGHT

BY THE TIME she left Reese's, Faye only had an hour before she was due to pick up Elliott. She could stop by the drugstore, then grab Elliott's favorite ice-cream cake as a treat for dinner. Those were the things she wanted to do.

Instead, she drove straight home. Ran upstairs, stripped down and jumped in the shower. Turning the water on as hot as she could stand it, she stood there, crying, until the hot water ran out.

She'd done what she had to do to be well for her son.

By the time she went to get him, she was in control once again. Ready for whatever he might need from her.

She was prepared to deal with a boy who'd just found out that the man he'd always believed to be his father was not. And that the man who'd fathered him was someone he barely knew.

In the long run, having Reese for a father was going to be great for Elliott. She believed that with all her heart.

In the short term—they had adjustments to make. Which meant she had to be willing to take Elliott's guff. To stand up to his tests. As it had been explained to her, he was, in part, horrible to her when he was struggling the most as a way to test her love. Would she stay through the worst of him?

As she escorted him out to the car, she was ready for anything.

Or so she thought.

The one thing she hadn't expected was total silence.

"We've had quite a day, huh?" she asked him. Sara had told her just to act normally. To let Elliott lead.

How did you act normally when you knew your son had just met his real father?

He shrugged. "It was okay."

"You're doing okay?"

Another shrug. "Sure. I guess."

"You guess?"

"You know, sure."

She had to start the car. Drive home. Fix dinner. Normal, Sara had said.

"Did you tell anyone that Ree…Dad is your dad?"

"Yeah. A couple of guys."

"What did they say?"

"It's cool."

"I just want you to know that if you want to see him, anytime you want to see him or spend time with him, it's fine with me. Just let me know and I'll take you over."

"He said he'll come get me tomorrow to go to the beach if it's okay with you."

She blanched. She'd been with Reese less than two hours ago and he hadn't said anything.

"When did he say that?" Whether it was right or not, she couldn't help the wave of betrayal that washed over her. Why hadn't Reese told her he'd had plans with their son?

"When I called him."

Her heart settled into a more even rhythm. "When did you call him?"

"When I was waiting for you."

Elliott sounded as though nothing more was happening than a trip to the beach with a friend.

Sara had said to take her lead from him.

She started the car.

"So...can I go with him?"

"Of course!" She put all the cheer she had into her voice. Elliott needed to spend time with his real father. To get to know him. To trust him. To learn from him.

She wanted this more than anything.

Which was why, as soon as her son was settled with a snack and his favorite TV show, she hid in her bathroom and cried some more.

She was finally getting the help Elliott needed.

And she'd never felt more alone in her life.

FAYE HAD JUST started to doze off that night when she heard Elliott get up. Not surprised, considering the change her son's life had taken that day, she threw off her covers. She and Reese were going to have to go over some things before Elliott stayed at his house.

He'd need dead-bolt locks on his doors and a way to protect determined little fists from breaking the window to get out.

When she'd been in Reese's house that afternoon, both details had slipped her mind. Because it wasn't real to her yet. The realization hit her between the eyes. She could decorate. But to think about dropping Elliott off for the night—giving his safekeeping over to another...

Hoping Elliott was headed for the kitchen and something to eat, she pulled on her summer robe and headed toward the hall, almost running into the skinny boy heading toward her.

She backed up, wondering where he was headed.

"Can I come in your room?"

He was awake. Wide awake. Looking her in the eye.

His gaze filled with fear.

No, not just fear. Worry laced with fear.

It had been a while since he'd been emotionally open to her. She was a little rusty on reading him.

"Of course you can," she told him. For the first six years of his life, Elliott had been strictly forbidden from visiting his parents' bedroom. It was a rule she'd upheld as firmly as Frank for fear that her son would inadvertently walk in on something hideous.

"You are always welcome to come to me, Elliott. I mean it when I say that. Always."

She followed him back in and when he climbed on the bed, scooting his legs under the covers, she acted like it was the most natural thing in the world to climb in after him.

He lay down, his head on the extra pillow on the other side of her bed. So she lay down, too.

Ever since leaving Frank, she'd kept night-lights on in every room, partly so she could see Elliott when he sleepwalked, but mostly to make sure her own demons didn't escape in the dark. She could see her son but didn't face him. Didn't want to push him too far. Or push him away.

"I'm scared."

Lying flat on her back, staring at the ceiling, she prayed for guidance. "Of what?"

"I want to go to the beach tomorrow and all, but…"

"But what?"

"Do you think other kids didn't like me because of my old dad?"

Listen to your heart. Let it guide you. Sara's words came back to her.

"No. Do you?"

"Sometimes."

It was the first she'd ever heard of it. Ever.

"Why? Did someone say something?"

"No."

"But you thought they didn't like you for some reason?"

"Well…"

She waited.

You were entrusted with this child to raise because something in the universe thinks you have what it takes to do so…

Something else she'd heard along the way.

"Frank isn't your father, Elliott. You aren't anything like him."

"But I sleepwalk. And junk."

"That's not your fault. No one blames you. And even so, you're working with Sara, right?"

"I guess."

He didn't sound convinced.

"What if he doesn't like me, Mom?"

Her eyes flooded with tears before she could stop herself. He was so young. So sweet. Her arms ached to hold him.

She turned toward him. "You're his son, Elliott. He's going to love you no matter what."

"My old dad didn't like me."

"Frank was a bad man, sweetie. The things he liked weren't good. You *are* good." Where the words came from, she didn't know.

"But what if Reese doesn't like me?"

"He'll like you, Elliott. You're funny and smart and interesting. You're good at pretty much everything when you try hard."

"I wasn't so good at making cakes." He laughed. "That splatter that hit your nose, remember?"

She'd forgotten. He'd been about four. He'd wanted to help in the kitchen and she'd let him hold the hand mixer in a bowl of cake batter for a second before she took over. She hadn't turned it on, hoping he'd be satisfied just to hold it.

Instead, he'd known how to turn it on. Full speed. By the time she'd taken the mixer and turned it off, there'd been chocolate batter all over the counter, the wall, their hair.

And under her nose.

"You dad is going to like you even if you aren't good at anything," she told him now. "Because he's your dad and that's just how it works."

"He won't like me if I'm mean to you."

Her entire being slowed down.

"How do you know that?"

"He told me."

"When?"

"Today when we were in the woods."

She wanted to know exactly what Reese had said. Word for word. Wanted to know like a kid in school who had a crush on a boy.

Like how the young Faye had wanted to know exactly what Reese had said when she'd had her friend ask him if he liked her.

She wanted to know why Reese had felt the need to speak to her son about his treatment of her. But didn't ask that, either. Elliott's relationship with Reese was sacred. Off-limits until one or the other wanted to share. She would not pry.

"If you tell him that I got mad at you sometimes, he won't like me."

Faye sat up. Pulled him up beside her. And practically touched her nose to his, she looked him so closely in the eye. "Elliott, in the first place, your father and I are a team where you are concerned. Our job is to help you grow up healthy and happy. Not to tattle on you or make you like one of us more than the other. In the second place, when a kid acts out, a father might have to get mad at him—punish him even by, you know, taking away a privilege like watching TV or something—but even then, he still likes him. More than that, he still loves him."

The boy nodded. His big blue eyes were starting to look tired. "Like you love me still even when I'm mean," he said.

"Exactly."

"So I just have to wait for Dad to know me enough to love me and then he'll like me."

"He already loves you, Elliott." Reese hadn't said so, but she knew he did. No matter how much both of them had changed or how far apart they'd grown from each other, she was positive Reese loved their son. "I can't explain it because I don't even understand it, but when a person has a child, they don't have to know that child to love them. It just happens automatically."

He seemed to think about that. Nodded. Then asked, "Do you like him?"

She'd been more prepared for the question that afternoon when she'd picked him up.

"Of course I do."

"Do you love him?"

How did she answer that one? Where was a truth that an eight-year-old would understand?

"Yes, Elliott, I do." She kept it short and simple. No other words came.

He nodded.

"Is that okay with you?"

He shrugged. "Yeah. I'm just glad you do because he loves you, too, and that way we can all get along."

Instead of fight. Or worse. Her son had horrendous conditioning. She and Reese had a huge challenge ahead of them. One they needed to actually talk about, instead of around. As soon as possible.

And then it hit her.

"You asked him if he loved me?" Her stomach swirled. Her heart pounded.

"Yeah. When he was telling me about knowing you before."

And the answer had been positive.

To appease the boy? Maybe. At least in part.

But Reese wouldn't out-and-out lie.

He'd told her that afternoon that when he'd gone out with Susan, he'd found that he hadn't been missing out on anything with Faye.

If only she'd gone to him with her fears, asked him about the other woman…asked him why he was behaving so oddly…

If only she'd nursed her broken heart in a less destructive way…

If-onlys were the path to bitterness. She wasn't going to let evil win. Not completely. Not where she could still make a difference.

"Can I go back to sleep in my room now?" Elliott had yawned twice.

"Of course." She'd hoped he'd stay. But was glad he wanted to go, too. Pulling back the covers, she let him climb out of bed and watched as he left the room. She wanted to go after him. Tuck him in. But she had a feeling that he'd feel like too much of a baby if she did so.

The last thing she wanted, as her son went off to spend a day with his father for the first time, was to have him feeling like a baby.

Or to have Reese thinking she'd raised his son to be one.

CHAPTER TWENTY-NINE

WHEN THE RING of his phone woke him, Reese was already halfway out of bed before he answered it. A firefighter first and foremost, he reached for a pair of jeans with his free hand.

"Reese?"

Fear sliced through him when he heard her voice.

He hadn't even looked at the caller ID. A middle of the night call meant a fire.

"Yeah? What's wrong? Is Elliott sick? Did he hurt himself sleepwalking?" Scenarios played through his mind as he continued to dress with one hand.

"Elliott's asleep in his bed," she said, which was when he realized she was completely calm. And that it was just after midnight.

"I'm sorry if I woke you. I needed to speak with you before you pick him up in the morning. Without him knowing..."

Elliott had called him earlier that evening to tell him his mother said it was fine if they went to the beach the next day. He'd insisted that the boy put his mother on the phone and Faye had confirmed her approval, as well as made the arrangements for a pickup time. He'd thought all was well between them.

As well as they were going to be for ex-lovers who'd just found out they were going to be raising their child together.

"Okay, I'm listening."

"He's worried you aren't going to like him but I think it's more than that. He's confused about our relationship and where he fits into it."

Everything stilled within him. "What did you tell him?"

"That we both want the same thing, for him to grow up healthy and happy, and that we are going to work together to see that happen."

He started breathing easier again. But, in jeans that were on and not zipped, no shirt, and barefoot, he went to the kitchen for a beer. Just in case.

"So what's the problem?"

"He asked me if I love you."

He gulped. Then, before she could say more, could tell him how she'd answered, he blurted, "He asked me, too."

"I know, he told me. And I gave him the same answer you did. The thing is…"

She was saying more. He was back on her answer. The same as his. And sipping his beer.

"…he's afraid, Reese…"

He tuned back in and wished to God he knew what they were talking about.

"Afraid of what?"

"I'm only guessing, but his only experience of a father in his life is someone who hurt me. And someone I tried to please so I wouldn't get hurt."

Setting the bottle down, Reese dropped to a kitchen chair, elbows on his knees, and stared at the floor. "He needs to know that I'm going to treat you well."

"I think so, yes."

"Words aren't going to convince him."

"No."

"Have I ever treated you badly?"

"No."

"So we should be okay, then."

"I think we need to be friendly with each other. Around him."

She was right, of course. He'd known where this was going.

They loved each other. Or had in another lifetime and some of it was still with them. "I'm good with that, if you are." For Elliott's sake.

"Me, too."

Picking up his beer, he took a big gulp. "Is that all then?"

"One more thing…"

He'd thought so. Meaning that he still knew her at least a little bit? "What?"

"We need some kind of system. So that we aren't blindsided by him like I was this afternoon when he said you'd take him to the beach. I hadn't even known he'd asked you."

He hadn't thought anything of the boy's call, other than to be a bit...pleased...that he'd received it. And so soon.

But he kind of saw her point.

"I need to tell him I'll talk to you about it," he said.

"I'd appreciate it if you would."

"All you have to do is ask, Faye. It's all you ever needed to do. You just never do." Why in the hell had he said that?

"Never? We've been co-parents for less than twenty-four hours."

"I meant in the past, and forget I said it. It was wrong. I didn't mean it."

"No, Reese, this is just what I'm talking about. If either one of us has stuff simmering beneath the surface, Elliott can be hurt by it. He's a smart kid and he's also incredibly sensitive. So tell me, what did you mean?"

It really was nothing. Frustration. But for the good of the boy, he tried to put into words why he thought he might have said it.

"It's...just...you make it hard for a guy...for me...to know what you expect from me, Faye. That's what I remember from the past. Never knowing what you needed. Like I was supposed to read your mind all the time. I'm a guy. So...all

I'm saying is…in the future…if you need something…just ask."

"You mean like I just did? When I called you tonight?"

No. He sipped his beer and thought about letting it go. "But you didn't, Faye. You told me that we needed a system. And waited for me to come up with what you really needed—for me to come to you when Elliott asks for something that requires your approval or input."

The silence that hung on the line had him helping himself to another gulp of beer.

"I used to do that to you? Make you guess all the time?"

"Worse, you just never said anything when I didn't get it right."

"So at least I've improved."

"Yeah." He'd give her that one.

"Good night, Reese."

"Night, Faye." It was only after he hung up that he realized he had a hard-on.

From talking to his abused ex-girlfriend.

A complication he very definitely did not need.

OVER THE NEXT two weeks, there were three more gasoline fires. Two small ones on the beach and a not-so-small one that took down a deserted barn on a property owned by an older couple. Thankfully, they were away visiting their great-grandchildren.

Some history was lost—plastic bins of memorabilia as well as the barn itself—but no one was hurt.

Faye tended to a stroke victim, four car accidents—one fatality—and a guy who'd nearly cut off his hand on a machine at work. She was on-site for two of the three gasoline fires. Those times at work, being a paramedic, were about the only times she felt strong.

And over the next two weeks, Elliott continued to withdraw. From the kids at the Stand—including Kyle—and from Reese, too.

That first Saturday that Reese and Elliott had gone to the beach, they'd only been gone a few minutes when they'd come back and asked her to go with them. It had been another anticlimactic day. Her and Reese sitting on the sand without much to say, watching Elliott, who played in the water. She'd cried herself to sleep that night.

She was no longer hoping the pain would ever go away. But at some point, she was going to be out of tears.

Some things weren't meant to heal.

Maybe for Elliott, too.

The past weekend, when Reese had invited him to go fishing—something Elliott had always wanted to do—he'd declined. Said he didn't want to go. Didn't like to fish.

She'd asked him if he wanted to invite Reese

to go out for pizza with them and he'd said no to that, too.

But he called his father almost every day. Faye didn't know what they talked about. And didn't ask.

Elliott had been sleepwalking as much as always. There were no more late-night visits to her room. No confidences. But the one person he didn't seem to withdraw from was her. And for the first time in years, he went two weeks without being angry with her.

She'd had no more meetings alone with Reese. No private conversations. And no time to talk when they were together with Elliott, showing him how friendly they were.

She dreamed about him constantly. And had been so turned on she'd woken up wet between her legs on two separate occasions. The first time, she'd been afraid she'd peed the bed. Had jumped up thoroughly embarrassed with herself until she realized what had happened.

She thought about talking to Bloom about the situation during her weekly session but didn't. She knew the source of the problem—a psyche trying to heal by regressing back to pre-abuse times.

The reason Reese was the only star of her nighttime shows was because he'd been her only love before Frank. Her only pre-abuse sexual experience.

She just hadn't realized quite how powerful her psyche could be.

Or that men weren't the only ones with wet dreams.

The only thing stable in her life was her job.

She and Reese avoided each other at the station as they'd done since she'd been hired on. Not so much that it was obvious. They just didn't end up in the same place at the same time unless they were on a call. And then only the scene mattered.

And yet, she felt him there. Every minute of every day. The father of her child in his office. Walking through the house. Working out.

Reese, the man who'd once been her whole world. Who might still have been if he hadn't failed to tell her when he was in crisis. If she hadn't changed the entire course of her life.

Reese, the man who didn't believe in forever love anymore. And her, an abused woman who couldn't give her love to him even if he did believe.

What a pair they made. Two damaged people trying to save their damaged child. Two people with more regrets than they could master.

And still, she yearned for him. Not just in a physical sense but…for him. She thought about him far more than she'd have liked, trying to see the young man who'd felt as though he had to read her mind. Felt as though he never knew what to do to please her.

She didn't really understand. He hadn't had to do anything. She'd loved being with him. Still, she went around and around in her mind, replaying memories. And figured he must be remembering incorrectly.

Or had he been misreading her back then? Perhaps he hadn't known her as well as she'd thought.

She wondered if he'd done anything about Elliott's space in his home. He'd been at work pretty much every day. And he'd been back in LA at least three times, working on gasoline fire forensics.

She wondered a lot of things. But had no answers. She was living in the eye of a tornado and had no shelter in which to hide.

Faye wasn't good without a plan. After two weeks of trying to step back—to let things unfold she set up a meeting with Sara.

And found that the counselor was equally surprised that Elliott wasn't showing any signs of change, other than phone calls with his father, and being less mean to her. The boy was more isolated than ever and wouldn't confide in anyone.

Unless...

Was he confiding in Reese? Did Reese know something he wasn't sharing? He'd checked in with Sara twice, as had been arranged, but only to say that there were no issues. Sara understood the phone calls between father and son were brief. Uneventful.

But Reese was new at the parenting thing. What if Elliott was giving him clues that he wasn't getting?

If you need something...just ask.

His words came back to her as she left Sara's office on the second Thursday after they'd told Elliott that Reese was his father.

He didn't want to read her mind. She shouldn't assume he knew these things.

Fine.

He was at work. She couldn't have conversations like this with him there. His rules, not hers. So after she'd finished housework, she called him. Asked if she could see him over lunch, expecting to have to convince him that the meeting was necessary.

Instead, he agreed immediately. Then suggested that it be someplace they wouldn't be overheard.

Not wanting to be trapped at her house or his, afraid of the intimacy, she suggested the beach.

He told her he knew of a food truck, said there were benches nearby where they could sit and eat. They'd be outside, could see the ocean.

When they'd arrived, all of the benches had been taken and somehow they ended up on the blanket she kept in the trunk of her car. She sat cross-legged with her blue sundress stretched over her knees, overlooking the ocean and eating the best grilled cheese sandwich she'd ever had.

A picnic. With a man she loved but was no longer close to. Awkward, to say the least. She'd thought the food would stick in her throat but it slid right down.

Until he looked at her with a gaze that seemed to take in far more than she was sharing.

"I've been thinking about you." His words could have been a come-on but the way he said them, as though assessing and finding something wrong, didn't sound like one.

But if he had something to get off his mind...

She waited. He didn't say anything more.

With half a sandwich sitting on the paper on her lap, she told him, "I had a meeting with Sara this morning."

He nodded. Seemed to be enjoying his sandwich.

"You aren't too warm here, in the sun?" In jeans and a polo shirt, he sure could be. Reese had always been a hot-blooded guy.

"I'm fine."

"Elliott's not improving, Reese. If anything he's showing signs of regressing."

He took another bite of his sandwich. Shrugged. "Sara said there'd be a period of adjustment. Any change...even good change...is stressful on kids."

He'd listened. She'd give him that.

"Here's the thing... I don't want to pry...but,

you know earlier, when I said we need to keep in touch about him…"

"I'm to call you if he asks to see me, make arrangements through you…"

"We need to be in touch regarding everything where he's concerned. At least at first."

"I have no problem with that."

"So… I have to ask…what do you two talk about? What's going on with him?"

"I figured you'd know that. I ask questions, he gives one-word answers and that's that."

Her heart fell a bit.

She couldn't help but remember the last time she and Reese had been on a picnic together. They really had been kids, back then. So unaware of the dangers around them. Or uncaring of them. They'd ended up naked that day.

Why she chose that moment to remember, she had no idea. But seeing him sitting there, his lips wrapping around toasted bread, she remembered the moist feel of them on nipples warmed by the sun.

"I'd hoped he wasn't saying anything to me or Sara because he was telling you," she finally said.

He shook his head. "We knew there'd be a period of adjustment," he said again.

"But he calls you almost every day. And has made it clear that he doesn't want me to overhear what he's saying. Maybe he's telling you something that would mean something more to Sara or me than it does to you."

Another shake of the head was her only response.

"Reese, you told me to ask if I wanted something."

This time he nodded. Either his sandwich was phenomenal or the man was starving. It used to be that the first couple of bites would take his edge off.

"So, I'm asking. What does Elliott talk to you about?"

"You."

Oh. No. Of course, she'd expected that her son might not want to stay with her if he had another choice.

But he'd come to her room the night he'd found out about Reese. He'd sought his comfort and security from her.

"What about me?"

When he dropped the last quarter of his sandwich and looked at her, Faye lost a bit of breath.

"He and I have an agreement," he said. "He has to call to report to me every day in terms of his treatment of you. If he's angry with you, he's to tell me. And then tell me how he handled the anger. If I find his behavior inappropriate, we discuss other choices. Whatever else happens with him, whatever you decide for his future, my son will not disrespect his mother."

She blinked a couple of times. She was not going to cry.

"What does he get in return?" she asked.

"Nothing. Other than learning to be a good man."

"But you said you had an agreement..." Like a tour of a fire truck in exchange for a phone call.

"I told him what I expected, and he agreed."

There he was with that expectation thing again. He was on the other side of it this time, but it was still there. The need to have expectations delineated.

She'd never known it had been an issue in their past, but maybe it had been.

"How's he been telling you he's doing?"

"Mostly fine. There were a couple of moments, but I'm sure you know about them already."

She shook her head. "His treatment of me is the only thing that's improved over the past couple of weeks. He's been great." Now she knew why.

"He said he raised his voice to you two nights ago. When you told him it was time for bed."

"He did. Because I was in the kitchen, doing dishes. I'd called out to him to get in his pajamas and get his teeth brushed. He'd called back, asking if he had to. I said yes. He said okay."

"Must have been his tone of voice then."

She shook her head. "Believe me, it was nothing like the one he uses to cut me to the quick."

"Another time was on Monday when he got on you for being late to pick him up."

"He just asked me where I'd been…"

"He said he complained at you."

"Nothing like he used to," she told him. "He said he'd been waiting but his tone was completely different than it used to be. And he didn't have the surly look on his face. I haven't seen that in a while."

Not since before her son had climbed into bed with her.

"I don't kid myself, Reese. I know he has issues where I'm concerned. Sara knows it, too. We're working through his anger with me. I'm also fully aware that there might be a time when he needs to be away from me for a while. He might need space. But I'm telling you, these past two weeks have been vastly different. Now I know why."

"Maybe."

"But the thing that's weird is that he thinks he's still being bad. He's reporting things to you that aren't bad at all."

"Why would he do that?"

She wished she knew. Feeling slightly panicky as she thought of her eight-year-old son's skewed world, she said, "Maybe to test you. To see how you react when he's acting out. To see if you'll still be around."

But somehow, she didn't think so.

"Seems like if that was the case, he'd do something worse than complain about you being late," Reese said.

"Maybe he doesn't want you to think there's no reason for the phone calls anymore. He wants to keep having them so he's making a reason."

"He can call me anytime he wants. He doesn't need a reason."

"He's eight, Reese. He's had a lot thrown at him. It's going to take a while before he just trusts. Or accepts."

"Which is why you probably shouldn't worry overly much yet about his apparent lack of progress."

He was right, of course. She knew that. And still…she worried.

But she didn't want to.

She also didn't want him to get up and leave. He'd finished his sandwich. She'd wrapped up hers.

The meeting was going to end and she wasn't done.

CHAPTER THIRTY

On Friday, Reese grabbed a bag of burritos and drove to Faye's house. If she wasn't home, he'd have enough for lunch and dinner.

He needed to see her without giving her a chance to do any damned planning. He wanted the real Faye—whoever that turned out to be.

This pussyfooting around, pretending that they didn't have an intense history, was nuts. It wasn't going to do the boy any good.

It sure as hell wasn't doing Reese any good.

And he didn't think it was good for Faye, either. When they'd walked back to their vehicles the day before at the beach, he'd been left with a very clear impression that something wasn't right for her.

He'd said he wasn't a mind reader. She'd said she would ask. She had.

So what was he doing in return? Other than keeping his distance? Leaving the major responsibility to her? She'd told him quite clearly she was concerned about their son. And he'd told her not to worry.

Big of him.

But it was more than that and he knew it.

Just as he knew, when he saw her car in the drive and then climbed the steps up to her apartment, that she wasn't going to be pleased to see him.

It occurred to him that she might have her hair down. No makeup on. Knew he had no business hoping so. He'd always preferred her first-thing-in-the-morning look but it wasn't his business to pay attention to her appearance now.

His body would get that straight eventually. He was determined about that.

He heard her on the other side of the door after his first knock. Figured she would look through the peephole. Steeled himself to look professional.

An office call with a bag of burritos.

When the door didn't immediately open, he showed her the bag. Second thought told him he had a better chance of making it in the door with her favorite fast-food weakness than he did as her employer. Or the father of her child.

The door opened.

He'd been right—her hair was down and she wasn't wearing any makeup. She was wearing her black Lycra shorts, tank bra and a translucent black-and-white top.

"I brought lunch," he said before she could send him on his way. Because he thought the chances were good that she would? "Payback for yesterday." When she'd suggested lunch.

"You bought yesterday."

"See it as a peace offering."

"I didn't realize we needed one."

He still had no idea what she needed.

"How about an apology?" He hadn't intended to meet her gaze on that one. It had just sort of happened.

He didn't like the emotion that surged between them. But it got him in the door.

"What are you apologizing for?" Faye asked as she brought them both ice tea. She sat with him on the couch, reaching into the bag of burritos and pulling out a wrapped bean-stuffed tortilla. Their glasses were on coasters on the coffee table, along with the bag.

Helping himself to lunch, he said, "For being such an ass when you first came to town."

"You have no reason to apologize. You had every right to be angry with me, Reese. You still do."

He wasn't all that hungry. Was more interested in looking around. "I'm not angry."

"You should be."

Her place was pristine. Everything in its own spot. He'd expected as much. He'd seen how she'd kept house for her father, and her half of the dorm room she and Carrie had shared. He'd kind of liked that about her. Made her feel…reliable. Like he could trust her.

"I'm the one who broke trust first, Faye."

Looking down, her burrito held suspended,

she shook her head. And then faced him. "We can't keep going back there. You were struggling. I should have come to you and asked what was going on. I should have given you the benefit of a doubt when I got that phone call."

"If I'd found myself attracted to Susan, I'd have slept with her that night."

"If you'd wanted to do that, you should have. You just should have let me know first."

"I had no idea what I wanted. Except that I wasn't ready to lose you. Which is why I didn't tell you." He wasn't proud of that but there it was.

When it was happening, he'd figured he'd tell her about it when all was said and done. Figured she'd be glad to hear the outcome.

He could have done so that Saturday morning. But he hadn't. He'd taken the easy way out, waiting for her to cool off. Waiting for her to contact him.

Of course, he'd had no way of knowing that she'd known about Susan. He'd thought they were just dealing with him not going to her party.

"I was also a bit peeved that you'd told me not to bother to come Saturday. I was going to show you I was just fine missing the whole weekend." He wasn't proud of that, either. But maybe...if they dealt with the unresolved issues between them, they could move on to some kind of friendship. For their son's sake.

It wouldn't be the same. Or be enough.

"I was being jealous and manipulative," she said. "I was trying to force you to come Friday by attaching Saturday to it, as well. I'm the one who made the critical mistake. You have no need to apologize." She moved her attention back to her burrito.

His gaze got tangled up with her breasts. Stayed there.

He remembered them. Their shape. Their size. The darkening around her nipple.

No others had ever stacked up to hers.

He'd missed them.

"For the past two weeks, I just can't get the thought out of my head of you unable to enjoy sex. I can't bear the thought of the passionate woman I knew being so hurt that she can no longer enjoy that passion."

Her shrug bugged him. More than he liked.

"It is what it is. Everything comes with a price. My drunken stupor cost a lot."

"No way, Faye. You getting drunk was one thing. What Frank did…that was criminal. And all on him. I just want you to know…in an attempt at full disclosure so we can move forward…that I'm struggling a bit with the whole thing."

"My God, Reese. You've just found out you're a father, then add to that that your ex was… sexually abused…of course you're struggling."

"No…" They had to get this out. Get past it. "I mean, yes, of course. All of that. And so much more. I just need you to know…now that I've opened my life to you and Elliott… I'm still attracted to you, Faye. I don't intend to act on it. Although, I'm tempted to help you discover that you still have that passion…" The idea that his actions had led to her pain was killing him. "But I'm not going to because we can't afford to mess up anything between us. We might lose our son altogether if we do."

Which was why he was there. To get them on solid ground before the fragile and tentative friendship between them erupted into something that would upset Elliott's security again.

Faye wasn't saying anything. Was still eating. He figured that must be a good sign. Hoped to God it was.

"I just think, us pretending that we aren't close, yet I know just what to bring you for lunch…and you know that I have to eat or I get grouchy…we are close, Faye. We've both told our son we love each other, for God's sake." Lord knew that one had been bugging him, too.

One fucking date and he'd blown everything. For himself. But even worse, for Faye. For their son.

"So…here I am. I care about you. I know you. I want to be a part of your life. If you need anything, you can call me. If you need a friend to talk to—even if it's not about Elliott, you can call me.

I'm here for you. And I will have your back from this point forward. All you have to do is ask."

Phew. It was out. All but one thing. "And I'm planning to let everyone at work know the truth about us—in that we were together in the past and my newfound son is your son, Elliott—assuming you're okay with that?"

He'd been staring at her slightly bent profile as she ate. Had noticed that she'd stopped chewing somewhere along the way. But he'd had to get it out.

"Faye?" She wasn't saying anything. Or moving.

In the next second, he knew why.

He'd made her cry again.

Damn.

SOMEHOW FAYE MADE it through lunch. She'd excused herself to the bathroom. A couple of minutes of cold compress to her eyes had helped. She wasn't exactly sure what she'd said to Reese when she'd returned, but she thought things were better between them. Wanted them to be.

He was still attracted to her!

Lord knew, she wanted to jump his bones, too.

But the minute her desire turned off would make things awkward all over again. Would make the regrets burn her again, like the acid they were.

He'd offered friendship.

Close friendship.

She'd take it.

She was to the point of feeling pretty good about things later that afternoon when her phone rang.

Elliott wasn't through at the Stand for another couple of hours. After his computer workshop a few Saturdays ago, he'd signed up for a basic programming course on Friday afternoons, offered through the Stand's computer repair shop and training program. That afternoon was the first class.

So why was she getting a call from The Lemonade Stand?

"Faye? This is Sara. Lila and I are here together. Faye, Elliott's gone missing. We think you should get here as quickly as you can…"

She barely heard the rest, that security was all over the ground, that the police had been called, that no one knew if he'd left the grounds. No security cameras showed him, so they were hoping not. He'd last been seen half an hour before when he'd asked to use the restroom.

There was more.

She didn't catch it.

REESE HAD JUST returned to work after the drills he'd put himself through in the fitness room when he saw Faye's name on his private line.

"Faye?"

He'd asked her to call. Hadn't been sure she ever would. But certainly hadn't expected it so soon.

"Reese? Come quickly. Please. Elliott's missing. I'm on my way to the Stand right now. Please, Reese? I need you. I can't do this. If something's happened to him…"

Keys in hand, he was already on his way out the door.

"Where are you?"

She named the street. Five minutes away from him.

"Pull over," he said, describing the parking lot he wanted her to find. "You're upset. Just stop driving. Now."

"Reese, did you hear me?"

He was in his car. "I heard you. I'm on my way, babe. In my car. I've got the lights. I'll get you there faster…"

Elliott was missing. He couldn't think about that now. First things first. "Faye? Please. Pull over. Now."

He was still three minutes away. Even with traffic clearing in front of him.

He wasn't going to lose another woman in a car accident. He wasn't going to lose Faye a second time.

"Faye?"

"I'm where you told me," she said. "Please hurry, Reese. We have to find him."

He saw her, parked right where she'd said. Waiting for him.

Because she needed him.

The force of knowing that—of never having known that before—hit him. Hard.

Faye needed him.

And that was all he'd ever needed from her.

FAYE WAS BARELY aware of the flashing lights on Reese's car as he got out and ran toward her.

What she knew was that his arms were open. Trembling, she ran into them. He hugged her. Tight. She hugged him back.

And with tears streaming down her face, pulled away.

"We have to get to the Stand."

He was already opening the passenger door of his car for her before hurrying around to his side. The car was in gear and pointing toward the road before she had her seat belt on. He waited to pull out until she was buckled.

"Tell me what they said." Reese was the calm to her frantic. He hadn't been a father for long, but he cared about Elliott. She didn't doubt that. Just as she knew that he had a talent for going to work when the tough jobs had to be done.

He'd always been that way.

She'd always loved that about him.

As quickly as she could, she told him everything Sara had said, adding, "I just can't figure it out. He's never done anything like this before. Not here and not before, either. He's not a take-flight type of kid."

"Could someone have taken him?"

"Frank, you mean?" She shook her head. "He didn't want him when we lived together. He gave up full custody without a blink."

"He might have received notice that we've applied for a birth certificate name change hearing."

Buildings and palm trees whizzed past. Cars pulled over for them as they sped up one road and down another.

"It's possible," she said, knowing she should have paid more attention to that part of the process. She'd never considered that Frank would care. "If he sees your name…he listened to me whine about you for hours the night we met."

She couldn't go there now. Couldn't afford to be pulled back.

"But he can't get into the Stand," she reminded both of them. "You know how impossible it is to get access if you aren't on the list…"

Even employees of approved companies couldn't get access to The Lemonade Stand without going through a full identity profile, checked against all Stand residents and outpatient clients.

"So chances are he's missing of his own accord," Reese said, maneuvering through pulled-over cars and around curves and corners like the pro he was. They were almost there already.

"That's what Sara and Lila think. But they're no less concerned. Where would he go? And why? There's really no telling what's on his mind. He's got no money. No way to take care of himself. He's clearly struggling."

"Don't sell him too short, Faye," Reese said. "He's a planner. And self-sufficient. Like his mom."

She almost laughed, except her heart was too frightened to find even a hint of humor.

"I'm not self-sufficient," she told him. "I have to fight, every day, to do what must be done. It's always been that way. If I were self-sufficient, I would have left Frank Walker the first time he put a strap on my body…"

There was more. She couldn't go on.

They'd arrived at The Lemonade Stand. She counted four police cars in the parking lots. Officers were standing outside the front door, and from their expressions, she guessed things weren't good.

"Let's go find our son."

Reese's words made her start to cry, but she didn't waver as she climbed out of his car, took the hand he offered and walked with him into the domestic violence shelter.

CHAPTER THIRTY-ONE

THE SCENE INSIDE The Lemonade Stand—officials conversing in hushed tones, groups of two and three dispersed throughout the inner lobby, waiting for direction—was familiar enough. Whether it was fire or rescue, Reese had been around this type of scene many, many times.

Even when his wife had been killed.

He'd never been here as a father, though.

And never with Faye.

But he had no doubt what Faye and their son needed from him.

Finding Managing Director Lila McDaniels standing with two plainclothes detectives, he headed in their direction. Sara had taken Faye to sit on a couch in a corner, to get information or offer comfort. He assumed both.

"Who's in charge?" he asked as he stepped up to the group uninvited.

"I am." The leather-bound ID the man flipped at him said he was Sam Larson.

"You're married to Dr. Bloom Larson?" Reese surmised, starting to feel like he had some real help. According to Faye, the man's wife had been a victim. He'd know the ropes, the responsibility Reese was now facing to take care of his own family. And the worry.

"I am. She's on her way." Sam nodded toward Faye.

"I need to speak with a boy named Kyle," Reese said to Sam. "He's a resident here with his mother."

He wasn't asking.

Safe house or not, a boy was missing and he'd gone missing from the inside.

Lila hesitated but with one look between Reese and Sam, she said, "I'll call him up here."

"I'd rather go to him," Reese said without further explanation.

"I'll go with him," Sam assured Lila.

Good. Everyone understood each other here.

He was going to find his son.

WITH BLOOM ON one side of her and Sara on the other, Faye sat on a couch in a small lobby just outside Lila's office—the official search headquarters.

Sam and Reese were questioning residents, she'd been told. Officers had been dispatched throughout the grounds and on the streets surrounding the Stand—most particularly the street that housed the Stand's businesses. All of them, the thrift store, the computer shop and others, had a private entrance and exit into the Stand. Residents trained and worked at the facilities.

If Elliott had managed to escape, it would have most likely been through one of those. But preliminary checks of surveillance cameras came up empty.

"Do they think he's still inside?" she asked the two women. They'd become as much like friends as professional counselors to her. Probably because she was a first responder, as well.

If she got through this…when she got through this…she was going to pursue a position on the high-risk team. Then she'd be working with them, not just needing their services. She'd like that. To be a friend instead of a client.

"I knew something was bothering him," she said. Sara had seen it, too. They all had. And they'd failed him. Poor Elliott.

"He knows you're there for him, Faye. You're a great mother. Have confidence in that. I can assure you that he does," Sara said.

"You've been open and honest with him," Bloom added. "You don't hide things from him. He knows that, too. Those are the kinds of things that give a child security."

"Then why didn't he come to me with whatever is bothering him?"

"I guess when we find out what that is, we'll know the answer," Bloom said.

"One thing I can tell you for sure," Sara said.

"You've raised a very self-sufficient young man. If Elliott is on a mission of his own, and all preliminary information points to that conclusion, then he has a plan. And when he does what he needs to do, he'll be back."

If he was safe. And able to get back.

"What if he's gone to find Frank? To make him pay for what he did to us?" That fear had been with her ever since Reese had mentioned the possibility of Frank taking Elliott. That hadn't rung true. But the other way around did.

"They have officers in San Diego locating your ex-husband right now," Sara said. "It's a matter of process. Any time someone goes missing, securing the abuser is the first point of business."

She hadn't known that. Or if she had, she'd forgotten.

"You two really don't have to sit here with me," she said. She wasn't in danger. Didn't need to take up the time of two very busy professionals.

"Would you rather be left alone?" Bloom asked.

Reese had said she never asked for help. Did she want to be left alone?

She looked at the two women.

"Why do I get the feeling that that wasn't a surface question?"

"I don't know. Why do you?" Bloom asked.

Did she want to be left alone?

Of course not. Not ever. But it happened. You got

left alone. Through no fault of your own, and sometimes, through no fault of anyone else's, either.

"I've been left alone my whole life," she said, feeling like she was going to cry again. Like she had tears stored so deeply inside her they'd be a part of her forever.

"Your mother dying when you were so young, you mean?"

Is that what she'd meant? This wasn't about her. It was about Elliott.

"It wasn't her fault," she said. "She loved me. She just got sick."

"I know."

"And Daddy loved me, too. I always knew that. He just had to work to pay the medical bills. And to support us."

"I know."

She heard the words but wasn't even sure which counselor was talking to her.

"And Reese...turns out he wasn't leaving me for another woman. He might have, but he liked me better."

But still, when he'd made the choice to two-time her, he'd left her. In the deepest sense. He'd taken away her ability to trust him.

"I thought he was the one person who'd never leave," she said. She felt the words leave her but didn't recognize the childlike voice.

"But he did."

Because he'd chosen to be unfaithful to her—

planning to sleep with the other woman if he'd wanted to.

"Yes."

He'd had struggles of his own, though. She knew that now. And she'd failed him, too, by not asking him what was going on. By not letting him know what she needed.

"I was so afraid of losing him, I didn't let myself need him." Her head hurt. Her heart burned. She heard a buzzing in her ears.

"And then your father died." A voice pulled her back.

Yes. In the midst of the Frank nightmare. Before she could mend the rift between them.

"I never got to tell him how wrong I was. How sorry I am. I never got to tell him how much I love him."

"He was a father. Just like you're a mother. When Elliott is his angriest, what do you do?"

She gave him space, letting him work out what he needed to work out. She never stopped loving him. Not ever.

She couldn't. No matter what.

And she knew.

Her father had loved her. Even during the Frank times.

Something else occurred to her. She looked from one woman to the other. These were women she relied on, trusted to tell her the truth. Not because they cared about her, but because they were paid to be there for her. As a result, she'd never worried about them leaving her.

"That's why I don't have friends, isn't it? I lost touch with Carrie as soon as I left school. I'm alone because I don't let myself need anyone."

"Is that what you think?" Bloom asked again.

"Isn't that what both of you think?"

Bloom Larson smiled. A small, sad smile but one filled with compassion, too. "I think it's a good possibility," she said.

"And being unable to allow sexual contact, is that part of this, too? If I let myself need Reese, would I be able to enjoy sex with him?"

She didn't realize what she'd said until she saw both women staring at her.

She wanted to have sex with Reese. And she knew he wanted her, too.

"I've loved him since I was sixteen," she said, as though she had to justify herself.

"Your lack of sexual response is a separate issue, Faye," Bloom said. "I've told you, though, there are things we can do when you're ready, and there are sessions with you and Reese, things the two of you can try…"

"But I might never be able to respond normally again…"

"You might not."

She should be devastated by that. In some ways she probably was. But those ways didn't matter nearly as much as loving and being loved.

To love and be loved…that was all Elliott had ever needed. To feel free to love.

"My son learned to be self-sufficient by my example," she said, thinking out loud. Reese had said so in the car. The counselors had said so. "Do you think he left because he thinks I don't need him?"

"There's no reason to jump to that conclusion. He knows you love him. You've proven that to him over and over."

Reese had known she loved him, too, but he'd also sensed she'd never been in with both feet. She'd never loved completely.

"Or did I teach him to be so much like me that he won't let himself need anyone? Is he gone because he's afraid he's going to need me, or Reese, too much?"

In an odd, sickening way, that made more sense.

"Again, there's no reason to jump to those conclusions."

No good to do so, more likely. The authorities were already working under the assumption that Elliott had left of his own accord. Whether it was because he was afraid to need his parents, because he thought they didn't need him or because he was going after other demons, it didn't change the fact that he was gone.

Tears filled her eyes and she didn't fight them. Looking between the two women, she said, "I need him. I need him to come back. I need Reese, too. I don't want to be alone."

She broke. Sobbed. "I don't want to be alone." The words were clear.

They were the last thing she remembered before arms wrapped around her from both sides as the storm hit her in full force.

CHAPTER THIRTY-TWO

ON THEIR WAY to meet with Kyle in his mother's bungalow, Reese had filled Detective Larson in on the older boy's relationship with Elliott. He'd also mentioned his own dealings with Kyle, including his suspicions about how Kyle was at a gasoline fire crime scene shortly after Elliott had set a fire.

The boy's mother had vouched for him. Reese had believed Kyle when he'd questioned him.

But something wasn't ringing true now as they sat with the boy in his mother's living room.

"I have no idea where Elliott is," Kyle said for at least the tenth time. It was clear to Reese that Sam Larson believed him. Reese didn't like the way the boy kept looking at his mother.

Maybe it was a natural reaction for a kid being questioned, except that Kyle hadn't done it the first time Reese had questioned him. And his mother had been in the room then, too.

Kyle told them he'd invited Elliott to play basketball that afternoon. Elliott had refused.

"It wasn't a big deal," the boy said. "He pretty much says no all the time now."

"Do you have any idea why?" Sam asked.

Shaking his head, Kyle said, "No, sir."

He leaned forward then to pick at his shoe. And Reese stared. It was the same brand that forensic evidence had said was present at one of his earlier crime scenes.

"What size is your shoe?" he asked. Reese had asked him this once before. He remembered the answer.

"Nine," Kyle said, looking up at him.

Reese's gaze traveled from the boy's face back down to his shoe but stopped midway when he noticed something else. In the boy's shirt pocket. Something with a small binding.

"What's in your pocket, Kyle?"

The boy pulled out a pack of matches. "Just these," he said.

Reese froze. The exact kind as the book he'd taken from his son. "Where'd you get those?"

"My brother owns that restaurant," Kyle's mother spoke up.

"Why are they in your pocket?"

"I don't know."

"I think you do."

Kyle's mother stood. "I think we're done here."

Sam and Reese stood, too.

"I don't think we are," Sam said.

It took everything Reese had not to haul the other boy out of his seat and demand answers. If he'd done something to Elliott…or sent that boy off to do something for him…

He took a deep breath. Got himself under control. For Faye's sake.

She needed him to bring her son back to her.

FAYE WAS SITTING with Sara and Lila about an hour after her breakdown when Lila's phone rang. It was Suzie.

"I've got Elliott!"

Faye heard the woman's words from three feet away, she'd spoken so loudly. She didn't hear the rest of the conversation but she heard what Lila told Sam when she called him seconds later.

"He was hiding on the steps inside the cellar door in the back of her house," Lila was saying into the phone, looking right at Faye. "She'd noticed it slightly ajar. Apparently it was darker in there than he thought it would be and he'd propped it open to get some light."

Why he'd run away remained to be seen. They'd deal with that later.

Faye was out the door, heading toward the parking lot where Reese had left his car without remembering to thank anyone who'd helped her.

She would. But right then, she had to get to Elliott.

Reese meeting her at the car could have been coincidence. Luck. Yet she'd known he'd be there. And that he'd have his lights flashing all the way back to her place.

They didn't speak.

There was too much to say and no time to say it.

No ability to think it, even. She had to see her son. To hold him in her arms. To tell him how much she loved him. And needed him.

And then ground him for life for running away.

REESE STOOD BACK in her driveway as Faye ran toward Elliott.

He watched as Faye swung her fifty-pound son off the ground and into her arms. Saw Elliott's tear-stained face over her shoulder. And swallowed.

Suzie was there. Sam Larson would be coming. Reese had a report to write. And everyone needed an explanation.

It was possible that Elliott was involved in something more than running away. Something he had yet to tell Faye.

Elliott and Kyle. Two boys with known anger issues, two boys with matches. One who'd set a fire in a bathroom trash, the other present at the scene of a gasoline fire. Kyle even wore the same brand of tennis shoe that had shown up at another gasoline crime scene.

Did he wear a different size because they'd been donated? Maybe the first pair had been too big for the boy.

They didn't know yet. But they would.

Faye had put Elliott down and was questioning

him. What was wrong? Why had he run away? Why hadn't he called her?

Elliott's answers were the same. He didn't know. The more Faye questioned, the harder he shook his head, and the more vehemently he said didn't know anything.

Reese's heart sank.

For Elliott. For Faye. For all of them.

His son might be in trouble. It was going to kill Faye.

But it wouldn't be the end of the world, one way or the other. He'd see to that.

Elliott was young, and at risk. He'd been misled by a kid he looked up to in a place he'd been sent to get help. He now had a new father looking out for him. A fire chief, who knew how to teach him why arson didn't solve anything.

Elliott was already in treatment. The judge would see that he hadn't been there long enough for it to work.

No life had been lost.

Reese would pay for the chickens. And the barn.

"You talk to them yet?" Sam had come up behind him.

He shook his head. He'd followed protocol and waited for the detective in charge. He wasn't going to let this one get messed up.

And he couldn't bear to be the one who told Faye that her son was possibly involved with an arsonist.

"Elliott was the only one who had regular access outside of The Lemonade Stand," Larson said as they watched mother and child for a moment more. Elliott was standing, Faye was holding him while he cried—his face pressed to her stomach.

She hadn't looked over at Reese.

Not once.

She knew something.

Or suspected, anyway.

"Elliott?" Reese said. "Detective Larson needs to speak with you."

"Do I gotta go to jail?"

"No," Reese said. It wouldn't be jail. If he had any power at all, it wouldn't be juvenile detention, either. Not even for one night.

"We can talk right here," Sam said, looking at the boy with a firm expression but talking with far more compassion than he'd shown Kyle.

Reese knew Faye wouldn't want their dirty laundry aired in the front yard. Leading his son and his…he didn't know what she was to him anymore…upstairs, he asked everyone to take a seat in the living room. Made certain he was standing right behind Faye and Elliott, holding each of them by a shoulder.

After murmuring something to Faye, Suzie had gone back to her part of the house.

Sam cleared his throat, and Reese held up a hand. Then he looked down at his boy with a raised brow.

He wanted to question Elliott himself after all.

When the detective nodded, he moved around the front of the couch, knelt and looked his son right in the eye.

"I need you tell me the truth, Elliott," he said. "We're in a serious situation here and it's up to you to do the hard thing."

Maybe he was putting too much on a troubled kid. All he knew was he had to save his family—and his family included Elliott.

Maybe they weren't traditional and wouldn't ever be. Maybe they lived in separate houses. But they were related, by blood and by heart. Faye and Elliott needed him. And he needed them, too.

Wide-eyed, Elliott just stared at him.

"Why did you run away today?"

"I was scared."

The words fell into the room with a crack. Faye stared at her son. Reese almost wished he'd let the detective do the questioning. Except that something told him Elliott would talk to him.

Maybe two weeks of nightly confessionals had helped.

"Of what?" he asked.

The boy shrugged, and Reese shook his head. He noticed that Faye wasn't intervening. She was trusting him to handle this.

"A shrug's not going to do it, buddy."

Elliott started to cry again. Leaned against Faye. She looked over at him and he shook his head.

"Elliott, I need you to tell me what's going on."

"I can't," he said. "It's the code."

"Code?"

"We talk about junk…it's secret…and no one tells."

"Are you talking about the group counseling rules?" Faye asked.

"Yeah."

"So you know something from counseling?"

"Sorta."

"Does it have to do with Kyle?" Reese asked, starting to get worked up himself. Could that be all this was? And Elliott wasn't in trouble at all?

Elliott's silence gave Reese a fair confirmation that Kyle was involved.

"Is Kyle setting fires, Elliott?" Sam asked.

"No."

"But you know who is, don't you?" the detective coaxed.

"I don't know." The boy looked at Reese, who moved over to sit next to him.

"You have to man up, son."

"If I do, I'll get in trouble. And if I don't, I'll get in trouble. And everyone's going to be mad at me no matter what and…"

"That's why you ran away," Reese said, understanding completely. He felt Faye's muscles relax even from one seat over. He met her gaze. Wanted to touch her face. Give her a soft, reassuring kiss.

"Kyle knows what's in my paper that I burned," Elliott said. "If I tell his, he's gonna tell mine."

"Did he tell you that?"

"Uh-huh." The boy sniffled. Wiped his nose with his arm. Reaching for a tissue from the table beside her, Faye handed it to her son.

Elliott blew his nose, wadded up the tissue and handed it back to her.

Sam settled back into an armchair across from them.

"Want me to tell you a trick I learned?" Reese asked, trying his damnedest to remember being eight.

At Elliott's nod, he continued, "I learned that if you have a secret that you know is going to be told, it's best just to tell it yourself. That way it gets told the way it really happened. The way you know it. Not like someone else thinks it."

"Do I gotta say it right now?" Elliott's gaze was for him alone.

Reese guessed that whatever the boy had written had been about his mother. Knowing what Elliott could possibly have witnessed, he said, "No, you don't. It can be in private, just me and you, when we're done here." He was winging it.

He was a fire chief, not a dad. But no one was arguing with him.

"Now, you need to tell us Kyle's secret that made you run away."

"Maybe he should tell you."

"He wouldn't," Sam said. "We already asked him after you went missing. We talked to both him and his mother."

The disappointed pout on Elliott's lips angered Reese on Elliott's behalf but gave him hope, too.

"She's the one that tells Kyle it's his job to take notes and remember stuff from Sara to help his brother. She says it's because Kyle is lucky that he's at the Stand and with her and his brother's too old."

Kyle had a brother. Reese looked at Sam. Sam nodded and stood. "I'm on it." The man left the room, his phone already out of its holster.

"Kyle's brother is setting fires, isn't he?" Reese asked.

And Elliott nodded.

CHAPTER THIRTY-THREE

FAYE TURNED FROM Elliott's doorway later that night, having been allowed to actually tuck her son into bed, to find Reese right there, watching her.

She'd left him in the living room. He'd said good-night to Elliott, told him he'd done the right thing that day. That Reese was proud of him.

She'd half expected him to have let himself out before she got back.

"You have to get to the station," she said. She understood his job. "You've got your arsonist."

Kyle's older brother, Matt, had been arrested before dinner that evening, at his aunt's house where he'd been staying. Both Kyle and his mother had been protecting him.

"If they'd asked for help rather than trying to help him themselves, he'd have had a better chance," Faye said. And got the connection, too.

"Probably."

"I feel bad for him. He was just as much a victim as they were, but he couldn't live at the Stand because he's too old."

"From what I hear, they're trying to get a separate, smaller facility for men," Reese said. "Sam mentioned it when he called to say that Kyle and his mother and brother were all in custody."

Matt had been charged with several counts of arson and destruction of property. Kyle and his mom were charged with obstructing justice. They might also be accountable for endangering a minor for the part they forced Elliott to play.

Elliott had come upon Kyle sneaking out to meet his older brother at the computer shop one day. That was when the older boy had started blackmailing him with things Elliott had said in counseling—saying he'd tell everyone what had happened to Faye.

Which was also why Elliott's anger with Faye had escalated. He'd been forced to keep her secret because she'd done what Frank told her to do.

She and Reese walked to her front door. So hard to believe it had been only that afternoon that Reese had shown up with a bag of burritos.

He turned at the end of the hall and headed toward the kitchen instead of going straight to the door. Started cleaning away the empty pizza box that had been left after the three of them had had dinner together.

Mom and Dad giving their son the love and support he needed from them. Letting him talk. Letting him tell them over and over again what Kyle had said. How Kyle had encouraged him to burn the paper he'd written his worst feelings on, so it would feel like he was burning away the feelings themselves.

"When Kyle gave Elliott those matches to burn his own paper in the bathroom trash can, he'd solidified Elliott's feeling that Kyle cared about him and was trying to help him," Faye said aloud.

Reese continued helping her clean up the kitchen. Wiping the table while she put the glasses in the dishwasher.

"You can go, Reese. I don't want to keep you from…"

She was doing it again. Pushing him away.

With water still running in the sink, she grabbed his arm. Turned him toward her. "I don't want you to leave. I want you to spend the night."

No strings attached if that was how he'd prefer it. She just didn't want to be alone that night. Or any other night, now that she was admitting the truth.

He reached around her to turn off the water.

"I always thought my father leaving was my fault," he said. Her hand was still on his arm but he didn't touch her. "From what I understood, he was happy with my mother until I came along. My mom tells this story that on the day my father left, there was a fire across the street from us. The two weren't related but she says I was fascinated by the fire. I've wondered if maybe I took the stress from the one to the other. I was just a baby. Maybe two. But apparently I've been fascinated by fire ever since."

She'd known him all those years. Thought she'd known everything about him. How could she have not known this?

"Talking to Elliott, I think I get some of what he's going through. I've always had this fear that I'd fail my loved ones like my father failed me."

Why was he telling her this?

Did he mean…was there hope…?

Didn't matter. He mattered. She wanted everything he'd give her.

"Today, when you said you needed me…" He stopped. Looked her in the eye. Rubbed her shoulder with his hand. "It all came home to me, Faye. My issue with my father got in the way of how I related to you."

She shook her head. "I think we were crossed from the beginning, Reese. With my mother dying, I always thought I had it all under control. But I realized today that my whole life, I've never let myself need anyone, not fully. I've never let myself believe in true love, or lasting love, because I was afraid it would leave. And then, after what I did when I lost you… I never wanted to love like that again. Where the pain of loss was so strong you completely lose your mind…"

"We were two single-parent kids who thought we understood each other because of that," he said, "but instead we both had issues we never talked about."

She nodded. Sighed. Finally. They'd reached their place of understanding. The place he'd said they'd need to find to be able to co-parent Elliott successfully.

It took their son to show them themselves.

"I'm guessing it was no mistake that today's experience showed us both a new view of ourselves," she said, half smiling. "Fate has a funny way of knocking you over the head when you're missing the boat."

He didn't return her smile. With his hand still rubbing her arm, he said, "I'm so sorry, Faye. Everything you went through because…"

She touched a finger to his lips. Liked the feel of them. Really, really liked it. *Remembered* it.

"A very smart woman said something to me this afternoon that made a lot of sense." Bloom Larson, while her husband had been out helping Reese find their son. "She commented on how I didn't blame you anymore. How I understood what drove you to do what you did. She said it sounded as though I'd completely forgiven you… and when I did a self-check, I found that she was right. I had. Then she asked me if I thought you'd forgiven me, too. She said it sure seemed that way, seeing us together…"

"As far as I'm concerned there's nothing to forgive you for, Faye. Yeah, once in your life you got drunk. But so do millions of other college kids. You were with people you trusted and had reason to trust. There's no way you could have foreseen what was coming…"

Tears flooded her eyes. She'd told herself, when Elliott was found, that she was done crying. "Bloom asked me why I could forgive you but couldn't give the same gift to myself. She said the regrets don't have to eat me alive if I could just forgive myself like I forgave you."

It was going to take some work. But she was up to it.

"And I think maybe the same is true for you. Not just about me, but about Tabitha."

His hand on her arm rubbed a little quicker. Not harder, just faster.

In direct rhythm with her heartbeat.

"Will you spend the night with me, Reese? I need you here. I don't want to be alone." She repeated the words. She'd get used to them. And constantly check herself, too. She wasn't going to become selfish and make it all about her needs, but she would ask him for what she needed.

This was so her. Always with a plan.

"Of course I will," he said without hesitation. And then, "I'll sleep on the couch."

She'd been about to say she'd take the couch in Elliott's room. But stopped herself.

"Dr. Larson tells me that there are things we

can do, things she can help us with that might take away my aversion to being…touched."

All movement stopped. He stared at her. "Are you saying that you want to try?"

"I think I am." Her mouth was dry, her heart pounding. "Ever since I came here, I've been having these dreams about you. Naked, hot dreams."

He moved closer. Reaching up, she unbuttoned the top button of his shirt. And felt a slow, pulling eagerness inside herself.

"Dr. Larson and Sara both said that it's probably my psyche regressing to an earlier time as a way to help me heal from—"

"You told both of them that you're having hot dreams about me?" He had a funny grin on his face.

She nodded. That wasn't the important part. She got a second button undone.

"And they said it's probably your psyche?"
She nodded.

"Probably? Like it's possible that it could be something else?"

He took another step closer. An inch only. Because he was already close enough to lean forward and touch her thigh to thigh.

She licked her lips. Her mouth was so dry she could hardly talk. "I guess." And then stepped back. "But we don't know, Reese, and it would be awful if we get to a point and you're all…you know…and I push you away. Just the thought of that happening breaks my heart."

"You want to know what breaks mine?" he asked.

She nodded.

"The fact that you're afraid of yourself as much as you're afraid you won't like my touch. Don't you see, Faye, it's not the sex. Hell, yes, I want it. Need it, even. But there are other ways for a guy to get what he needs with his wife—without you having to accommodate me."

His words were so sensitive. So cute. The old Reese would have talked about boners and…other things.

"What I want you to know, to believe, is that I love you for you, not for your body, or my access to it."

Now that was a little more like it. Her eyes teared up. But she smiled, too.

"You aren't any less to me now, Faye, than you ever were. In the ways that matter, you're so much more. You need me," he finished. As if that said it all.

"I love you, Reese." She'd told her son. It was time to tell him.

"I love you, too."

Reaching up to kiss him was natural. This was Reese. Her lips were on his before she realized she'd reached for him. His mouth opened, his tongue against hers in a dance that was so familiar she fell into it. Into him.

Her breasts ached.

She was wet.

Her hands were on his chest, where she'd unbuttoned his shirt. Touching his skin.

And only then noticed that, other than with his mouth, he hadn't touched her.

She pulled back. Looked up at him.

"We have a son who's got issues with…" he said.

She couldn't believe she hadn't thought of Elliott. With Frank, Elliott had been a constant on her mind. Say what he wanted so he wouldn't get louder. Do what he wanted so he'd be done.

Thoughts of Frank ruined the mood.

But she took Reese's hand. "Let's go to my room," she told him. Maybe the moment would come back. She hoped it would.

She dreaded being in there with him and feeling tight and dry.

Her room was the larger of the two bedrooms, but still, it wasn't big. The bed was just a regular double, not a queen or king. There was one dresser. Two nightstands. A few things on the walls. None of it was hers. The place had come furnished.

He stood at the door.

"Is Elliott used to seeing your door closed?"

If she hadn't already been head over heels in love with this man, she'd just fallen. Completely. Forever.

"No," she said. "If he wakes up and sees it closed, it's going to scare him. And if he has a nightmare, I need to hear him."

Reese was Elliott's father. He cared.

It was okay that she put her son first.

"Then the door stays open. At least until we can buy a monitor and then explain to him that a mom and dad's door is closed so they don't wake their kids if they talk. But that if he ever needs to come in, he's always welcome. If we happened to be doing anything, the monitor would let us know he's up and on his way in, right?"

She nodded. Loving him so much it hurt.

"So." He started to unbutton his shirt further. One button. "Does that TV work?"

It was an older model on the dresser.

"It gets cable," she told him, walking over to him. Going for the next button. Waiting to see his navel again. The freckle that she'd always kissed right next to it.

His hand over hers stopped her.

"You want to watch TV in bed?" He finished unbuttoning his shirt and pulled the tails out of his pants.

TV. The thought of it made her weak with relief. She nodded.

"You should probably get ready for bed then."

She found him a toothbrush—she had a couple of new ones in the cupboard from when she'd found a three-pack on sale. In the past, they'd shared one whenever one of them had stayed over.

While she was in the bathroom, she quickly donned the T-shirt and cotton pajama shorts she normally wore to bed.

They weren't sexy. At all.

She went back to her room.

The first thing her gaze sought was that open bedroom door. She hadn't doubted that it would be open. She'd just looked. As she did every night for the past two years.

Reese was already in bed, propped up on a pillow as he flipped through channels.

She couldn't remember the number of times they'd watched TV in bed. It had always been after sex. And a snack that had usually involved chocolate.

Her first thought was to apologize for her attire, but she stopped herself.

She climbed under the covers. Embarrassed. Excited.

But not afraid.

Her foot touched his leg.

And she got wet again. Almost instantly.

Her door was open.

As was their son's.

Reese had found an old movie. Didn't seem to

notice that, for the first time in nine years, they were in bed together.

She couldn't think of anything else.

She remembered every single inch of his body. How it looked. How it felt.

"I wish it was nine years ago and I could slide on top of you and just do it," she told him.

He reached for her. Pulled her down beside him. Settled her head on his shoulder. Another familiar position, from even before they ever had sex. Back when they'd been in love but not lovers. And still later, too, on Sunday afternoons in the park or watching sports on TV.

"It'll come, babe," he said. "One way or another, it'll come."

She hoped he was right. Because in the bathroom, she'd been thinking about having another baby someday. A pregnancy he could share in every step of the way. A birth he could be present for.

He broke into her thoughts. "I have something to ask you."

"What?"

"Something I wanted to ask a million times back then..."

"What?" she asked again, really curious now.

"Will you marry me, Faye? As soon as humanly possible? As in, let's go to Reno this weekend and make it happen? With Elliott there as our witness, best man and...to walk you up the aisle?"

She sat up. "You don't know if I'll ever be able to…"

He sat up, too. "Don't you get it, Faye? I don't care. I mean, I care for your sake. I want you happy and enjoying every aspect of life, but as for the rest of it… I know what it feels like to make love to you. If we have to use…other means…I'll use those memories. Even the feel of your hand on me would be heaven. And I'll find a way to give you the same pleasure, if you want it. Trust me. We'll find a way."

He could touch her right then and she'd probably explode. As long as he wasn't on top of her. Or…

She didn't dry up.

Even thinking about being entered, she didn't dry up.

"You didn't answer my question."

She didn't want to be a burden. Didn't want to worry about being left.

She didn't want to live without Reese. She didn't want him to live alone, either. Or to be hurt.

And Elliott…

"Yes," she said. "Yes. Yes. Yes. I will marry you. This weekend. In Reno."

It wasn't the proposal she'd once dreamed of. Or the wedding she used to envision for them. It was so much more.

It was right.

"I will love you forever," she told him.

"And I will be with you forever," he said, looking her in the eye. "Even if something happens to me, I will be here in spirit, Faye. Always and forever."

Faye wanted to protect herself. To hold back.

But she laid her body down on top of his, placed her lips on his, and gave him the very last, hidden piece of her heart.

For all their sakes.

* * * * *

Be sure to check out the other recent books in Tara Taylor Quinn's
WHERE SECRETS ARE SAFE *miniseries*

HIS FIRST CHOICE
THE PROMISE HE MADE HER
HER SECRET LIFE

All available now from
Harlequin Superromance.

And look for the next
WHERE SECRETS ARE SAFE *book*
from Tara Taylor Quinn,
coming in August 2017!

Get 2 Free Books,
Plus 2 Free Gifts—
just for trying the Reader Service!

HP17R

Get 2 Free Books,

Plus 2 Free Gifts—

just for trying the Reader Service!

HARLEQUIN

HEARTWARMING™

READERSERVICE.COM

Manage your account online!

- Review your order history
- Manage your payments
- Update your address

> ### We've designed the Reader Service website just for you.

Enjoy all the features!

- Discover new series available to you, and read excerpts from any series.
- Respond to mailings and special monthly offers.
- Browse the Bonus Bucks catalog and online-only exculsives.
- Share your feedback.

Visit us at:

ReaderService.com

RS16R